F Anstey

The Talking Horse and Other Stories

F Anstey

The Talking Horse and Other Stories

ISBN/EAN: 9783743397972

Manufactured in Europe, USA, Canada, Australia, Japa

Cover: Foto ©Andreas Hilbeck / pixelio.de

Manufactured and distributed by brebook publishing software (www.brebook.com)

F Anstey

The Talking Horse and Other Stories

THE TALKING HORSE

AND OTHER TALES

BY

F. ANSTEY

AUTHOR OF 'VICE VERSÂ' 'THE GIANT'S ROBE'
'THE PARIAH' ETC.

SECOND EDITION

LONDON
SMITH, ELDER, & CO., 15 WATERLOO PLACE
1892

PREFACE

THESE STORIES originally appeared in 'Macmillan's,' 'Longman's,' 'Atalanta,' 'The Cornhill,' 'The Graphic,' 'Aunt Judy's,' 'The Reflector,' and Unwin's 'Christmas Annual,' respectively.

F. A.

CONTENTS

IT was on the way to Sandown Park that I met him first, on that horribly wet July afternoon when Bendigo won the Eclipse Stakes. He sat opposite to me in the train going down, and my attention was first attracted to him by the marked contrast between his appearance and his attire : he had not thought fit to adopt the regulation costume for such occasions, and I think I never saw a man who had made himself more aggressively horsey. The mark of the beast was sprinkled over his linen : he wore snaffle sleeve-links, a hard hunting-hat, a Newmarket coat, and extremely tight trousers. And with all this, he fell as far short of the genuine sportsman as any stage super who ever wore his spurs upside down in a hunting-chorus. His expression was mild and inoffensive, and his watery pale eyes and receding chin gave one the idea that he was hardly to be trusted astride anything more spirited than a gold-headed cane. And yet, somehow, he aroused compassion rather than any sense of the ludicrous : he had that look of shrinking self-effacement which comes of a recent humiliation, and, in spite of all extravagances, he was obviously a

B

gentleman; while something in his manner indicated
that his natural tendency would, once at all events,
have been to avoid any kind of extremes.

He puzzled and interested me so much that I did
my best to enter into conversation with him, only to
be baffled by the jerky embarrassment with which he
met all advances, and when we got out at Esher,
curiosity led me to keep him still in view.

Evidently he had not come with any intention of
making money. He avoided the grand stand, with
the bookmakers huddling in couples, like hoarse love-
birds; he kept away from the members' inclosure,
where the Guards' band was endeavouring to defy the
elements which emptied their vials into the brazen
instruments; he drifted listlessly about the course
till the clearing-bell rang, and it seemed as if he was
searching for some one whom he only wished to discover in order to avoid.

Sandown, it must be admitted, was not as gay as
usual that day, with its 'deluged park' and 'unsum-
mer'd sky,' its waterproofed toilettes and massed umbrellas, whose sides gleamed livid as they caught the
light—but there was a general determination to ignore
the unseasonable dampness as far as possible, and an
excitement over the main event of the day which no
downpour could quench.

The Ten Thousand was run : ladies with marvel-
lously confected bonnets lowered their umbrellas without a murmur, and smart men on drags shook hands

effusively as, amidst a frantic roar of delight, Bendigo strode past the post. The moment after, I looked round for my incongruous stranger, and saw him engaged in a well-meant attempt to press a currant bun upon a carriage-horse tethered to one of the trees—a feat of abstraction which, at such a time, was only surpassed by that of Archimedes at the sack of Syracuse.

After that I could no longer control my curiosity— I felt I must speak to him again, and I made an opportunity later, as we stood alone on a stand which commanded the finish of one of the shorter courses, by suggesting that he should share my umbrella.

Before accepting he glanced suspiciously at me through the rills that streamed from his unprotected hat-brim. 'I'm afraid,' I said, 'it is rather like shutting the stable-door after the steed is stolen.'

He started. 'He *was* stolen, then,' he cried; 'so you have heard?'

I explained that I had only used an old proverb which I thought might appeal to him, and he sighed heavily.

'I was misled for the moment,' he said: 'you have guessed, then, that I have been accustomed to horses?'

'You have hardly made any great secret of it.'

'The fact is,' he said, instantly understanding this allusion to his costume, 'I—I put on these things so as not to lose the habit of riding altogether—1 have not been on horseback lately. At one time I used to ride constantly—constantly. I was a regular attendant in Rotten Row—until something occurred which shook my nerve, and I am only waiting now for the shock to subside.'

I did not like to ask any questions, and we walked back to the station, and travelled up to Waterloo in company, without any further reference to the subject.

As we were parting, however, he said, ' I wonder if you would care to hear my full story some day? I cannot help thinking it would interest you, and it would be a relief to me.'

I was ready enough to hear whatever he chose to tell me; and persuaded him to dine with me at my rooms that evening, and unbosom himself afterwards, which he did to an extent for which I confess I was unprepared.

That he himself implicitly believed in his own story, I could not doubt; and he told it throughout with the oddest mixture of vanity and modesty, and an obvious struggle between a dim perception of his own absurdity and the determination to spare himself in no single particular, which, though it did not overcome my scepticism, could not fail to enlist sympathy. But for all that, by the time he entered upon the more sensational part of his case, I was driven to form conclusions respecting it which, as they will probably force themselves upon the reader's own mind, I need not anticipate here.

I give the story, as far as possible, in the words of its author ; and have only to add that it would never have been published here without his full consent and approval.

'My name,' said he, 'is Gustavus Pulvertoft. I have no occupation, and six hundred a year. I lived a quiet and contented bachelor until I was twenty-eight, and then I met Diana Chetwynd for the first time. We were spending Christmas at the same country-house, and it did not take me long to become the most devoted of her many adorers. She was one of the most variously accomplished girls I had ever met. She was a skilled musician, a brilliant amateur actress ; she could give most men thirty out of a hundred at billiards, and her judgment and daring across the most difficult country had won her the warm admiration of all hunting-men. And she was neither fast nor horsey, seeming to find but little pleasure in the society of mere sportsmen, to whose conversation she infinitely preferred that of persons who, like myself, were rather agreeable than athletic. I was not at that time, whatever I may be now, without my share of good looks, and for some reason it pleased Miss Chetwynd to show me a degree of favour which she accorded to no other member of the house-party.

It was annoying to feel that my unfamiliarity
with the open-air sports in which she delighted de-
barred me from her company to so great an extent;
for it often happened that I scarcely saw her until the
evening, when I sometimes had the bliss of sitting
next to her at dinner; but on these occasions I could
not help seeing that she found some pleasure in my
society.

I don't think I have mentioned that, besides being
exquisitely lovely, Diana was an heiress, and it was
not without a sense of my own presumption that I
allowed myself to entertain the hope of winning her
at some future day. Still, I was not absolutely pen-
niless, and she was her own mistress, and I had some
cause, as I have said, for believing that she was, at
least, not ill-disposed towards me. It seemed a favourable sign, for instance, when she asked me one day
why it was I never rode. I replied that I had not
ridden for years—though I did not add that the exact
number of those years was twenty-eight.

'Oh, but you must take it up again!' she said,
with the prettiest air of imperiousness. 'You ought
to ride in the Row next season.'

'If I did,' I said, 'would you let me ride with you
sometimes?'

'We should meet, of course,' she said; 'and it is
such a pity not to keep up your riding—you lose so
much by not doing so.'

Was I wrong in taking this as an intimation that,

by following her advice, I should not lose my reward?
If you had seen her face as she spoke, you would .
have thought as I did then—as I do now.

And so, with this incentive, I overcame any
private misgivings, and soon after my return to town
attended a fashionable riding-school near Hyde Park,
with the fixed determination to acquire the whole art
and mystery of horsemanship.

That I found learning a pleasure I cannot conscientiously declare. I have passed happier hours
than those I spent in cantering round four bare white-
washed walls on a snorting horse, with my inter-
dicted stirrups crossed upon the saddle. The riding-
master informed me from time to time that I was
getting on, and I knew instinctively when I was
coming off; but I must have made some progress, for
my instructor became more encouraging. 'Why,
when you come here first, Mr. Pulvertoft, sir, you
were like a pair o' tongs on a wall, as they say;
whereas now—well, you can tell yourself how you
are,' he would say; though, even then, I occasionally
had reason to regret that I was *not* on a wall. However, I persevered, inspired by the thought that each
fresh horse I crossed (and some were very fresh indeed) represented one more barrier surmounted
between myself and Diana, and encouraged by the
discovery, after repeated experiments, that tan was
rather soothing to fall upon than otherwise.

When I walked in the Row, where a few horsemen

were performing as harbingers of spring, I criticised
their riding, which I thought indifferent, as they
neglected nearly all the rules. I began to anticipate a day when I should exhibit a purer and more
classic style of equestrianism. And one morning I saw
Diana, who pulled up her dancing mare to ask me if
I had remembered her advice, and I felt proudly able
to reply that I should certainly make my appearance
in the Row before very long.

From that day I was perpetually questioning my
riding-master as to when he considered I should be
ripe enough for Rotten Row. He was dubious, but
not actually dissuasive. ' It's like this, you see, sir,'
he explained, ' if you get hold of a quiet, steady horse
—why, you won't come to no harm ; but if you go out
on an animal that will take advantage of you, Mr.
Pulvertoft, why, you'll be all no-how on him, sir.'

They would have móunted me at the school ; but
I knew most of the stud there, and none of them quite
came up to my ideal of a ' quiet, steady horse ; ' so I
went to a neighbouring job-master, from whom I had
occasionally hired a brougham, and asked to be shown
an animal he could recommend to one who had not
had much practice lately. He admitted candidly
enough that most of his horses ' took a deal of riding,'
but added that it so happened that he had one just
then which would suit me ' down to the ground '—a
phrase which grated unpleasantly on my nerves,
though I consented to see the horse. His aspect

impressed me most favourably. He was a chestnut of noble proportions, with a hogged mane; but what reassured me was the expression of his eye, indicating as it did a self-respect and sagacity which one would hardly expect for seven and sixpence an hour.

'You won't get a showier Park 'ack than what he is, not to be so quiet,' said his owner. 'He's what you may call a kind 'oss, and as gentle—you could ride him on a packthread.'

I considered reins safer, but I was powerfully drawn towards the horse: he seemed to me to be sensible that he had a character to lose, and to possess too high an intelligence wilfully to forfeit his testimonials. With hardly a second thought, I engaged him for the following afternoon.

I mounted at the stables, with just a passing qualm, perhaps, while my stirrup-leathers were being adjusted, and a little awkwardness in taking up my reins, which were more twisted than I could have wished; however, at length, I found myself embarked on the stream of traffic on the back of the chestnut—whose name, by the way, was Brutus.

Shall I ever forget the pride and ecstasy of finding that I had my steed under perfect control, that we threaded the maze of carriages with absolute security? I turned him into the Park, and clucked my tongue: he broke into a canter, and how shall I describe my delight at the discovery that it was not uncomfortable? I said 'Woa,' and he stopped, so gradually that my equilibrium was not seriously disturbed ; he trotted, and still I accommodated myself to his movements without any positive inconvenience. I could have embraced him for gratitude : never before had I been upon a beast whose paces were so easy, whose behaviour was so considerate. I could ride at last ! or, which amounted to the same thing, I could ride the horse I was on, and I would 'use no other.' I was about to meet Diana Chetwynd, and need not fear even to encounter her critical eyes.

We had crossed the Serpentine bridge, and were just turning in upon the Ride, when—and here I am only too conscious that what I am about to say may strike you as almost incredible—when I heard an unfamiliar voice addressing me with, 'I say—you !' and the moment afterwards realised that it proceeded from my own horse !

I am not ashamed to own that I was as nearly off as possible ; for a more practised rider than I could pretend to be might have a difficulty in preserving his equanimity in this all but unparalleled situation. I was too much engaged in feeling for my left stirrup to make any reply, and presently the horse spoke once more. 'I say,' he inquired, and I failed to discern the slightest trace of respect in his tone—'do you think you can ride ?' You can judge for yourself how disconcerting the inquiry must have been from such lips : I felt rooted to the saddle—a sensation which, with me, was sufficiently rare. I looked round in helpless bewilderment, at the shimmering Serpentine, and the white houses in Park Lane gleaming out of a lilac haze, at the cocoa-coloured Row, and the flash of distant carriage-wheels in the sunlight : all looked as usual—and yet, there was I on the back of a horse which had just inquired 'whether I thought I could ride ' !

'I have had two dozen lessons at a riding-school,' I said at last, with rather a flabby dignity.

'I should hardly have suspected it,' was his brutal retort. 'You are evidently one of the hopeless cases.'

I was deeply hurt, the more so because I could not deny that he had some claim to be a judge. 'I —I thought we were getting on so nicely together,' I faltered, and all he said in reply to that was, '*Did* you ? '

'Do you know,' I began, striving to be conversational, 'I never was on a horse that talked before.'

'You are enough to make any horse talk,' he answered ; 'but I suppose I *am* an exception.'

'I think you must be,' said I. 'The only horses I ever heard of as possessing the gift of speech were the Houyhnhnms.'

'How do you know I am not one of them ? ' he replied.

'If you are, you will understand that I took the liberty of mounting you under a very pardonable mistake ; and if you will have the goodness to . stand still, I will no longer detain you.'

'Not so fast,' said he: 'I want to know something more about you first. I should say now you
were a man with plenty of oats.'

'I am—well off,' I said. How I wished I was!

'I have long been looking out for a proprietor
who would not overwork me: now, of course, I don't
know, but you scarcely strike me as a *hard* rider.'

'I do not think I could be fairly accused of that,'
I answered, with all the consciousness of innocence.

'Just so—then buy me.'

'No,' I gasped: 'after the extremely candid
opinion you were good enough to express of my
riding, I'm surprised that you should even suggest
such a thing.'

'Oh, I will put up with that—you will suit me
well enough, I dare say.'

'You must excuse me. I prefer to keep my spare
cash for worthier objects; and, with your permission,
I will spend the remainder of the afternoon on foot.'

'You will do nothing of the sort,' said he.

'If you won't stop, and let me get off properly,'
I said with firmness, 'I shall *roll* off.' There were
some promenaders within easy hail; but how was I
to word a call for help, how explain such a dilemma
as mine?

'You will only reduce me to the painful necessity
of rolling on you,' he replied. 'You must see that
you are to a certain extent in my power. Suppose it
occurred to me to leap those rails and take you into

the Serpentine, or to run away and upset a mounted
policeman with you—do you think you could offer
much opposition ? '

I could not honestly assert that I did.   ' You were
introduced to me,' I said reproachfully, ' as a *kind*
horse ! '

' And so I am—apart from matters of business.
Come, will you buy, or be bolted with ?   I hate in-
decision ! '

' Buy ! ' I said, with commercial promptness.   ' If
you will take me back, I will arrange about it at
once.'

It is needless to say that my one idea was to get
safely off his back : after which, neither honour nor
law could require me to execute a contract extorted
from me by threats.   But, as we were going down
the mews, he said reflectively, ' I've been thinking—it
will be better for all parties, if you make your offer to
my proprietor *before* you dismount.'   I was too vexed
to speak : this animal's infernal intelligence had fore-
seen my manœuvre—he meant to foil it, if he could.

And then we clattered in under the glass-roofed
yard of the livery stables ; and the job-master, who
was alone there, cast his eyes up at the sickly-faced
clock, as if he were comparing its pallor with my own.
' Why, you *are* home early, sir,' he said.   ' You didn't
find the 'orse too much for you, did you ? '   He said
this without any suspicion of the real truth ; and, indeed, I may say, once for all, that this weird horse—

Houyhnhnm, or whatever else he might be—admitted
no one but myself into the secret of his marvellous
gifts, and in all his conversations with me, managed
(though how, I cannot pretend to say) to avoid being
overheard.

'Oh, dear no,' I protested, 'he carried me admirably—admirably!' and I made an attempt to slip off.

No such thing: Brutus instantly jogged my
memory, and me, by the slightest suggestion of a
'buck.'

'He's a grand 'orse, sir, isn't he?' said the job-
master complacently.

'M—magnificent!' I agreed, with a jerk. 'Will
you go to his head, please?'

But the horse backed into the centre of the yard,
where he plunged with a quiet obstinacy. 'I like him
so much,' I called out, as I clung to the saddle, 'that
I want to know if you're at all inclined to part with
him?' Here Brutus became calm and attentive.

'Would you be inclined to make me a orfer for
him, sir?'

'Yes,' I said faintly. 'About how much would
he be?'

'You step into my orfice here, sir,' said he, 'and
we'll talk it over.'

I should have been only too willing, for there was
no room there for the horse, but the suspicious
animal would not hear of it: he began to revolve
immediately.

'Let us settle it now—here,' I said, 'I can't wait.'

The job-master stroked away a grin. No doubt there *was* something unbusinesslike and unpractical in such precipitation, especially as combined with my appearance at the time.

'Well, you 'ave took a voilent fancy to the 'orse and no mistake, sir,' he remarked.

'I never crossed a handsomer creature,' I said; which was hardly a prudent remark for an intending purchaser, but then, there was the animal himself to be conciliated.

'I don't know, really, as I can do without him just at this time of year,' said the man. 'I'm under-'orsed as it is for the work I've got to do.'

A sweet relief stole over me: I had done all that could be expected of me. 'I'm very sorry to hear that,' I said, preparing to dismount. 'That *is* a disappointment; but if you can't there's an end of it.'

'Don't you be afraid,' said Brutus, '*he'll* sell me readily enough: make him an offer, quick!'

'I'll give you thirty guineas for him, come!' I said, knowing well enough that he would not take twice the money.

'I thought a gentleman like you would have had more insight into the value of a 'orse,' he said: 'why, his action alone is worth that, sir.'

'You couldn't let me have the action without the

horse, I suppose ? ' I said, and I must have intended some joke.

It is unnecessary to prolong a painful scene. Brutus ran me up steadily from sum to sum, until his owner said at last : ' Well, we won't 'aggle, sir, call it a hundred.'

I had to call it a hundred, and what is more, it *was* a hundred. I took him without a warranty, without even a veterinary opinion. I could have been induced to take my purchase away then and there, as if I had been buying a canary, so unaccustomed was I to transactions of this kind, and I am afraid the job-master considered me little better than a fool.

So I found myself the involuntary possessor of a Houyhnhnm, or something even worse, and I walked back to my rooms in Park Street in a state of stupor. What was I to do with him ? To ride an animal so brutally plainspoken would be a continual penance ; and yet, I should have to keep him, for I knew he was cunning enough to outwit any attempt to dispose of him. And to this, Love and Ambition had led me ! I could not, after all I had said, approach Diana with any confidence as a mere pedestrian : the fact that I was in possession of a healthy horse which I never rode, would be sure to leak out in time, and how was I to account for it ? I could see no way, and I groaned under an embarrassment which I dared not confide to the friendliest ear. I hated the monster that had saddled himself upon me, and looked in vain for any mode of escape.

I had to provide Brutus with stabling in another part of the town, for he proved exceedingly difficult to please : he found fault with everything, and I only wonder he did not demand that his stable should be fitted up with blue china and mezzotints. In his new quarters I left him for some days to his own devices : a course which I was glad to find, on visiting him again, had considerably reduced his arrogance. He wanted to go in the Row and see the other horses, and it did not at all meet his views to be exercised there by a stableman at unfashionable hours. So he proposed a compromise. If I would only consent to mount him, he engaged to treat me with forbearance, and pointed out that he could give me, as he expressed it, various 'tips' which would improve my seat. I was not blind to the advantages of such an arrangement. It is not every one who secures a riding-master in the person of his own horse ; the horse is essentially a generous animal, and I felt that I might trust to Brutus's honour. And to do him justice, he observed the compact with strict good faith. Some of his 'tips,' it is true, very nearly tipped me off, but their result was to bring us closer together ; our relations were less strained ; it seemed to me that I gained more mastery over him every day, and was less stiff afterwards.

But I was not allowed to enjoy this illusion long.

C

One day when I innocently asked him if he found my hands improving, he turned upon me his off sardonic eye. 'You'll *never* improve, old sack-of-beans' (for he had come to address me with a freedom I burned to resent); 'hands! why, you're sawing my mouth off all the time. And your feet "home," and tickling me under my shoulders at every stride—why, I'm half ashamed to be seen about with you.'

I was deeply hurt. 'I will spare you for the future,' I said coldly; 'this is my last appearance.'

'Nonsense,' he said, 'you needn't show temper over it. Surely, if I can put up with it, *you* can! But we will make a new compact.' (I never knew such a beast as he was for bargains!) 'You only worry me by interfering with the reins. Let 'em out, and leave everything to me. Just mention from time to time where you want to go, and I'll attend to it,— if I've nothing better to do.'

I felt that such an understanding was destructive of all dignity, subverting, as it did, the natural relations between horse and rider; but I had hardly any self-respect left, and I consented, since I saw no way of refusing. And on the whole, I cannot say, even now, that I had any grave reason for finding fault with the use Brutus made of my concessions; he showed more tact than I could have expected in disguising the merely nominal nature of my authority.

I had only one serious complaint against him,

which was that he had a habit of breaking suddenly
away, with a merely formal apology, to exchange
equine civilities with some cob or mare, to whose
owner I was a perfect stranger, thus driving me to
invent the most desperate excuses to cover my seeming intrusion : but I managed to account for it in
various ways, and even made a few acquaintances in
this irregular and involuntary manner.   I could have
wished he had been a less susceptible animal, for,
though his flirtations were merely Platonic, it is
rather humiliating to have to play ' gooseberry ' to
one's own horse—a part which I was constantly being
called upon to perform !

As it happened, Diana was away in Paris that
Easter, and we had not met since my appearance in
the Row ; but I knew she would be in town again
shortly, and with consummate diplomacy I began to
excite Brutus's curiosity by sundry careless, half-
slighting allusions to Miss Chetwynd's little mare,
Wild Rose. ' She's too frisky for my taste,' I said,
' but she's been a good deal admired, though I dare
say you wouldn't be particularly struck by her.'

So that, on the first afternoon of Diana's return
to the Row, I found it easy, under cover of giving
Brutus an opportunity of forming an opinion, to pre-
vail on him to carry me to her side.   Diana, who was
with a certain Lady Verney, her chaperon, welcomed
me with a charming smile.

' I had no idea you could ride so well,' she said,

'you manage that beautiful horse of yours so very easily—with such light hands, too.'

This was not irony, for I could now give my whole mind to my seat; and, as I never interfered at all with the steering apparatus, my hands must have seemed the perfection of lightness.

'He wants delicate handling,' I answered carelessly, 'but he goes very well with *me*.'

'I wish you would let me try his paces some morning, Pulvertoft,' struck in a Colonel Cockshott, who was riding with them, and whom I knew slightly: 'I've a notion he would go better on the curb.'

'I shall be very happy,' I began, when, just in time, I noticed a warning depression in Brutus's ears. The Colonel rode about sixteen stone, and with spurs! 'I mean,' I added hastily, 'I should have been—only, to tell you the truth, I couldn't conscientiously trust any one on him but myself.'

'My dear fellow!' said the Colonel, who I could see was offended, 'I've not met many horses in my time that I couldn't get upon terms with.'

'I think Mr. Pulvertoft is *quite* right,' said Diana. 'When a horse gets accustomed to one he does so resent a strange hand: it spoils his temper for days. I never will lend Wild Rose to anybody for that very reason!'

The Colonel fell back in the rear in a decided sulk. 'Poor dear Colonel Cockshott!' said Diana, 'he is so proud of his riding, but *I* think he dragoons a horse. I don't call that *riding*, do you?'

'Well—hardly,' I agreed, with easy disparagement. 'I never believe in ruling a horse by fear.'

'I suppose you are very fond of yours?' she said.

'Fond is not the word!' I exclaimed—and it certainly was not.

'I am not sure that what I said about lending Wild Rose would apply to *you*,' she said. 'I think you would be gentle with her.'

I was certain that I should treat her with all consideration; but as I doubted whether she would wholly reciprocate it, I said with much presence of mind, that I should regard riding her as akin to profanation.

As Brutus and I were going home, he observed that it was a good thing I had not agreed to lend him to the Colonel.

'Yes,' I said, determined to improve the occasion, 'you might not have found him as considerate as— well, as some people!'

'I meant it was a good thing for *you*!' he hinted darkly, and I did not care to ask for an explanation. 'What did you mean,' he resumed, 'by saying that I should not admire Wild Rose? Why, she is charming—charming!'

'In that case,' I said, 'I don't mind riding with her mistress occasionally—to oblige you.'

'You don't mind!' he said; 'you will *have* to, my boy,—and every afternoon!'

I suppressed a chuckle: after all, man *is* the nobler animal. I could manage a horse—in my own way. My little *ruse* had succeeded: I should have no more forced introductions to mystified strangers.

And now for some weeks my life passed in a happy dream. I only lived for those hours in the Row, where Brutus turned as naturally to Wild Rose as the sunflower to the sun, and Diana and I grew more intimate every day. Happiness and security made me almost witty. I was merciless in my raillery of the eccentric exhibitions of horsemanship which were to be met with, and Diana was provoked by my comments to the sweetest silvery laughter. As for Colonel Cockshott, whom I had once suspected of a desire to be my rival, he had long become a 'negligible quantity;' and if I delayed in asking Diana to trust me with her sweet self, it was only because I found an epicurean pleasure in prolonging a suspense that was so little uncertain.

And then, without warning, my riding was interrupted for a while. Brutus was discovered, much to his annoyance, to have a saddle-raw, and was even so unjust as to lay the blame on me, though, for my own part, I thought it a mark of apt, though tardy, retribution. I was not disposed to tempt Fortune upon any other mount, but I could not keep away from the Row, nevertheless, and appeared there on foot. I saw Diana riding with the Colonel, who seemed to think his opportunity had come at last; but whenever she passed the railings on which I leaned, she would raise her eyebrows and draw her mouth down into a little curve of resigned boredom, which completely reassured me. Still, I was very glad when Brutus was well again, and we were cantering down the Row once more, both in the highest spirits.

'I never heard the horses here *whinny* so much as they do this season,' I said, by way of making conversation. 'Can you account for it at all?' For he sometimes gave me pieces of information which enabled me to impress Diana afterwards by my intimate knowledge of horses.

'Whinnying?' he said. 'They're *laughing*, that's what they're doing—and no wonder!'

'Oh!' said I, 'and what's the joke?'

'Why, *you* are!' he replied. 'You don't suppose you take *them* in, do you? They know all about you, bless your heart!'

'Oh, do they?' I said blankly. This brute took a positive pleasure, I believe, in reducing my self-esteem.

'I dare say it has got about through Wild Rose,' he continued. 'She was immensely tickled when I told her. I'm afraid she must have been feeling rather dull all these days, by the bye.'

I felt an unworthy impulse to take his conceit down as he had lowered mine.

'Not so very, I think,' I said. 'She seemed to me to find that brown hunter of Colonel Cockshott's a very agreeable substitute.'

Late as it is for reparation, I must acknowledge with shame that in uttering this insinuation, I did that poor little mare (for whom I entertained the highest respect) a shameful injustice; and I should like to state here, in the most solemn and emphatic manner, my sincere belief that, from first to last, she conducted herself in a manner that should have shielded her from all calumny.

It was only a mean desire to retaliate, a petty and ignoble spite, that prompted me thus to poison Brutus's confidence, and I regretted the words as soon as I had uttered them.

'That beast!' he said, starting as if I had touched him with a whip—a thing I never used—'why, he hasn't two ideas in his great fiddle-head. The only sort of officer _he_ ought to carry is a Salvationist!'

'I grant he has not your personal advantages and charm of manner,' I said. 'No doubt I was wrong to say anything about it.'

'No,' he said, 'you—you have done me a service,' and he relapsed into a sombre silence.

I was riding with Diana as usual, and was about to express my delight at being able to resume our companionship, when her mare drew slightly ahead and lashed out suddenly, catching me on the left leg, and causing intense agony for the moment.

Diana showed the sweetest concern, imploring me to go home in a cab at once, while her groom took charge of Brutus. I declined the cab; but, as my leg was really painful, and Brutus was showing an impatience I dared not disregard, I had to leave her side.

On our way home, Brutus said moodily, ' It is all over between us—you saw that ? '

' I felt it ! ' I replied. ' She nearly broke my leg.'

' It was intended for me,' he said. ' It was her way of signifying that we had better be strangers for the future. I taxed her with her faithlessness; she denied it, of course—every mare does; we had an explanation, and everything is at an end ! '

I did not ride him again for some days, and when I did, I found him steeped in Byronic gloom. He even wanted at first to keep entirely on the Bayswater side of the Park, though I succeeded in arguing him out of such weakness. ' Be a horse ! ' I said. ' Show her you don't care. You only flatter her by betraying your feelings.'

This was a subtlety that had evidently not occurred to him, but he was intelligent enough to feel the force of what I said. ' You are right,' he admitted ; ' you are not quite a fool in some respects. She shall see how little I care ! '

Naturally, after this, I expected to accompany

Diana as usual, and it was a bitter disappointment to me to find that Brutus would not hear of doing so. He had an old acquaintance in the Park, a dapple-grey, who, probably from some early disappointment was a confirmed cynic, and whose society he thought would be congenial just then. The grey was ridden regularly by a certain Miss Gittens, whose appearance as she titupped laboriously up and down had often furnished Diana and myself with amusement.

And now, in spite of all my efforts, Brutus made straight to the grey. I was not in such difficulties as might have been expected, for I happened to know Miss Gittens slightly, as a lady no longer in the bloom of youth, who still retained a wiry form of girlishness. Though rather disliking her than not, I found it necessary just then to throw some slight effusion into my greeting. She, not unnaturally perhaps, was flattered by my preference, and begged me to give her a little instruction in riding, which—Heaven forgive me for it !—I took upon myself to do.

Even now I scarcely see how I could have acted otherwise : I could not leave her side until Brutus had exhausted the pleasures of cynicism with his grey friend, and the time had to be filled up somehow. But, oh, the torture of seeing Diana at a distance, and knowing that only a miserable misunderstanding between our respective steeds kept us apart, feeling constrained even to avoid looking in her direction, lest she should summon me to her side !

One day, as I was riding with Miss Gittens, she glanced coyly at me over her sharp right shoulder, and said, 'Do you know, only such a little while ago, I never even dreamed that we should ever become as intimate as we are now; it seems almost incredible, does it not?'

'You must not say so,' I replied. 'Surely there is nothing singular in my helping you a little with your riding?' Though it struck me that it would have been very singular if I had.

'Perhaps not singular,' she murmured, looking modestly down her nose; 'but will you think me very unmaidenly if I confess that, to me, those lessons have developed a dawning danger?'

'You are perfectly safe on the grey,' I said.

'I—I was not thinking of the grey,' she returned. 'Dear Mr. Pulvertoft, I must speak frankly—a girl has so many things to consider, and I am afraid you have made me forget how wrongly and thoughtlessly I have been behaving of late. I cannot help suspecting that you must have some motive in seeking my society in so—so marked a manner.'

'Miss Gittens,' said I, 'I can disguise nothing: I have.'

'And you have not been merely amusing yourself all this time?'

'Before Heaven,' I cried with fervour, 'I have *not*!'

'You are not one of those false men who give their

bridle-reins a shake, and ride off with "Adieu for evermore ! "—tell me you are not ? '

I might shake *my* bridle-reins till I was tired and nothing would come of it unless Brutus was in the humour to depart; so that I was able to assure her with truth that I was not at all that kind of person.

' Then why not let your heart speak ? '

' There is such a thing,' I said gloomily, ' as a heart that is gagged.'

' Can no word, no hint of mine loosen the gag ? ' she wished to know. ' What, you are silent still ? Then, Mr. Pulvertoft, though I may seem harsh and cruel in saying it, our pleasant intercourse must end —we must ride together no more ! '

No more ? What would Brutus say to that ? I was horrified. ' Miss Gittens,' I said in great agitation, ' I entreat you to unsay those words. I—I am afraid I could not undertake to accept such a dismissal. Surely, after that, you will not insist ! '

She sighed. ' I am a weak, foolish girl,' she said; ' you are only too able to overcome my judgment. There, Mr. Pulvertoft, look happy again— I relent. You may stay if you will ! '

You must believe that I felt thoroughly ashamed of myself, for I could not be blind to the encouragement which, though I sought to confine my words to strict truth, I was innocently affording. But, with a horse like mine, what was a man to do ? What would you have done yourself ? As soon as was prudent, I hinted to Brutus that his confidences had lasted long enough ; and as he trotted away with me, he remarked, ' I thought you were never going.' Was he weary of the grey already ? My heart leaped. ' Brutus,' I said thickly, ' are you strong enough to bear a great joy ? '

' Speak out,' he said, ' and do try to keep those heels out of my ribs.'

' I cannot see you suffer,' I told him, with a sense of my own hypocrisy all the time. ' I must tell you—circumstances have come to my knowledge which lead me to believe that we have both judged Wild Rose too hastily. I am sure that her heart is yours still. She is only longing to tell you that she has never really swerved from her allegiance.'

' It is too late now,' he said, and the back of his head looked inflexibly obstinate ; ' we have kept asunder too long.'

' No,' I said, ' listen. I take more interest in you than you are, perhaps, aware of, and I have thought of a little plan for bringing you together again. What if I find an opportunity to see the lady she belongs to—we have not met lately, as you know, and I do not pretend that I desire a renewal of our intimacy——'

' You like the one on the grey best ; I saw that long ago,' he said ; and I left him in his error.

' In any case, for your sake, I will sacrifice myself,' I said magnanimously. ' I will begin to-morrow.

Come, you will not let your lives be wrecked by a foolish lovers' quarrel?'

He made a little half-hearted opposition, but finally, as I knew he would, consented. I had gained my point: I was free from Miss Gittens at last!

That evening I met Diana in the hall of a house in Eaton Square. She was going downstairs as I was making my way to the ball-room, and greeted me with a rather cool little nod.

'You have quite deserted me lately,' she said, smiling, but I could read the reproach in her eyes, 'you never ride with us now.'

My throat was swelling with passionate eloquence —and I could not get any of it out.

'No, I never do,' was all my stupid tongue could find to say.

'You have discovered a more congenial companion,' said cruel Diana.

'Miss Chetwynd,' I said eagerly, 'you don't know how I have been wishing—! Will you let me ride with you to-morrow, as—as you used to do?'

'You are quite sure you won't be afraid of my naughty Wild Rose?' she said. 'I have given her such a scolding, that I think she is thoroughly ashamed of herself.'

'You thought it was *that* that kept me!' I cried. 'Oh, if I could tell you!'

She smiled: she was my dear, friendly Diana again.

'You shall tell me all about it to-morrow,' she said. 'You will not have another opportunity, because we are going to Aix on Friday. And now, good-night. I am stopping the way, and the linkman is getting quite excited over it.'

She passed on, and the carriage rolled away with her, and I was too happy to mind very much—had she not forgiven me? Should we not meet to-morrow? I should have two whole hours to declare myself in, and this time I would dally with Fortune no longer.

How excited I was the following day: how fearful, when the morning broke grey and lowering: how grateful, when the benignant sun shone out later, and promised a brilliant afternoon: how carefully I dressed, and what a price I paid for the flower for my buttonhole!

So we cantered on to the Row, as goodly a couple (if I may be pardoned this retrospective vanity) as any there; and by and by, I saw, with the quick eye of a lover, Diana's willowy form in the distance. She was not alone, but I knew that the Colonel would soon have to yield his place to me.

As soon as she saw me, she urged her mare to a trot, and came towards me with the loveliest faint blush and dawning smile of welcome, when, all at once, Brutus came to a dead stop, which nearly threw me on his neck, and stood quivering in every limb.

' Do you see that ? ' he said hoarsely. ' And I was about to forgive her ! '

I saw : my insinuation, baseless enough at the beginning, was now but too well justified. Colonel Cockshott was on his raw-boned brown hunter, and even my brief acquaintance with horses enabled me to see that Wild Rose no longer regarded him with her former indifference.

Diana and the Colonel had reined up and seemed waiting for me—would Brutus never move ? ' Show your pride,' I said in an agonised whisper, ' Treat her with the contempt she deserves ! '

' I will,' he said between his bit and clenched teeth.

And then Miss Gittens came bumping by on the grey, and, before I could interfere, my Houyhnhnm was off like a shot in pursuit. I saw Diana's sweet, surprised face : I heard the Colonel's jarring laugh as I passed, and I—I could only bow in mortified appeal, and long for a gulf to leap into like Curtius !

I don't know what I said to Miss Gittens. I believe I made myself recklessly amiable, and I remember she lingered over parting in a horribly emotional manner. I was too miserable to mind : all the time I was seeing Diana's astonished eyes, hearing Colonel Cockshott's heartless laugh. Brutus made a kind of explanation on our way home : ' You meant well,' he said, ' but you see you were wrong. Your proposed sacrifice, for which I am just as grateful to you as if it had been effected, was useless. All I could do in return was to take you where your true inclination lay. I, too, can be unselfish.'

I was too dejected to curse his unselfishness. 1 did not even trouble myself to explain what it had probably cost me. I only felt drearily that I had had my last ride, I had had enough of horsemanship for ever !

That evening I went to the theatre, I wanted to deaden thought for the moment; and during one of the intervals I saw Lady Verney in the stalls, and went up to speak to her. 'Your niece is not with you?' I said; 'I thought I should have had a chance of—of saying good-bye to her before she left for the continent.'

I had a lingering hope that she might ask me to lunch, that I might have one more opportunity of explaining.

'Oh,' said Lady Verney, 'but that is all changed; we are not going—at least, not yet.'

'Not going !' I cried, incredulous for very joy.

'No, it is all very sudden; but,—well, you are almost like an old friend, and you are sure to hear it sooner or later. I only knew myself this afternoon, when she came in from her ride. Colonel Cockshott has proposed and she has accepted him. We're *so* pleased about it. Wasn't dear Mrs. —— delightful in that last act ? I positively saw real tears on her face ! '

D

If I had waited much longer she would have seen a similar display of realism on mine. But I went back and sat the interval out, and listened critically to the classical selection of chamber-music from the orchestra, and saw the rest of the play, though I have no notion how it ended.

All that night my heart was slowly consumed by a dull rage that grew with every sleepless hour; but the object of my resentment was not Diana. She had only done what as a woman she was amply justified in doing after the pointed slight I had apparently inflicted upon her. Her punishment was sufficient already, for, of course, I guessed that she had only accepted the Colonel under the first intolerable sting of desertion. No: I reserved all my wrath for Brutus, who had betrayed me at the moment of triumph. I planned revenge. Cost what it might I would ride him once more. In the eyes of the law I was his master. I would exercise my legal rights to the full.

The afternoon came at last. I was in a white heat of anger, though as I ascended to the saddle there were bystanders who put a more uncharitable construction upon my complexion.

Brutus cast an uneasy eye at my heels as we started: ' What are those things you've got on ? ' he inquired.

' Spurs,' I replied curtly.

' You shouldn't wear them till you have learnt to

turn your toes in,' he said.   'And a whip, too !   May
I ask what that is for ? '

'We will discuss that presently,' I said very coldly;
for I did not want to have a scene with my horse in
the street.

When we came round by the statue of Achilles
and on to the Ride, I shortened my reins, and got a
better hold of the whip, while I found that, from some
cause I cannot explain, the roof of my mouth grew
uncomfortably dry.

'I should be glad of a little quiet talk with you, if
you've no objection,' I began.

'I am quite at your disposal,' he said, champing
his bit with a touch of irony.

'First, let me tell you,' I said, 'that I have lost
my only love for ever.'

'Well,' he retorted flippantly, 'you won't die of it.
So have I.   We must endeavour to console one another ! '

I still maintained a deadly calm.   'You seem un-
aware that you are the sole cause of my calamity,' I
said.   'Had you only consented to face Wild Rose
yesterday, I should have been a happy man by this
time ! '

'How was I to know that, when you let me think
all your affections were given to the elderly thing who
is trotted out by my friend the grey ? '

'We won't argue, please,' I said hastily.   'It is
enough that your infernal egotism and self-will have

ruined my happiness. I have allowed you to usurp the rule, to reverse our natural positions. I shall do so no more. I intend to teach you a lesson you will never forget.'

For a horse, he certainly had a keen sense of humour. I thought the girths would have snapped.

'And when do you intend to begin?' he asked, as soon as he could speak.

I looked in front of me : there were Diana and her accepted lover riding towards us; and so natural is dissimulation, even to the sweetest and best women, that no one would have suspected from her radiant face that her gaiety covered an aching heart.

'I intend to begin *now*,' I said. 'Monster, demon, whatever you are that have held me in thrall so long, I have broken my chains! I have been a coward long enough. You may kill me if you like. I rather hope you will; but first I mean to pay you back some of the humiliation with which you have loaded me. I intend to thrash you as long as I remain in the saddle.'

I have been told by eye-witnesses that the chastisement was of brief duration, but while it lasted, I flatter myself, it was severe. I laid into him with a stout whip, of whose effectiveness I had assured myself by experiments upon my own legs. I dug my borrowed spurs into his flanks. I jerked his mouth. I dare say he was almost as much surprised as pained. But he *was* pained!

I was about to continue my practical rebuke, when

my victim suddenly evaded my grasp; and for one
vivid second I seemed to be gazing upon a birdseye
view of his back; and then there was a crash, and I
lay, buzzing like a bee, in an iridescent fog, and each
colour meant a different pain, and they faded at last
into darkness, and I remember no more.

'It was weeks,' concluded Mr. Pulvertoft, 'before
that darkness lifted and revealed me to myself as a
strapped and bandaged invalid. But—and this is perhaps the most curious part of my narrative—almost
the first sounds that reached my ears were those of
wedding bells; and I knew, without requiring to be
told, that they were ringing for Diana's marriage with
the Colonel. *That* showed there wasn't much the
matter with me, didn't it? Why, I can hear them
everywhere now. I don't think she ought to have
had them rung at Sandown though: it was just a
little ostentatious, so long after the ceremony; don't
you think so?'

'Yes—yes,' I said; 'but you never told me what
became of the horse.'

'Ah! the horse—yes. I am looking for him.
I'm not so angry with him as I was, and I don't like
to ask too many questions at the stables, for fear they
may tell me one day that they had to shoot him while I
was so ill. You knew I was ill, I dare say?' he broke
off: 'there were bulletins about me in the papers.
Look here.'

He handed me a cutting on which I read:

'THE RECENT ACCIDENT IN ROTTEN ROW.—There is no change as yet in Mr. Pulvertoft's condition. The unfortunate gentleman is still lying unconscious at his rooms in Park Street; and his medical attendants fear that, even if he recovers his physical strength, the brain will be permanently injured.'

'But that was all nonsense!' said Mr. Pulvertoft, with a little nervous laugh, 'it wasn't injured a bit, or how could I remember everything so clearly as I do, you know?'

And this was an argument that was, of course, unanswerable.

THE GOOD LITTLE GIRL

A STORY FOR CHILDREN

HER name was Priscilla Prodgers, and she was a very good little girl indeed. So good was she, in fact, that she could not help being aware of it herself, and that is a stage to which very many quite excellent persons never succeed in attaining. She was only just a child, it is true, but she had read a great many beautiful story-books, and so she knew what a powerful reforming influence a childish and innocent remark, or a youthful example, or a happy combination of both, can exert over grown-up people. And early in life—she was but eleven at the date of this history—early in life she had seen clearly that her mission was to reform her family and relatives generally. This was a heavy task for one so young, particularly in Priscilla's case, for, besides a father, mother, brother, and sister, in whom she could not but discern many and serious failings, she possessed an aunt who was addicted to insincerity, two female cousins whose selfishness and unamiability were painful to witness, and a male cousin who talked slang and was so

worldly that he habitually went about in yellow
boots! Nevertheless Priscilla did not flinch, although,
for some reason, her earnest and unremitting efforts
had hitherto failed to produce any deep impression.
At times she thought this was owing to the fact that
she tried to reform all her family together, and that
her best plan would be to take each one separately,
and devote her whole energies to improving that
person alone. But then she never could make up
her mind which member of the family to begin with.
It is small wonder that she often felt a little dis-
heartened, but even that was a cheering symptom,
for in the books it is generally just when the little
heroine becomes most discouraged that the seemingly
impenitent relative exhibits the first sign of softening.

So Priscilla persevered: sometimes with merely a
shocked glance of disapproval, which she had practised before the looking-glass until she could do it
perfectly; sometimes with some tender, tactful little
hint. 'Don't you think, dear papa,' she would say
softly, on a Sunday morning, 'don't you *think* you
could write your newspaper article on some *other* day
—is it a work of *real* necessity?' Or she would ask
her mother, who was certainly fond of wearing pretty
things. 'How much bread for poor starving people
would the price of your new bonnet buy, mother?
I should *so* like to work it out on my little slate!'

Then she would remind her brother Alick that it
would be so much better if, instead of wasting his

time in playing with silly little tin soldiers, he would try to learn as much as he could before he was sent to school; while she was never tired of quoting to her sister Betty the line, 'Be good, sweet maid, and let who will be clever!' which Betty, quite unjustly, interpreted to mean that Priscilla thought but poorly of her sister's intellectual capacity. Once when, as a great treat, the children were allowed to read 'Ivanhoe' aloud, Priscilla declined to participate until she had conscientiously read up the whole Norman period in her English history; and on another occasion she cried bitterly on hearing that her mother had arranged for them to learn dancing, and even endured bread and water for an entire day rather than consent to acquire an accomplishment which she feared, from what she had read, would prove a snare. On the second day—well, there was roast beef and Yorkshire pudding for dinner, and Priscilla yielded; but she made the resolution—and kept it too—that, if she went to the dancing class, she would firmly refuse to take the slightest pains to learn a single step.

I only mention all these traits to show that Priscilla really was an unusually good child, which makes it the more sad and strange that her family should have profited so little by her example. She was neither loved nor respected as she ought to have been, I am grieved to say. Her papa, when he was not angry, made the cruellest fun of her mild reproofs; her mother continued to spend money on dresses and bonnets, and even allowed the maid to say that her mistress was 'not at home,' when she was merely unwilling to receive visitors. Alick and Betty, too, only grew more exasperated when Priscilla urged them to keep their tempers, and altogether she could not help feeling how wasted and thrown away she was in such a circle.

But she never quite lost heart; her papa was a literary man and wrote tales, some of which she feared were not as true as they affected to be, while he invariably neglected to insert a moral in any of them; frequently she dropped little remarks before him with apparent carelessness, in the hope that he might put them in print—but he never did; she never could recognise herself as a character in any of his stories, and so at last she gave up reading them at all!

But one morning she came more near to giving up in utter despair than ever before. Only the previous day she had been so hopeful! her father had really seemed to be beginning to appreciate his little daughter, and had presented her with sixpence in the new coinage to put in her money-box. This had emboldened her to such a degree that, happening on the following morning to hear him ejaculate 'Confound it!' she had, pressing one hand to her beating heart and laying the other hand softly upon his shoulder (which is the proper attitude on these occasions), reminded him that such an expression was scarcely less reprehensible than actual bad language. Upon which her hard-hearted papa had told her, almost sharply, '*not to be a little prig!*'

Priscilla forgave him, of course, and freely, because he was her father and it was her duty to bear with him; but she felt the injustice deeply, for all that. Then, when she went up into the nursery, Alick and Betty made a frantic uproar, merely because she insisted on teaching them the moves in chess, when they perversely wanted to play Halma! So, feeling baffled and sick at heart, she had put on her hat and run out all alone to a quiet lane near her home, where she could soothe her troubled mind by thinking over the ingratitude and lack of appreciation with which her efforts were met.

She had not gone very far up the lane when she saw, seated on a bench, a bent old woman in a poke-bonnet with a crutch-handled stick in her hands, and this old woman Priscilla (who was very quick of observation) instantly guessed to be a fairy—in which, as it fell out, she was perfectly right.

'Good day, my pretty child!' croaked the old dame.

'Good-day to you, ma'am!' answered Priscilla politely (for she knew that it was not only right but prudent to be civil to fairies, particularly when they take the form of old women). 'But, if you please, you mustn't call me pretty—because I am not. At least,' she added, for she prided herself upon her truthfulness, 'not *exactly* pretty. And I should hate to be always thinking about my looks, like poor Milly —she's our housemaid, you know—and I so often have to tell her that she did not make her *own* face.'

'I don't alarm you, I see,' said the old crone; 'but possibly you're not aware that you're talking to a fairy ?'

'Oh, yes, I am—but I'm not a bit afraid, because, you see, fairies can only hurt *bad* children.'

'Ah, and you're a good little child—that's not difficult to see !'

'They don't see it at home !' said Priscilla, with a sad little sigh, 'or they would listen more when I I tell them of things they oughtn't to do.'

'And what things do they do that they oughtn't to, my child—if you don't mind telling me ?'

'Oh, I don't mind in the *least !*' Priscilla hastened to assure her ; and then she told the old woman all her family's faults, and the trial it was to bear with them and go on trying to induce them to mend their ways. 'And papa is getting worse than ever,' she concluded dolefully ; 'only fancy, this very morning he called me a little prig !'

'Tut, tut !' said the fairy sympathetically, 'deary, deary me ! So he called you *that*, did he ?—"a little prig"! And *you*, too ! Ah, the world's coming to a pretty pass ! I suppose, now, your papa and the rest of them have got it into their heads that you are too young and too inexperienced to set up as their adviser—is that it ?'

'I'm afraid so,' admitted Priscilla; 'but we mustn't blame them,' she added gently, 'we must remember that they don't know any better—mustn't we, ma'am?'

'You sweet child!' said the old lady with enthusiasm; 'I must see if I can't do something to help you, though I'm not the fairy I used to be—still, there are tricks I can manage still, if I'm put to it. What you want is something that will prove to them that they ought to pay more attention to you, eh?—something there can be no possible mistake about?'

'Yes!' cried Priscilla eagerly, 'and—and—how would it be if you changed them into something else, just to *show* them, and then I could ask for them to be transformed back again, you know?'

'What an ingenious little thing you are!' exclaimed the fairy; 'but, let us see—if you came home and found your cruel papa doing duty as the family hatstand, or strutting about as a Cochin China fowl——'

'Oh, *yes*; and I'd feed him every day, till he was sorry!' interrupted the warmhearted little girl impulsively.

'Ah, but you're so hasty, my dear. Who would write all the clever articles and tales to earn bread and meat for you all?—fowls can't use a pen. No, we must find a prettier trick than that—there *was* one I seem to remember, long, long ago, performing for a good little ill-used girl, just like you, my dearie, just like you! Now what was it? some gift I gave her whenever she opened her lips——'

'Why, *I* remember—how funny that you should have forgotten! Whenever she opened her lips, roses, and diamonds, and rubies fell out. That would be the very thing! Then they'd *have* to attend to me! Oh, do be a kind old fairy and give me a gift like that—do, *do!*'

'Now, don't be so impetuous! You forget that this is not the time of year for roses, and, as for jewels, well, I don't think I can be very far wrong in supposing that you open your lips pretty frequently in the course of the day?'

'Alick does call me a "mag,"' said Priscilla; 'but that's wrong, because I never speak without having something to say. I don't think people ought to—it may do so *much* harm; mayn't it?'

'Undoubtedly. But, anyhow, if we made it *every* time you opened your lips, you would soon ruin me in precious stones, that's plain! No, I think we had better say that the jewels shall only drop when you are saying something you wish to be particularly improving—how will that do?'

'Very nicely indeed, ma'am, thank you,' said Priscilla, 'because, you see, it comes to just the same thing.'

'Ah, well, try to be as economical of your good things as you can—remember that in these hard times a poor old fairy's riches are not as inexhaustible as they used to be.'

'And jewels really will drop out?'

'Whenever they are wanted to "point a moral and adorn a tale,"' said the old woman (who, for a fairy, was particularly well-read). 'There, run along home, do, and scatter your pearls before your relations.'

It need scarcely be said that Priscilla was only too willing to obey; she ran all the way home with a light heart, eager to exhibit her wonderful gift. 'How surprised they will be!' she was thinking. 'If it had been Betty, instead of me, I suppose she would have come back talking toads! It would have been a good lesson for her—but still, toads are nasty things, and it would have been rather unpleasant for the rest of us. I think I won't tell Betty *where* I met the fairy.'

She came in and took her place demurely at the family luncheon, which was the children's dinner; they were all seated already, including her father, who had got through most of his writing in the course of the morning.

'Now make haste and eat your dinner, Priscilla,' said her mother, 'or it will be quite cold.'

'I always let it get a little cold, mother,' replied the good little girl, 'so that I mayn't come to think too much about eating, you know.'

As she uttered this remark, she felt a jewel pro-

ducing itself in some mysterious way from the tip of
her tongue, and saw it fall with a clatter into her
plate.   'I'll pretend not to notice anything,' she
thought.

'Hullo !' exclaimed Alick, pausing in the act of
mastication, 'I say—*Prissie !*'

'If you ask mother, I'm sure she will tell you that
it is most ill-mannered to speak with your mouth full,'
said Priscilla, her speech greatly impeded by an
immense emerald.

'I like that !' exclaimed her rude brother ; 'who's
speaking with their mouth full *now* ?'

'"*Their*" is not grammar, dear,' was Priscilla's
only reply to this taunt, as she delicately ejected a
pearl, 'you should say *her* mouth full.'   For Priscilla's
grammar was as good as her principles.

'But really, Priscilla, dear,' said her mother, who
felt some embarrassment at so novel an experience as
being obliged to find fault with her little daughter,
'you should not eat sweets just before dinner, and—
and couldn't you get rid of them in some other
manner ?'

'Sweets !' cried Priscilla, considerably annoyed
at being so misunderstood, 'they are not *sweets,*
mother.   Look !'   And she offered to submit one for
inspection.

'If I may venture to express an opinion,' observed
her father, 'I would rather that a child of mine
should suck sweets than coloured beads, and in either

case I object to having them prominently forced upon my notice at meal-times. But I daresay I'm wrong. I generally am.'

'Papa is quite right, dear,' said her mother, 'it *is* such a dangerous habit—suppose you were to swallow one, you know! Put them in the fire, like a good girl, and go on with your dinner.'

Priscilla rose without a word, her cheeks crimsoning, and dropped the pearl, ruby, and emerald, with great accuracy, into the very centre of the fire. This done, she returned to her seat, and went on with her dinner in silence, though her feelings prevented her from eating very much.

'If they choose to think my pearls are only beads, or jujubes, or acidulated drops,' she said to herself, bitterly, 'I won't waste any more on them, that's all! I won't open my lips again, except to say quite ordinary things—so *there* !'

If Priscilla had not been such a very good little girl, you might almost have thought she was in a temper; but she was not; her feelings were wounded, that was all, which is quite a different thing.

That afternoon, her aunt Margarine, Mrs. Hoyle, came to call. She was the aunt whom we have already mentioned as being given to insincerity; she was not well off, and had a tendency to flatter people; but Priscilla was fond of her notwithstanding, and she had never detected her in any insincerity towards herself. She was sent into the drawing-room to enter-

E

tain her aunt until her mother was ready to come
down, and her aunt, as usual, overwhelmed her with
affectionate admiration. 'How pretty and well you
are looking, my pet!' she began, 'and oh, what a
beautiful frock you have on!'

'The little silkworms wore it before I did, aunt,'
said Priscilla, modestly.

'How sweet of you to say so! But they never
looked half so well in it, I'll be bou—— Why, my
child, you've dropped a stone out of a brooch or something. Look—on the carpet there!'

'Oh,' said Priscilla, carelessly, 'it was out of my
mouth—not out of a brooch, I never wear jewellery.
I think jewellery makes people grow so conceited;
don't you, Aunt Margarine?'

'Yes, indeed, dearest—indeed you are *so* right!'
said her aunt (who wore a cameo-brooch as large as a
tart upon her cloak), 'and—and surely that can't be a
diamond in your lap?'

'Oh, yes, it is. I met a fairy this morning in the
lane, and so——' and here Priscilla proceeded to nar-
rate her wonderful experience. 'I thought it might
perhaps make papa and mamma value me a little
more than they do,' she said wistfully, as she finished
her story, 'but they don't take the least notice; they
made me put the jewels on the fire—they did, really!'

'What blindness!' cried her aunt; 'how *can*
people shut their eyes to such a treasure? And—
and may I just have *one* look? What, you really

don't want them?—I may keep them for my very
own? You precious love! Ah, I know a humble
home where you would be appreciated at your proper
worth. What would I not give for my poor naughty
Belle and Cathie to have the advantage of seeing
more of such a cousin!'

'I don't know whether I could do them much
good,' said Priscilla, 'but I would try my best.'

'I am sure you would!' said Aunt Margarine,
'and now, dearest sweet, I am going to ask your dear
mamma to spare you to us for just a little while; we
must both beg very hard.'

'I'll go and tell nurse to pack my things now, and
then I can go away with you,' said the little girl.

When her mother heard of the invitation, she
consented quite willingly. 'To tell you the truth,
Margarine,' she said, 'I shall be very glad for the
child to have a change. She seems a little unhappy
at home with us, and she behaved most unlike her
usual self at lunch; it *can't* be natural for a child of
her age to chew large glass beads. Did your Cathie
and Belle ever do such a thing?'

'Never,' said Aunt Margarine, coughing. 'It is
a habit that certainly ought to be checked, and I
promise you, my dear Lucy, that if you will only
trust Priscilla to me, I will take away anything of
that kind the very moment I find it. And I do think,
poor as we are, we shall manage to make her feel at
home. We are all so fond of your sweet Priscilla!'

So the end of it was that Priscilla went to stay with her aunt that very afternoon, and her family bore the parting with the greatest composure.

'I can't give you nice food, or a pretty bedroom to sleep in such as you have at home,' said her kind aunt. 'We are very plain people, my pet; but at least we can promise you a warm welcome.'

'Oh, auntie,' protested Priscilla, 'you mustn't think I mind a little hardship! Why, if beds weren't hard and food not nicely cooked now and then, we should soon grow too luxurious to do our duty, and that would be so very bad for us!'

'Oh, what *beauties!*' cried her aunt, involuntarily, as she stooped to recover several sparkling gems from the floor of the cab. 'I mean—it's better to pick them up, dear, don't you think? they might get in people's *way*, you know. What a blessing you will be in our simple home! I want you to do all you can to instruct your cousins; don't be afraid of telling them of any faults you may happen to see. Poor Cathie and Belle, I fear they are very far from being all they should be!' and Aunt Margarine heaved a sigh.

'Never mind, auntie; they will be better in time, I am sure. *I* wasn't *always* a good girl.'

Priscilla thoroughly enjoyed the first few days of her visit; even her aunt was only too grateful for instruction, and begged that Priscilla would tell her, quite candidly, of any shortcomings she might notice. And Priscilla, very kindly and considerately, always *did* tell her. Belle and Catherine were less docile, and she saw that it would take her some time to win their esteem and affection; but this was just what Priscilla liked: it was the usual experience of the heroines in the books, and much more interesting, too, than conquering her cousins' hearts at once.

Still, both Catherine and Belle persistently hardened their hearts against their gentle little cousin in the unkindest way; they would scarcely speak to her, and chose to make a grievance out of the fact that one or other of them was obliged, by their mother's strict orders, to be constantly in attendance upon her, in order to pick up and bring Mrs. Hoyle all the jewels that Priscilla scattered in profusion wherever she went.

'If you would only carry a plate about with you, Priscilla,' complained Belle one day, 'you could catch the jewels in that.'

'But I don't *want* to catch the jewels, dear Belle,' said Priscilla, with a playful but very sweet smile; 'if other people prize such things, that is not my fault, is it? *Jewels* do not make people any happier, Belle!'

'I should think not!' exclaimed Belle. 'I'm sure my back perfectly aches with stooping, and so does Cathie's. There! that big topaz has just gone and rolled under the sideboard, and mother will be *so* angry if I don't get it out! It is too bad of you, Priscilla! *I* believe you do it on purpose!'

'Ah, you will know me better some day, dear,' was the gentle response.

'Well, at all events, I think you might be naughty just now and then, Prissie, and give Cathie and me a half-holiday.'

'I would do anything else to please you, dear, but not that; you must not ask me to do what is impossible.'

Alas! not even this angelic behaviour, not even the loving admonitions, the tender rebukes, the shocked reproaches that fell, accompanied by perfect cascades of jewels, from the lips of our pattern little Priscilla, succeeded in removing the utterly unfounded prejudices of her cousins, though it was some consolation to feel that she was gradually acquiring a most beneficial influence over her aunt, who called Priscilla 'her little conscience.' For, you see, Priscilla's conscience had so little to do on her own account that it was always at the service of other people, and indeed quite enjoyed being useful, as was only natural to a conscientious conscience which felt that it could never have been created to be idle.

Very soon another responsibility was added to little Priscilla's burdens. Her cousin Dick, the worldly one with the yellow boots, came home after his annual holiday, which, as he was the junior clerk in a large bank, he was obliged to take rather late in the year. She had looked forward to his return with some excitement. Dick, she knew, was frivolous and reckless in his habits—he went to the theatre occasionally and frequently spent an evening in playing billiards and smoking cigars at a friend's house. There would be real credit in reforming poor cousin Dick.

He was not long, of course, in hearing of Priscilla's marvellous endowment, and upon the first occasion they were alone together treated her with a respect and admiration which he had very certainly never shown her before.

'You're wonderful, Prissie!' he said; 'I'd no idea you had it in you!'

'Nor had I, Dick; but it shows that even a little girl can do something.'

'I should rather think so! and—and the way you look—as grave as a judge all the time! Prissie, I wish you'd tell me how you manage it, I wouldn't tell a soul.'

'But I don't know, Dick. I only talk and the jewels come—that is all.'

'You artful little girl! you can keep a secret, I see, but so can I. And you might tell me how you do the trick. What put you up to the dodge? I'm to be trusted, I assure you.'

'Dick, you can't—you mustn't—think there is any trickery about it! How can you believe I could be such a wicked little girl as to play tricks? It was an old fairy that gave me the gift. I'm sure I don't know why—unless she thought that I was a good child and deserved to be encouraged.'

'By Jove!' cried Dick, 'I never knew you were half such fun!'

'I am not fun, Dick. I think fun is generally so very vulgar, and oh, I wish you wouldn't say "by Jove!" Surely you know he was a heathen god!'

'I seem to have heard of him in some such capacity,' said Dick. 'I say, Prissie, what a ripping big ruby!'

'Ah, Dick, Dick, you are like the others! I'm afraid you think more of the jewels than of any words I may say—and yet *jewels* are common enough!'

'They seem to be with you. Pearls, too, and such fine ones! Here, Priscilla, take them; they're your property.'

Priscilla put her hands behind her: 'No, indeed, Dick, they are of no use to me. Keep them, please; they may help to remind you of what I have said.'

'It's awfully kind of you,' said Dick, looking really touched. 'Then—since you put it in that way—thanks, I will, Priscilla. I'll have them made into a horse-shoe pin.'

'You mustn't let it make you too fond of dress, then,' said Priscilla; 'but I'm afraid you're that already, Dick.'

'A diamond!' he cried; 'go on, Priscilla, I'm listening—pitch into me, it will do me a *lot* of good!'

But Priscilla thought it wisest to say no more just then.

That night, after Priscilla and Cathie and Belle had gone to bed, Dick and his mother sat up talking until a late hour.

'Is dear little cousin Priscilla to be a permanency in this establishment?' began her cousin, stifling a yawn, for there had been a rather copious flow of precious stones during the evening.

'Well, I shall keep her with us as long as I can,' said Mrs. Hoyle, 'she's such a darling, and they don't seem to want her at home. I'm sure, limited as my means are, I'm most happy to have such a visitor.'

'She seems to pay her way—only her way is a trifle trying at times, isn't it? She lectured me for half an hour on end without a single check!'

'Are you sure you picked them all up, dear boy?'

'Got a few of the best in my waistcoat-pocket now. I'm afraid I scrunched a pearl or two, though: they were all over the place, you know. I suppose you've been collecting too, mater?'

'I picked up one or two,' said his mother; 'I should think I must have nearly enough now to fill a bandbox. And that brings me to what I wanted to consult you about, Richard. How are we to dispose of them? She has given them all to me.'

'You haven't done anything with them yet, then?'

'How could I? I have been obliged to stay at home: I've been so afraid of letting that precious

child go out of my sight for a single hour, for fear
some unscrupulous persons might get hold of her. I
thought that perhaps, when you came home, you
would dispose of the jewels for me.'

'But, mater,' protested Dick, 'I can't go about
asking who'll buy a whole bandbox full of jewels!'

'Oh, very well, then; I suppose we must go on
living this hugger-mugger life when we have the
means of being as rich as princes, just because you
are too lazy and selfish to take a little trouble!'

'I know something about these things,' said Dick.
'I know a fellow who's a diamond merchant, and it's
not so easy to sell a lot of valuable stones as you
seem to imagine, mother. And then Priscilla really
overdoes it, you know—why, if she goes on like this,
she'll make diamonds as cheap as currants!'

'*I* should have thought that was a reason for
selling them as soon as possible; but I'm only a
woman, and of course *my* opinion is worth nothing!
Still, you might take some of the biggest to your
friend, and accept whatever he'll give you for them—
there are plenty more, you needn't haggle over the
price.'

'He'd want to know all about them, and what
should I say? I can't tell him a cousin of mine
produces them whenever she feels disposed.'

'You could say they have been in the family for
some time, and you are obliged to part with them; I
don't ask you to tell a falsehood, Richard.'

'Well, to tell you the honest truth,' said Dick,
'I'd rather have nothing to do with it. I'm not
proud, but I shouldn't like it to get about among our
fellows at the bank that I went about hawking diamonds.'

'But, you stupid, undutiful boy, don't you see that
you could leave the bank—you need never do anything
any more—we should all live rich and happy somewhere in the country, if we could only sell those jewels!
And you won't do that one little thing!'

'Well,' said Dick, ' I'll think over it. I'll see what
I can do.'

And his mother knew that it was perfectly useless
to urge him any further: for, in some things, Dick was
as obstinate as a mule, and, in others, far too easy-
going and careless ever to succeed in life. He had
promised to think over it, however, and she had to
be contented with that.

On the evening following this conversation cousin
Dick entered the sitting-room the moment after his
return from the City, and found his mother to all
appearances alone.

'What a dear sweet little guileless angel cousin
Priscilla is, to be sure!' was his first remark.

'Then you *have* sold some of the stones!' cried
Aunt Margarine. ' Sit down, like a good boy, and tell
me all about it.'

'Well,' said Dick, 'I took the finest diamonds and
rubies and pearls that escaped from that saintlike

child last night in the course of some extremely dis-
paraging comments on my character and pursuits—
I took those jewels to Faycett and Rosewater's in New
Bond Street—you know the shop, on the right-hand
side as you go up——'

'Oh, go on, Dick; go on—never mind *where* it is—
how much did you get for them ? '

'I'm coming to that; keep cool, dear mamma.
Well, I went in, and I saw the manager, and I said:
" I want you to make these up into a horse-shoe scarf-
pin for me." '

'You said that ! You never tried to sell one ? Oh,
Dick, you are too provoking ! '

'Hold on, mater; I haven't done yet. So the
manager—a very gentlemanly person, rather thin on
the top of the head—not that that affects his business
capacities; for, after all——'

'Dick, do you want to drive me frantic ! '

'I can't conceive any domestic occurrence which
would be more distressing or generally inconvenient,
mother dear. You do interrupt a fellow so ! I
forgot where I was now—oh, the manager, ah yes !
Well, the manager said, " We shall be very happy
to have the stones made in any design you may
select "—jewellery, by the way, seems to exercise a
most refining influence upon the manners : this man
had the deportment of a duke—" you may select,"
he said ; " but of course I need not tell you that none
of these stones are genuine." '

'Not genuine!' cried Aunt Margarine excitedly.
'They must be—he was lying!'

'West-end jewellers never lie,' said Dick; 'but
naturally, when he said that, I told him I should like
to have some proof of his assertion. "Will you take
the risk of testing?" said he. "Test away, my dear
man!" said I. So he brought a little wheel near the
emerald—"whizz!" and away went the emerald!
Then he let a drop of something fall on the ruby—and
it fizzled up for all the world like pink champagne.
"Go on, don't mind *me*!" I told him, so he touched
the diamond with an electric wire—"phit!" and there
was only something that looked like the ash of a
shocking bad cigar. Then the pearls—and they
popped like so many air-balloons. "Are you
satisfied?" he asked.

' "Oh, perfectly," ' said I, "you needn't trouble
about the horse-shoe pin now. Good evening," and
so I came away, after thanking him for his very
amusing scientific experiments.'

'And do you believe that the jewels are all shams,
Dick?—do you really?'

'I think it so probable that nothing on earth will
induce me to offer a single one for sale. I should
never hear the last of it at the bank. No, mater,
dear little Priscilla's sparkling conversation may be
unspeakably precious from a moral point of view, but
it has no commercial value. Those jewels are bogus
—shams every stone of them!'

. Now, all this time our heroine had been sitting unperceived in a corner behind a window-curtain, reading 'The Wide, Wide World,' a work which she was never weary of perusing. Some children would have come forward earlier, but Priscilla was never a forward child, and she remained as quiet as a little mouse up to the moment when she could control her feelings no longer.

'It isn't true!' she cried passionately, bursting out of her retreat and confronting her cousin; 'it's cruel and unkind to say my jewels are shams! They are real—they are, they *are!*'

'Hullo, Prissie!' said her abandoned cousin; 'so you combine jewel-dropping with eaves-dropping, eh?'

'How dare you!' cried Aunt Margarine, almost beside herself, 'you odious little prying minx, setting up to teach your elders and your betters with your cut and dried priggish maxims! When I think how I have petted and indulged you all this time, and borne with the abominable litter you left in every room you entered—and now to find you are only a little, conceited, hypocritical impostor—oh, *why* haven't I words to express my contempt for such conduct—why am I dumb at such a moment as this?'

'Come, mother,' said her son soothingly, 'that's not such a bad beginning; I should call it fairly fluent and expressive, myself.'

'Be quiet, Dick! I'm speaking to this wicked child, who has obtained our love and sympathy and attention on false pretences, for which she ought to be put in prison—yes, in *prison*, for such a heartless trick on relatives who can ill afford to be so cruelly disappointed ! '

' But, aunt ! ' expostulated poor Priscilla, ' you always said you only kept the jewels as souvenirs, and that it did you so much good to hear me talk ! '

' Don't argue with *me*, miss ! If I had known the stones were wretched tawdry imitations, do you imagine for an instant—— ? '

' Now, mother,' said Dick, ' be fair—they were uncommonly good imitations, you must admit that ! '

' Indeed, indeed I thought they were real, the fairy never told me ! '

' After all,' said Dick, ' it's not Priscilla's fault. She can't help it if the stones aren't real, and she made up for quality by quantity anyhow; didn't you, Prissie ? '

Hold your tongue, Richard ; she *could* help it, she knew it all the time, and she's a hateful, sanctimonious little stuck-up viper, and so I tell her to her face ! '

Priscilla could scarcely believe that kind, indulgent, smooth-spoken Aunt Margarine could be addressing such words to her ; it frightened her so much that she did not dare to answer, and just then Cathie and Belle came into the room.

' Oh, mother,' they began penitently, ' we're *so*

sorry, but we couldn't find dear Prissie anywhere, so we haven't picked up anything the whole afternoon !'

'Ah, my poor darlings, you shall never be your cousin's slaves any more. Don't go near her, she's a naughty, deceitful wretch; her jewels are false, my sweet loves, false! She has imposed upon us all, she does not deserve to associate with you !'

'I always said Prissie's jewels looked like the things you get on crackers !' said Belle, tossing her head.

'Now we shall have a little rest, I hope,' chimed in Cathie.

'I shall send her home to her parents this very night,' declared Aunt Margarine; 'she shall not stay here to pervert our happy household with her miserable *gewyaws !*'

Here Priscilla found her tongue. 'Do you think I *want* to stay ?' she said proudly; 'I see now that you only wanted to have me here because—because of the horrid jewels, and I never knew they were false, and I let you have them all, every one, you know I did; and I wanted you to mind what I said and not trouble about picking them up, but you *would* do it ! And now you all turn round upon me like this ! What have I done to be treated so ? What have I done ?'

'Bravo, Prissie !' cried Dick. 'Mother, if you ask me, I think it serves us all jolly well right, and it's a downright shame to bullyrag poor Prissie in this way!'

'I *don't* ask you,' retorted his mother, sharply; 'so you will kindly keep your opinions to yourself.'

'Tra-la-la!' sang rude Dick, 'we are a united family—we are, we are, we *are*!'—a vulgar refrain he had picked up at one of the burlesque theatres he was only too fond of frequenting.

But Priscilla came to him and held out her hand quite gratefully and humbly. 'Thank you, Dick,' she said; '*you* are kind, at all events. And I am sorry you couldn't have your horse-shoe pin!'

'Oh, *hang* the horse-shoe pin!' exclaimed Dick, and poor Priscilla was so thoroughly cast down that she quite forgot to reprove him.

She was not sent home that night after all, for Dick protested against it in such strong terms that even Aunt Margarine saw that she must give way; but early on the following morning Priscilla quitted her aunt's house, leaving her belongings to be sent on after her.

She had not far to walk, and it so happened that her way led through the identical lane in which she had met the fairy. Wonderful to relate, there, on the very same stone and in precisely the same attitude, sat the old lady, peering out from under her poke-bonnet, and resting her knotty old hands on her crutch-handled stick!

Priscilla walked past with her head in the air,

F

pretending not to notice her, for she considered that the fairy had played her a most malicious and ill-natured trick.

'Heyday!' said the old lady (it is only fairies who can permit themselves such old-fashioned expressions nowadays). 'Heyday, why, here's my good little girl again! Isn't she going to speak to me?'

'No, she's not,' said Priscilla—but she found herself compelled to stop, notwithstanding.

'Why, what's all this about? You're not going to sulk with me, my dear, are you?'

'I think you're a very cruel, bad, unkind old woman for deceiving me like this!'

'Goodness me! Why, didn't the jewels come, after all?'

'Yes—they came, only they were all horrid artificial ones—and it is a shame, it *is*!' cried poor Priscilla from her bursting heart.

'Artificial, were they? that really is very odd! Can you account for that at all, now?'

'Of course I can't! You told me that they would drop out whenever I said anything to improve people —and I was *always* saying *something* improving! Aunt had a bandbox in her room quite full of them.'

'Ah, you've been very industrious, evidently; it's unfortunate your jewels should all have been artificial —most unfortunate. I don't know how to explain it, unless'—(and here the old lady looked up queerly from under her white eyelashes), 'unless your goodness was artificial too ?'

'How do you mean?' asked Priscilla, feeling strangely uncomfortable. 'I'm sure I've never done anything the least bit naughty—how can my goodness possibly be artificial ?'

'Ah, that I can't explain; but I know this—that people who are really good are generally the last persons to suspect it, and the moment they become aware of it and begin to think how good they are, and how bad everybody else is, why, somehow or other, their goodness crumbles away and leaves only a sort of outside shell behind it. And—I'm very old, and of course I may be mistaken—but I think (I only say I *think*, mind) that a little girl so young as you must have some faults hidden about her somewhere, and that perhaps on the whole she would be better employed in trying to find them out and cure them before she attempted to correct those of other people. And I'm sure it can't be good for any child to be always seeing herself in a little picture, just as she likes to fancy other people see her. Very many pretty books are written about good little girls, and it is quite true that children may exercise a great influence for good—more than they can ever tell, perhaps—but only just so long as they remain natural and unconscious, and not unwholesome little pragmatical prigesses; for then they make themselves and other people worse than they might have been. But of course, my dear, you never made such a mistake as that!'

Priscilla turned very red, and began to scrape one of her feet against the other; she was thinking, and her thoughts were not at all pleasant ones.

'Oh, fairy,' she said at last, 'I'm afraid that's just what I *did* do. I was always thinking how good I was and putting everybody—papa, mamma, Alick, Betty, Aunt Margarine, Cathie, Belle, and even poor cousin Dick—right! I have been a horrid little hateful prig, and that's why all the jewels were rubbish. But, oh, shall I have to go on talking sham diamonds and things all the rest of my life?'

'That,' said the fairy, 'depends entirely on yourself. You have the remedy in your own hands—or lips.'

'Ah, you mean I needn't talk at all? But I must —sometimes. I couldn't bear to be dumb as long as I lived—and it would look so odd, too!'

'I never said you were not to open your lips at all. But can't you try to talk simply and naturally —not like little girls or boys in any story-books what-ever—not to "show off" or improve people; only as a girl would talk who remembers that, after all, her elders are quite as likely as she is to know what they ought or ought not to do and say?'

'I shall forget sometimes, I know I shall!' said Priscilla disconsolately.

'If you do, there will be something to remind you, you know. And by and by, perhaps, as you grow up you may, quite by accident, say something sincere and noble and true—and then a jewel will fall which will really be of value! '

' No! ' cried Priscilla, ' no, *please*! Oh, fairy, let me off that! If I *must* drop them, let them be false ones to punish me—not real. I don't want to be rewarded any more for being good—if I ever am really good! '

' Come,' said the fairy, with a much pleasanter smile, ' you are not a hopeless case, at all events. It shall be as you wish, then, and perhaps it will be the wisest arrangement for all parties. Now run away home, and see how little use you can make of your fairy gift.'

Priscilla found her family still at breakfast.

' Why,' observed her father, raising his eyebrows as she entered the room, ' here's our little monitor— (or is it *monitress*, eh, Priscilla ?)—back again. Children, we shall all have to mind our p's and q's— and, indeed, our entire alphabet, now! '

' I'm sure,' said her mother, kissing her fondly, ' Priscilla knows we're all delighted to have her home! '

' *I'm* not,' said Alick, with all a boy's engaging candour.

' Nor am I,' added Betty, ' it's been ever so much nicer at home while she's been away! '

Priscilla burst into tears as she hid her face upon

her mother's protecting shoulder. 'It's true!' she sobbed, 'I don't deserve that you should be glad to see me — I've been hateful and horrid, I know —but, oh, if you'll only forgive me and love me and put up with me a little, I'll try not to preach and be a prig any more—I will truly!'

And at this her father called her to his side and embraced her with a fervour he had not shown for a very long time.

.   .   .   .   .   .

I should not like to go so far as to assert that no imitation diamond, ruby, pearl, or emerald ever proceeded from Priscilla's lips again. Habits are not cured in a day, and fairies—however old they may be—are still fairies; so it *did* occasionally happen that a mock jewel made an unwelcome appearance after one of Priscilla's more unguarded utterances. But she was always frightfully ashamed and abashed by such an accident, and buried the imitation stones immediately in a corner of the garden. And as time went on the jewels grew smaller and smaller, and frequently dissolved upon her tongue, leaving a faintly bitter taste, until at last they ceased altogether and Priscilla became as pleasant and unaffected a girl as she who may now be finishing this history.

Aunt Margarine never sent back the contents of that bandbox; she kept the biggest stones and had a brooch made of them, while, as she never mentioned that they were false, no one out of the family ever so much as suspected it.

But, for all that, she always declared that her niece Priscilla had bitterly disappointed her expectations—which was perhaps the truest thing that Aunt Margarine ever said.

A MATTER OF TASTE

PART I

It is a little singular that, upon an engagement becoming known and being discussed by the friends and acquaintances of the persons principally concerned, by far the most usual tone of comment should be a sorrowing wonder. That particular alliance is generally the very last that anybody ever expected. 'What made him choose *her*, of all people,' and 'What on earth she could see in *him*,' are declared insoluble problems. It is confidently predicted that the engagement will never come to anything, or that, if such a marriage ever does take place, it is most unlikely to prove a success.

Sometimes, in the case of female friends, this ton is even perceptible under their warmest felicitations, and through the smiling mask of compliment shine eyes moist with the most irritating quality of compassion. 'So glad! so delighted! But why, *why* didn't you consult *me*?'—this complicated expression might be rendered : ' I could have saved you from this—I *was* so pleased to hear of it ! '

And yet, in the majority of cases, these unions are not found to turn out so very badly after all, and the misguided couple seem really to have gauged their own hearts and their possibilities of happiness together more accurately than the most clear-sighted of their acquaintances.

The announcement that Ella Hylton had accepted George Chapman provoked the customary sensation and surprise in their respective sets, and perhaps with rather more justification than usual.

Miss Hylton had undeniable beauty of a spiritual and rather *exalté* type, and was generally understood to be highly cultivated. She had spent a year at Somerville, though she had gone down without trying for a place in either ' Mods.' or ' Greats,' thereby preserving, if not increasing, her reputation for superiority. She had lived all her life among cultured people ; she was devoted to music and regularly attended the Richter Concerts, though she could seldom be induced to play in public ; she had a feeling for art, though she neither painted nor drew ; a love of literature strong enough to deter her from all amateur efforts in that direction. In art, music and literature she was impatient of mediocrity ; and, while she was as fond as most girls of the pleasures which upper middle-class society can offer, she reverenced intellect, and preferred the conversation of the plainest celebrity to

the platitudes of the mere dancing-man, no matter
how handsome of feature and perfect of step he might
be.

George Chapman was certainly not a mere dancing-
man, his waltzing being rather conscientious than
dreamlike, and he was only tolerably good-looking.
On the other hand, he was not celebrated in any way,
and even his mother and sisters had never considered
him brilliant. He had been educated at Rugby and
Trinity, Cambridge, where he rowed a fairly good oar,
on principle, and took a middle second in the Moral
Science Tripos. Now he was in a solicitor's office,
where he was receiving a good salary, and was valued
as a steady, sensible young fellow, who could be
thoroughly depended upon. He was fond of his profession, and had acquired a considerable knowledge
of its details; apart from it he had no very decided
tastes; he lived a quiet, regular life, and dined out and
went to dances in moderation; his manner, though
he was nearly twenty-six, was still rather boyishly
blunt.

What there was in him that had found favour in
Ella Hylton's fastidious eyes the narrator is not rash
enough to attempt to particularise. But it may be
suggested that the most unlikely people may possess
their fairy rose and ring which render them irresistible
to at least one heart, if they only have faith to believe
in and luck to perceive their power.

So, early in the year, George had plucked up

courage to propose to Miss Hylton, after meeting and secretly adoring her for some months past, and she, to the general astonishment, had accepted him.

He had a private income—not a large one—of his own, and had saved out of it. She was entitled under her grandmother's will to a sum which made her an heiress in a modest way, and thus there was no reason why the engagement should be a long one, and, though no date had been definitely fixed for the marriage, it was understood that it should take place at some time before the end of the summer.

Soon after the engagement, however, an invalid aunt with whom Ella had always been a great favourite was ordered to the south of France, and implored her to go with her; which Ella, who had a real affection for her relative, as well as a strong sense of duty, had consented to do.

This was a misfortune in one of two ways: it either curtailed that most necessary and most delightful period during which *fiancés* discover one another's idiosyncrasies and weaknesses, or it made it necessary to postpone the marriage.

George naturally preferred the former, as the more endurable evil; but Ella's letters from abroad began to hint more and more plainly at delay. Her aunt might remain on the Continent all the summer, and she could not possibly leave her; there was so much to be done after her return that could not be done in a hurry; they had not even begun to furnish the

pretty little house on Campden Hill that was to be
their new home—it would be better to wait till
November, or even later.

The mere idea was alarming to George, and he
remonstrated as far as he dared; but Ella remained
firm, and he grew desperate.

He might have spared himself the trouble. About
the middle of June Ella's aunt—who, of course, had
had to leave the Riviera—grew tired of travelling,
and Ella, to George's intense satisfaction, returned to
her mother's house in Linden Gardens, Notting.
Hill.

And now, when our story opens, George, who had
managed to get away from office-work two hours
before his usual time, was hurrying towards Linden
Gardens as fast as a hansom could take him, to see
his betrothed for the first time after their long
separation.

He was eager, naturally, and a little nervous.
Would Ella still persist in her wish for delay? or
would he be able to convince her that there were no
obstacles in the way? He felt he had strong argu-
ments on his side, if only—and here was the real seat
of his anxiety—if only her objections were not raised
from some other motive! She might have been
trying to prepare him for a final rupture, and then—
' Well,' he concluded, with his customary good sense,.
' no use meeting trouble halfway—in five minutes I
shall know for certain ! '

. . . . . .

At the same moment Mrs. Hylton and her daughter Flossie, a vivacious girl in the transitionary sixteen-year-old stage, were in the drawing-room at Linden Gardens. It was the ordinary double drawing-room of a London house, but everything in it was beautiful and harmonious. The eye was vaguely rested by the delicate and subdued colour of walls and hangings; cabinets, antique Persian pottery, rare bits of china, all occupied the precise place in which their decorative value was most felt; a room, in short, of exceptional individuality and distinction.

Flossie was standing at the window, from which a glimpse could just be caught of fresh green foliage and the lodge-gates, with the bustle of the traffic in the High Street beyond; Mrs. Hylton was writing at a Flemish bureau in the corner.

'I suppose,' said Flossie meditatively, as she fingered a piece of old stained glass that was hanging in the window, 'we shall have George here this afternoon.'

Mrs. Hylton raised her head. She had a striking face, tinted a clear olive, with a high wave of silver hair crowning the forehead; her eyebrows were dark, and so were the brilliant eyes; the nose was aquiline, and the thin, well-cut mouth a little hard. She was a woman who had been much admired in her time, and who still retained a certain attraction, though some were apt to find her somewhat cold and unsympathetic.

Her daughter Ella, for example, was always secretly a little in awe of her mother, who, however, had no terrors for audacious, outspoken Flossie.

'If he comes, Flossie, he will be very welcome,' she said, 'but I hardly expect him yet. George is not likely to neglect his duties, even for Ella.'

Flossie pursed her mouth rather scornfully: 'Oh, George is immaculate!' she murmured.

'If he was, it would hardly be a reproach,' said her mother, catching the word; 'but, at all events, George has thoroughly good principles, and is sure to succeed in the world. I have every reason to be pleased.'

'Every reason?—ah! but *are* you pleased? Mother, dear, you know he's as dull as dull!'

'Ella does not find him so—and, Flossie, I don't like to hear you say such things, even in Ella's absence.'

'Oh, I never abuse him to Ella; it wouldn't be any use: she's firmly convinced that he's perfection—at least she was before she went away.'

'Why? do you mean that she has altered?—have you seen any sign of it, Flossie?'

Mrs. Hylton made this inquiry sharply, but not as if such a circumstance would be altogether displeasing to her.

'Oh, no; only she hasn't seen him for so long, you know. Perhaps, when she comes to look at him with fresh eyes, she'll notice things more. Ah, here *is*

George, just getting out of a hansom—so he has played truant for once ! There's one thing I *do* think Ella might do—persuade him to shave off some of those straggly whiskers. I wonder why he never seems to get a hat or anything else like other people's ! '

Presently George was announced. He was slightly above middle height, broad-shouldered and fresh-coloured; the obnoxious whiskers did indeed cover more of his cheeks than modern fashion prescribes for men of his age, and had evidently never known a razor ; he wore a turn-down collar and a necktie of a rather crude red ; his clothes were neat and well brushed, but not remarkable for their cut.

'Well, my dear George,' said Mrs. Hylton, 'we have seen very little of you while Ella has been away.'

'I know,' he said awkwardly ; 'I've had a lot of things to look after in one way and another.'

'What ? after your work at the office was over ! ' cried Flossie incredulously.

'Yes—after that ; it's taken up my time a good deal.'

'And so you couldn't spare any to call here—I see ! ' said Flossie. 'George,' she added, with a sudden diversion, 'I wonder you aren't afraid of catching cold ! How *can* you go about in such absurdly thin boots as those ? '

'These ? ' he said, inspecting them doubtfully— they were strong, sensible boots with notched and projecting soles of ponderous thickness—' why, what's the matter with them, Flossie, eh? Don't you think they're strong enough for walking in? '

' No, George; they're the very things for an after-noon dance, and quite a lot of couples could dance in them, you see. But for walking—ah, I'm afraid you sacrifice too much to appearances.'

' I don't, really ! ' George protested in all good faith ; ' now *do* I, Mrs. Hylton ? '

' Flossie is making fun of you, George ; you mustn't mind her impertinence.'

' Oh, is that all ? Do you know, I really thought for the moment that she meant they were too small for me ! You like getting a rise out of me, Flossie, don't you ? '

And he laughed with such genuine and good-natured amusement that the young lady felt somehow a little small, and almost ashamed, although it took the form of suppressed irritation. ' He really ought not to come here in such things,' she said to herself ; ' and I don't believe that, even now, he sees what I meant.'

Just at this point Ella came in, with the least touch of shyness, perhaps, at meeting him before wit-nesses after so long an absence ; but she only looked the more charming in consequence, and, demure as her greeting was, her pretty eyes had a sparkle of pleasure that scattered all George Chapman's fears to the winds. Even Flossie felt instinctively that straggly-whiskered, red-necktied, thick-booted George had lost none of his divinity for Ella.

They did not seem to have much to say to one another, notwithstanding; possibly because Ella was called upon to dispense the tea which had just been brought in. George sat nursing the hat which Flossie found so objectionable, while he balanced a teacup with the anxious eye of a juggler out of practice, and the conversation flagged. At last, under pretence of renewing his tea, most of which he had squandered upon a Persian rug, he crossed to Ella: 'I say,' he suggested, 'don't you think you could come out for a little while? I've such lots to tell you and—and I want you to go somewhere with me.'

Mrs. Hylton made no objection, beyond stipulating that Ella must not be allowed to tire herself after her journey, and so, a few minutes later, Miss Hylton came down in her pretty summer hat and light cape, and she and George were allowed to set out.

Once outside the house, he drew a long breath of mingled relief and pleasure: 'By Jove, Ella, I am glad to get you back again! I say, how jolly you do look in that hat! Now, do you know where I'm going to take you?'

'It will be quietest in the Gardens,' said Ella.

'Ah, but that's not where you're going now,' he said with a delicious assumption of authority; 'you're coming with me to see a certain house on Campden Hill you may have heard of.'

G

' That will be delightful. I do want to see our dear
little house again very much. And, George, we will
go carefully over all the rooms, and settle what can
be done with each of them. Then we can begin directly;
we haven't too much time.'

' Perhaps,' he said with a conscious laugh, ' it
won't take so much time as you think.'

' Oh, but it *must*—to do properly. And while I've
been away I've had some splendid ideas for some of
the rooms—I've planned them out so beautifully. You
know that delightful little room at the back ?—the one
I said should be your own den, with the window all
festooned with creepers and looking out on the garden
—well—— ?'

' Take my advice,' he said, ' and don't make any
plans till you see it. And as for plans, these furnishing fellows do all that—they don't care to be bothered
with plans.'

' They will have to carry out ours, though. I shall
love settling how it is all to be—it will be such fun.'

' You wouldn't call it fun if you knew what it was
like, I can tell you.'

' But I *do* know. Mother and I rearranged most
of the rooms at home only last year—so you see I have
some experience. And what experience can *you* have
had, if you please ? '

Ella had a mental vision as she spoke of the house
in Dawson Place when George lived with his mother
and sisters—a house in which furniture and every-

thing else were commonplace and *bourgeois* to the last
degree, and where nothing could have been altered
since his boyhood ; indeed she had often secretly
pitied him for having to live in such surroundings,
and admired the filial patience that had made him
endure them so long.

'I've had my share, Ella, and I should be very
sorry for you to have all the worry and bother I've
been through over it ! '

'But when, George ? How ? I don't understand.'

'Ah, that's my secret ! ' he said provokingly ; 'and
you know, Ella, if we began furnishing now, it would
take no end of a time, with all these wonderful plans
of yours, and—and I couldn't stand having to wait
till next November for you—I couldn't do it ! '

'Mother thinks the marriage need not be put off
now,' said Ella simply, 'and we shall have six weeks
till then ; the house can be quite ready for us by the
time we want it.'

'Six weeks ! ' he said impatiently, 'what's six
weeks ? You've no idea what these chaps are, Ella !
And then there are all your own things to get, and
they would take up most of your time. No, we should
have had to put it off, whatever you may say. And
that would mean another separation—for, of course,
you would go away in August, and I should have to
stay in town : the office wouldn't give me my fortnight
twice over—honeymoon or no honeymoon ! '

Ella looked completely puzzled. 'But what are
you trying to prove *now*, George ? '

'I was only showing you that, even though you
have come back earlier, we couldn't possibly have got
things ready in time, if I hadn't——' but here he
stopped. 'No, I want that to be a surprise for you,
Ella ; you'll see presently,' he added.

Ella's delicate eyebrows contracted. 'I like to be
prepared for my surprises, please, George. Tell me
now.'

They had turned up one of the quiet streets leading
to the hill. They were so near the house that George
thought he might abandon further mystery, not to
mention that he was only too anxious to reveal his
secret.

'Well, then, Ella, if you must have it,' he said
triumphantly, 'the house is very nearly ready *now*—
what do you think of that ? '

'Do you mean that—that it is furnished,
George ?'

'Papered, painted, decorated, furnished—everything, from top to bottom ! I thought that would
surprise you, Ella ! '

'I think,' she answered slowly, 'you might have
told me you were doing it.'

'What ! before it was all done ? That would have
spoilt it all, dear. I should have written, though, if
you hadn't been coming home so soon. And now it's
finished I must say it looks uncommonly jolly. I'm

sure you'll be pleased with it—it looks quite a different place.'

She tried to smile : 'And did you do it all your-self, George ? '

'Well, no—not exactly. I flatter myself I know how to see that the work's properly done, and all that ; but there are some things I don't pretend to be much of a hand at, so I got certain ladies to give me some wrinkles.'

Ella felt relieved. She was disappointed, it is true—hurt, even, at having been deprived of any voice in the matter. She had been looking forward so much to carrying out her pet schemes, to enjoying her friends' admiration of the wonders wrought by her artistic invention. And she had never thought of George, somehow, as likely to have any strikingly original ideas on the subject of decoration, although she liked him none the less for that.

But it was something that he had had the good sense to take her mother and Flossie into his confidence : she knew she could trust them to preserve him from any serious mistakes.

'You see,' said George, half apologetically, ' I would ever so much rather have waited till you came back, only I couldn't tell when that would be. I really couldn't help myself. You're sure you don't mind about it ? If you only knew how I worked over it, rushing about from one place to another, as soon as I could get away from the office, picking up bits of

furniture here and there, standing over those beggars
of painters and keeping 'em at it, and working out
estimates and seeing foremen and managers and all
kinds of chaps! I used to get home dead-tired of an
evening; but I didn't mind that : I felt it was all bringing you nearer to me, darling, and that made everything a pleasure !'

There was such honest affection in his look and
voice; he had so evidently intended to please her, and
had been in such manifest dread of any further
separation from her, that she was completely disarmed.

'Dear George,' she said gently, 'I am so sorry
you took all the trouble on yourself; it was very, very
good of you to care so much, and I know I shall be
delighted with the house.'

'Well,' said George, 'I'm not much afraid about
that, because I expect our tastes are pretty much the
same in most things.'

They were by this time at the house, and George,
after a little fumbling with his as yet unfamiliar
latchkey, threw open the door with a flourish and
said, 'There you are, little woman ! Walk in and you'll
see what you shall see ! '

No sooner was Ella inside the hall than her heart
sank : 'Looks neat and nice, doesn't it ? ' said George
cheerfully. 'You'd almost take that paper for real
marble, wouldn't you ? See how well they've done
those veins. I like this yellowish colour better than

green, don't you ? It looks so cool in summer. That's
a good strong hall-lamp—not what you call high art,
exactly—but gives a rattling good light, and that's
the main thing. Here, I'll light it up for you—confound it! they haven't turned the gas on yet. However, there's too much sunshine for it to show much,
if they had. This linoleum is a capital thing : you
might scrub as long as you liked and you'd never get
that pattern out ! '

'No,' Ella agreed, with a tragic little smile, 'it—it
looks as if it would last.'

'Last ! I should just think so ! And here's a hatstand—you could almost swear it was carved wood of
some sort, but it's only cast-iron painted ; indestruct-
ible, you see ; they told me that was the latest dodge
—wonderful how cheaply they turn them out, isn't
it ? '

'I thought you said you were helped ? '

'Oh, I didn't want any help *here*—this is only the
passage, you know ! '

Yes, it was only the passage—and yet she had
been picturing such a charming entrance, with a
draped arch, a graceful lamp, a fresh bright paper, a
small buffet of genuine old oak, and so on. She suppressed a sigh as she passed on ; after all, so long as
the rooms themselves were all right, it did not so very
much matter, and she knew that her mother's taste
could be trusted.

But on the threshold of the dining-room she

stopped aghast. The walls had been distempered a
particularly hideous drab; the curtains were mustard
yellow; the carpet was a dull brown; the mottled
marble mantelpiece, for which she had been intending
to substitute one in walnut wood with tiles, still shone
in slabs of petrified brawn; there was a huge maho-
gany sideboard of a kind she had only seen in old-
fashioned hotels.

'Comfortable, eh?' remarked George. 'Lots of
wear in those curtains!'

Unhappily there was, as Ella was only too well
aware. 'You did *this* room yourself too, then,
George?' she managed to say, without betraying
herself by her voice.

'Yes, I chose everything here. You see, Ella, we
shall only use this room for meals.'

'Only for meals, yes,' she acquiesced with a
shudder; 'but—George, surely you said mother had
helped you with the rooms?'

'What! your mother? No, Ella; her notions are
rather too grand for me. It was Jessie and Carrie I
meant. Just come and see what they've made of my
den.'

Ella followed. The window—which had commanded such a cheerful outlook into one of the
pretty gardens, with a pink thorn, a laburnum-tree
or two, and some sycamores which still flourish fresh
and fair on Campden Hill—was obscured now by

some detestable contrivance in transparent paper
imitating stained glass.

'That was the girls' notion,' said George, following the direction of her eyes ; ' they fixed it all themselves—it was their present to me. Pretty of them to
think of it, wasn't it ?   I call it an immense improvement, and, you see, it's stuck on with some patent
cement varnish, so it can't rub off.   You get the effect
better if you stand here —*now*, see how well the colours
come out in the sun ! '

If only they *would* come out!   But what could she
do but stand and admire hypocritically ? Her eyes, in
spite of herself, seemed drawn to that bright-hued
sham intersected by black lines intended to represent
leading ; of the room itself she only saw vaguely that
it was not unworthy of the window.

'Nothing to what they've done with the drawing-
room ! ' said innocent George, beaming ; ' come along,
darling, you'll scarcely know the place.'

And Ella, reduced to a condition of stony stupor,
followed to the drawing-room.   She did not know the
place, indeed.   It was a quaintly-shaped, irregular
room, with French windows opening upon the garden
on one side and a deep bow-window on another ; when
she had last seen it, the walls were covered with a
paper so pleasing in tone and design that she had
almost decided to retain it.   That paper was gone,
and in its place a gaudy semi-Chinese pattern of
unknown birds, flying and perching on sprawling

branches laden with impossible flowers. And then
the furniture—the 'elegant drawing-room suite' in
brilliant plush and shiny satin, the cheap cabinets,
and the ready-made black and gilt overmantel, with
its panels of swans, hawthorn-blossom, and landscapes
sketchily daubed on dead gold—surely it had all been
transferred bodily from the stage of some carelessly
mounted farcical comedy !

Ella's horrified gaze gradually took in other
features—the china monkeys swinging on cords, the
porcelain parrots hanging in great brass rings, huge
misshapen terra-cotta jars and pots, dead grass in
bloated drain-pipes, tambourines, beribboned and
painted with kittens and robins, enormous wooden
sabots, gilded Japanese fans, a woolly white rug and a
bright Kidderminster carpet.

'*Oh*, George !' burst involuntarily from her
lips.

' I knew you'd be pleased !' he said complacently ;
' but I mustn't take all the credit myself. It was like
this, you see : I felt all right enough about the other
rooms, but the drawing-room—that's *your* room, and
I was awfully afraid of not having it exactly as it
ought to be. So I went to the girls, and I said, " *You*
know all about these things—just make it what you
think Ella will like, and then we can't go wrong !"
We had that Grosvenor Gallery paper down first of
all. "Choose something bright and cheerful," I said,
and I don't think they've chosen badly. Then the

pottery and china and all that—those are the girls'
presents to *you*, with their best love.'

' It—it's very good of them,' said poor Ella, on
the verge of tears.

' Oh, they think a lot of you! They were rather
nervous about doing anything at first, for fear you
mightn't like it; but I told them they needn't be
afraid. " What I like, Ella will like," I said ; and, I
must say, no one could wish to see a prettier drawing-
room than they've turned it into—they've a good deal
of taste, those two girls.'

Ella stood there in a kind of dreary dream. What
had happened to the world since she came into this
house? What was this change in her? She was
afraid to speak, lest the intense rebellious anger she
felt should gain the mastery. Was it she that had
these wicked thoughts of George—poor, kind, unsus-
pecting, loving George? She felt a little faint, for the
windows were closed and the room stuffy with the
odour of the new furniture and the atmosphere of the
workshop; everything here seemed to her commonplace and repulsive.

' How about those plans of yours now, Ella, eh? '
cried George.

This was too much; her overtried patience broke
down. 'George! ' she cried impulsively, and her voice
sounded hoarse and strange to her own ear ; ' George!
I must speak—I must tell you!——' and then she
checked herself. She must keep command of herself, or

she could not, without utter loss of dignity, find the
words that were to sting him into a sense of what he
had done and allowed to be done. Before she could
go on, George had drawn her to him, and was patting
her shoulder tenderly. 'I know, dear little girl,' he
said, 'I know; don't try to tell me anything. I'm so
awfully glad you're pleased; but all the money and
pains in the world wouldn't make the place good
enough for my Ella!'

She released herself with a little cry of impotent
despair. How could she say the sharp, cruel speeches
that were struggling to reach her tongue now? It
was no use; she was a coward; she simply had not
the courage to undeceive him here, on the very first
day of their reunion, too!

'You haven't been upstairs yet,' said George,
dropping sentiment abruptly; 'shall we go up?'

Ella assented submissively, much as even this cost
her; but it was better, she reflected, to get it over and
know the very worst. However, she was spared this
ordeal for the present; as they returned to the hall,
they found themselves suddenly face to face with a
dingy man, whose face was surrounded by a fringe of
black whiskers and crowned by a shock of fleecy
hair.

'Who on earth are you?' demanded George, as
the man rose from the kitchen-stairs.

'No offence, sir and lady! Peagrum, that's *my*
name, fust shop round the corner as you go into

Silver Street, plumber and sanitry hengineer, gas-
fittin' and hartistic decorating, bell-'anging in all
its branches. I received instructions from Mr. Jones
that I was to look into a little matter o' leakage in
the back-kitchen sink ; also to see what taps, if hany,
required seein' to, and gen'ally to put things straight
like. So I come round, 'aving the keys, jest to cast a
heye over them, as I may term it, preliminry to com-
mencing work in the course of a week or so, as soon
as I'm at libity to attend to it pussonally.'

'Oh, the landlord sent you ? All right, then.'

'Correct, sir,' said the plumber affably. 'While I've
been 'ere, I took the freedom of going all over this
little 'ouse, and a nice cosy little 'ouse you've made of
it, for such a nouse as it is ! You've done it up very
tysty—very tysty you've done this little 'ouse up ; and
I've some claim to speak, seein' as how I've had the
decoration throughout of a many 'ouses in my time,
likewise mansions. You ain't been too ambitious,
which is the error most parties falls into with small
'ouses. Now the parties as 'ad the place before you
—by the name o' Rummles—well, I daresay they
satisfied theirselves, but the 'ouse never looked right
—not to *my* taste, it didn't ! '

'George, get rid of this person ! ' said Ella rapidly,
under her breath, in French. Unfortunately, George's
acquaintance with that tongue was about on a par
with the plumber's, and he remained passive.

The plumber now proceeded to put down his

mechanic's straw-bag upon the hall-table, which he did with great care, as if it were of priceless stuff and contained fragile articles ; having done this, he posed himself with one elbow resting on the post at the foot of the staircase, like a grimy statue of Shakespeare.

'Ah,' he said, shaking his touzled head, ' this ain't the fust time I've been 'ere in my puffessional capacity, not by a long way. Not by a long way, it ain't. Mr. Rummles, him as I mentioned to you afore, and a nice pleasant-spoken gentleman he was, too—in the tea trade—Mr. Rummles, he allus sent round for me whenever there was hany odd jobs as wanted doin', and in course I was allus pleased to get 'em, be they hodd or hotherwise.'

'Er-exactly,' said George, as soon as he could put in a word ; ' but you see, this lady and I——'

The plumber, however, did not abandon his position, and seemed determined that they should hear him :

'I know, sir—I see how things were with you with 'arf a glance ; but afore we go any further, it's right you should know 'oo I am and all about me. Jest 'ear what I'm goin' to tell you, for it's somethink out of the common way, though gospel-truth. It's a melinkly reflection for a man in my station of life, but '—and here he lowered his voice to a solemn pitch—' I've never set foot inside of this 'ere 'ouse without somethink 'appens more or less immejit. Ah, it's true, though. Seems almost like as if I

brought a fatality in along o' me. Don't you interrupt; you wait till I'm done, and see if I'm talking
at random or without facks to support me. Well, *fust*
time as ever I was sent for 'ere was in regard to
drains, as they couldn't flush satisfactory. I did my
work and come away. Not three weeks arter, Miss
Rummles, the heldest gell, was took ill with typhoid.
Never the same young lady again—nor yet she never
won't be neither, not if she lives to a nundered. " Nothing very hodd about *that*? " says you. Wait a bit.
Next time, it was the kitching copper as had got all
furred up like. I tinkered that up to rights, and come
away. Well, afore I'd even made out my account,
that identical copper blew up and scalded the cook
dreadful! " Coppers will play these games," you sez.
All right, then; but you let me finish. Third time
there was a flaw in one of the gas-brackets in the
spare room. I soddered it up and I come away.
Soon arterwards, a day or two as it might be, Mrs.
Rummles 'ad 'er mar a-stayin' with her, and the old
lady slep in that very room, and was laid up weeks!
" Curus," says I, when I come to 'ear of it, " *very*
curus! " and it set me a-thinkin'. Last time but one
—'ere, lemme see—that was a bell-'anging job, I *think*
—no, I'm wrong, it was drains agen, so it were—
drains it was agen. And the *next* thing I 'eard was
that Mrs. Rummles was a-layin' at death's door with
the diffthery! The last time—ah, I recklect well, I
was called in to see if somethink wasn't wrong with

the ballcock in the top cistin. I see there *was* some-think, and I come away as usual. That day week, old Mr. Rummles was took with a fit on the floor in the back droring-room, which broke up the 'ouse!

'Now, I think, as fair-minded and unprejudiced parties, you'll agree with me that there was some-thing more'n hordinary coinside-ency in all that. I declare to you!' avowed the plumber, with a gloomy relish and a candour that was possibly begotten of beer, 'I declare to you there's times when I do honestly believe as I carry a curse along with me whenever I visits this 'ere partickler 'ouse! and, though it's agen my own hinterests, I deem it on'y my dooty, as a honest man, to mention it!'

Under any other circumstances, the plumber's compliments on her taste and his lugubrious as-sumption of character of the Destroying Angel would have sorely tried, if not completely upset, Ella's gravity; as it was, she was too wretched to have more than a passing and quite unappreciative sense of his absurdity. George, having the quality of mind which makes jokes more readily than sees them, took him quite seriously.

'Well,' he answered solemnly, 'I hope you won't bring *us* bad luck, at all events!'

'*I* 'ope so, sir, I'm sure. I '*ope* so. It will not be by any desire on my part, more partickler when you're just settin' up 'ousekeepin' with your good lady 'ere. But there's no tellin' in these matters.

That's where it is, you see—there's no tellin'. And, arter all my experence, with the best intentions in the world, I can't go and guarantee to you as nothink won't come of it. I wish I could, but, as a honest man, I can't. If it's to be,' moralised this fatalistic plumber, 'it *is* to be, and that's all about it, and no hefforts on my part or yours won't make hany difference, will they, sir ? '

'Well, well,' said George, plainly ill at ease, 'that will do, my friend. Now, Ella, what do you say— shall we go upstairs ? '

'Not now,' she gasped, 'let us go away—. Oh, George, take me outside, please ! '

'Dash that confounded fool of a plumber ! ' said George, irritably, when they were in the street again ; 'wonder if he thinks I'm going to employ him after that ! Not that it isn't all bosh, of course—— Why, Ella, you're not tired, are you ? '

'I—I think I am a little—do you mind if we drive home ? '

Ella was very silent during their short drive. When they reached Linden Gardens she said, ' I think we must say good-bye here, George. I feel as if I were going to have a headache.'

'You poor little girl ! ' he said, looking rather crestfallen, for he had been counting upon going in and being invited to remain for dinner, 'it's been rather too much for you, going over the house and

H

all that—or was it that beastly plumber with his rigmaroles?'

'It wasn't the plumber,' she said hurriedly, as the door was opened, 'and—good-bye, George.'

'How easily girls do get knocked up!' thought George, as he walked homeward, 'a little pleasant excitement like this and she seems quite upset. She was delighted with the house, though, that's one blessing, and I mustn't forget to tell the girls how touched she was by their presents. What a darling she is, and how happy we shall be together!'

PART II

ONCE safely at home, Ella hastened upstairs to her own room, where, if the truth must be told, she employed the half-hour before dinner in unintermittent sobbing, into which temper largely entered. 'He has spoilt it all for me! How *could* he—oh, how could he?' ran the burden of her moan. At the dinner-table, though pale and silent, she had recovered composure.

'A pleasant walk, Ella?' inquired her mother, with rather formal interest.

'Yes, very,' replied Ella, trusting she would not be questioned further.

'I believe I know where you went!' cried indiscreet Flossie. 'You went to look at your new home—now, *didn't* you ? Ah, I thought so ! I suppose you have quite made up your minds how you mean to do the rooms ? '

' Quite.'

' We might go round to all the best places to-morrow,' said Mrs. Hylton, ' and see some papers and hangings—there were some lovely patterns in Blank's windows the other day.'

' And, Ella,' added Flossie, ' I've been out with Andrews after school several times, to Tottenham Court Road, and Wardour Street, and Oxford Street—oh, everywhere, hunting up old furniture, and I can show you where they have some beautiful things—not shams, but really good ! '

' You know, Ella,' said Mrs. Hylton, observing that she did not answer, ' I want you to have a pretty house, and you and George must order exactly what you like; but I think you will find I may be some help to you in choosing.'

' Thank you, mother,' said Ella, without any animation ; ' I—I don't think we shall want much.'

' You will want all that young people in your position do want, I suppose,' said Mrs. Hylton, a little impatiently ; ' and of course you understand that the bills are to be my affair.'

' Thank you, mother,' murmured Ella again. She didn't feel able to tell them just yet how this had all been forestalled ; she felt that she would infallibly break down if she tried.

'You seem a little overdone to-night, my dear,' said her mother frigidly; she was naturally hurt at the very uneffusive way in which her good offices had been met.

'I have such a dreadful headache,' pleaded Ella. 'I—I think I overtired myself this afternoon.'

'Then you were very foolish, after travelling all yesterday, as you did. I don't wonder that George was ashamed to come in. You had better go to bed early, and I will send Andrews in to you with some of my sleeping mixture.'

Ella was glad enough to obey, though the draught took some time to operate; she felt as if no happiness or peace of mind were possible for her till George had been persuaded to undo his work.

Surely he could not refuse when he knew that her mother was prepared to do everything for them at her own expense!

And here it began to dawn upon her what this would entail! George's words came back to her as if she heard them actually spoken. Did he not say that the house had been furnished out of his savings?

What was she asking him to do? To dismantle it entirely; to humiliate himself by going round to all the people he had dealt with, asking them as a favour to take back their goods, or else he must sell them as best he could for a fraction of their cost. Who was to refund him all he had so uselessly spent? Could she ask her mother to do so? Would he even consent to such an arrangement if it was proposed?

Then his sisters—how could she avoid offending them irreparably, perhaps involving George in a quarrel with his family, if she were to carry her point?

As she realised, for the first time, the inevitable consequences of success, she asked herself in despair what she ought to do—where her plain duty lay?

Did she love George—or was it all delusion, and was he less to her than mere superfluities, the fringe of life?

She did love him, in spite of any passing disloyalty of thought. She felt his sterling worth and goodness, even his weaknesses had something lovable in them for her.

And he had been planning, spending, working all this time to give her pleasure, and this was his reward! She had been within an ace of letting him see the cruel ingratitude that was in her heart! 'What a selfish wretch I have been!' she thought; 'but I won't be—no, I won't! George shall *not* be snubbed, hurt, estranged from his family on my account!'

No, she would suffer—she alone—and in silence. Never by a word would she betray to him the pain his well-intentioned action cost her. Not even to her mother and Flossie would she permit herself to utter the least complaint, lest they should insist upon opening George's eyes !

So, having arrived at this heroic resolve, in which she found a touch of the sublime that almost consoled her, the tears dried on her cheeks and Ella fell asleep at last.

Some readers, no doubt—though possibly few of our heroine's sex—will smile scornfully at this crumpled rose-leaf agony, this tempest in a Dresden teacup; and the writer is not concerned to deny that the situation has its ludicrous side.

But, for a girl brought up as Ella Hylton had been, in an artistic *milieu*, her eye insensibly trained to love all that was beautiful in colour and form, to be almost morbidly sensitive to ugliness and vulgarity— it was a very real and bitter struggle, a hard-won victory to come to such a decision as she formed. Life, Heaven knows, contains worse trials and deeper tragedies than this ; but at least Ella's happy life had as yet known no harder.

And, so far, she must be given the credit of having conquered.

Resolution is, no doubt, half the battle. Unfortunately, Ella's resolution, though she hardly perceived this at present, could not be effected by one isolated and final act, but by a long chain of daily and hourly forbearances, the first break in which would undo all that had gone before.

How she bore the test we are going to see.

She woke the next morning to a sense that her life had somehow lost its savour; the exaltation of her resolve overnight had gone off and left her spirits flat and dead; but she came down, nevertheless, determined to be staunch and true to George under all provocations.

'Have you and George decided when you would like your wedding to be?' asked her mother, after breakfast, 'because we ought to have the invitations printed very soon.'

'Not yet,' faltered Ella, and the words might have passed either as an answer or an appeal.

'I think it should be some time before the end of next month, or people will be going out of town.'

'I suppose so,' was the reply, so listlessly given that Mrs. Hylton glanced keenly at her daughter.

'What do you feel about it yourself, Ella?'

'I? oh, I—I've no feeling. Perhaps, if we waited—no, it doesn't matter—let it be when you and George wish, mother, please!'

Mrs. Hylton gave a sharp, annoyed little laugh: 'Really, my dear, if you can't get up any more interest in it than that, I think it would certainly be wiser to wait!'

It was more than indifference that Ella felt—a wild aversion to beginning the new life that but lately had seemed so mysteriously sweet and strange; she was frightened by it, ashamed of it, but she could not help herself. She made no answer, nor did Mrs. Hylton again refer to the subject.

But Ella's worst tribulations had yet to come. That afternoon, as she and her mother and Flossie were sitting in the drawing-room, 'Mrs. and the Miss Chapmans' were announced. Evidently they had deemed it incumbent on them to pay a state visit as soon as possible after Ella's return.

Ella returned their effusive greetings as dutifully as she could. She had never succeeded in cultivating a very lively affection for them; to-day she found them barely endurable.

Mrs. Chapman was a stout, dewlapped old lady, with dull eyes and pachydermatous folds in her face. She had a husky voice and a funereal manner. Jessie, her eldest daughter, was not altogether uncomely in a commonplace way: she was dark-haired, high-coloured, loud-voiced—generally sprightly and voluble and overpowering; she was in such a hurry to speak that her words tripped one another up, and she had a meaningless and, to Ella, highly irritating little laugh.

Carrie was plain and colourless, content to admire and echo her sister.

After some conversation on Ella's Continental experiences, Jessie suddenly, as Ella's uneasy instinct foresaw, turned to Mrs. Hylton. 'Of course, Ella told you what a surprise she had at Campden Hill yesterday? Weren't you electrified?'

'No doubt I should have been,' said Mrs. Hylton,

who detested Jessie, 'only Ella did not think fit to mention it.'

'Oh, I wonder at that! I hope I wasn't going to betray the secrets of the prison-house?' Jessie was fond of using stock phrases to give lightness and sparkle to her conversation. 'Ella, the idea of your keeping it all to yourself, you sly puss! But tell me—would you ever have believed Tumps'—his. sisters called George 'Tumps'—'could be capable of such independent behaviour?'

'No,' said Ella, ' I—indeed I never should!'

'Ha, ha! nor should we! You would have screamed to see him fussing about—wasn't he killing over it, Carrie?'

'Oh, he was, Jessie!'

'My son,' explained Mrs. Chapman to Mrs. Hylton, 'is so wonderfully energetic and practical. I have never known him fail to carry through anything he has once undertaken—he inherits that from his poor dear father.'

'I don't quite gather what your brother George has been doing, even now?' said Mrs. Hylton to Jessie.

'Oh, but my lips are sealed. Wild horses sha'n't drag any more from me! Don't be afraid, Ella, I won't spoil sport!'

'There is no sport to spoil,' said Ella. 'Mother, it is only that—that George has furnished the house while I have been away.'

'Really?' said Mrs. Hylton politely; 'that *is* energetic of him, indeed!'

'Poor dear Tumps came home so proud of your approval,' said Jessie to Ella, 'and we were awfully relieved to find you didn't think we'd made the house quite too dreadful—weren't we, Carrie?'

'Yes, indeed, Jessie.'

'Of course,' observed the latter young lady, 'it's always so hard to hit upon another person's taste exactly—especially in furnishing.'

'Impossible, I should have thought,' from Mrs. Hylton.

'I hope Ella is of a different opinion—what do *you* say, dearest?'

'Oh,' cried Ella hastily, with splendid mendacity, 'I—I liked it all very much, and—and it was so much too kind of you and Carrie. I've never thanked you for—for all the things you gave me!'

'Oh, *those*! they ain't worth thanking for—just a few little artistic odds and ends. They set off a room, you know—give it a finish.'

'Young people nowadays,' croaked old Mrs. Chapman lugubriously in Mrs. Hylton's courteously inclined ear, 'think so much of luxury and ornament. I'm sure when I married my dear husband, we——'

'Now, mater dear, you really *mustn't*!' interrupted the irrepressible Jessie; 'Mrs. Hylton is on *our* side, you know. She likes pretty things about her—don't you, Mrs. Hylton? And, talking of that, Ella,

I hope you thought our glyco-vitrine decoration a success? We were perfectly surprised ourselves to see how well it came out! Just transparent coloured paper, Mrs. Hylton, and you cut it into sheets, and gum it on the window-panes, and really, unless you were told or came quite close, you would declare it was real stained glass! You ought to try some of it on your windows, Mrs. Hylton. I'll tell you where you can get it—you go down——'

'I'm afraid I'm old-fashioned, my dear,' said Mrs. Hylton, stiffly; 'if I cannot have the reality, I prefer to do without even the best imitations.'

'Why, you're deserting us, I declare! Ella, you must take her to see the window, and then perhaps she will change her opinion.'

'I always tell my girls,' said Mrs. Chapman, in her woolly voice, 'when I am dead and gone they can make any alterations they please, but while I am spared to them I like everything about the house to be kept exactly as it was in their poor father's life-time.'

'*Isn't* she a dear conservative old mummy?' said Jessie to Ella in an audible aside. 'Why, I do believe she won't see anything to admire in your little house —at least, if she does, the dear old lady, she'd sooner die than admit it!'

The Chapmans went at last, and before they were out of the house Mrs. Hylton, with an effort to seem unconcerned, said: 'And so, Ella, you and George

have done without my help? Of course you know
your own affairs best; still, I should have thought—
I should certainly have thought—that I might have
been of some assistance to you—if only in pecu-
niary matters.'

'George preferred that you should not be troubled,'
stammered Ella.

'I am not blaming him. I respect him for wishing to be independent. I own to being a little surprised that you should not have told me of this
before, though, Ella. But for that chattering girl, I
presume I should have been left to discover it for
myself. I wonder you cannot bring yourself to be a
little more open with your mother, my dear.'

'Oh, mother!' cried Ella in despair, 'indeed I
was going to tell you—only, I did not know myself
till yesterday. At least, that is——' she broke off
lamely, fearing to reflect on George.

'I find it hard to believe that George would act
without consulting you in any way. It is strange
enough that he should have undertaken to furnish
the house in your absence.'

'But if I couldn't be there!' pleaded Ella—'and
I couldn't.'

'Naturally, as you were on the Continent, you
couldn't be on Campden Hill at the same time; you
need not be absurd, Ella. But what I want to know
is this—have you had a voice in the matter, or have
you not?'

'N—not much,' confessed Ella, hanging her head.

'So I suspected, and I think George ought to be ashamed of himself. I never heard of such a thing, and I shall make a point of seeing the house and satisfying myself that it is fit for a daughter of mine to inhabit.'

'Mother!' exclaimed Ella, springing up excitedly, 'you don't understand. Why should you choose to suppose that the house is not pretty? It is not done as *you* would do it, because poor George hadn't much money to spend; but if I am satisfied, why should you come between us? And I *am* satisfied—quite, quite satisfied; he has done it all beautifully, and I will not have a single thing altered! After all, it is *his* house —our house—and nobody else has any right to interfere—not even you, mother!'

Mrs. Hylton shrugged her shoulders. 'Oh, my dear, if that is the way you think proper to speak to me, it is time to change the subject. Pray understand that I shall not dream of interfering. I am very glad that you are so satisfied.' And by-and-by she left the room majestically.

When she had gone, Flossie, who had been listening open-eyed to all that had taken place, came and stood in front of Ella's chair.

'Ella, tell me,' she said, 'has George really furnished the house exactly as you like—*really* now?'

'Haven't I said so, Flossie? Why should you doubt it?'

'Oh, I don't know; I was wondering, that was all!'

'Really!' cried Ella angrily, 'anyone would think poor George was a sort of barbarian, who couldn't be expected to know anything, or trusted to do anything!'

'I'm sure I never *said* so, Ella. But how clever of him to choose just the right things! And, Ella, do all the colours and things go well together? I always thought most men didn't notice much about all that. And are the new mantelpieces pretty? Oh, and where did he go for the papers and the carpets?'

'Flossie, I wish you wouldn't tease so. Can't you see I have a headache? I can't answer so many questions, and I won't! Once for all, everything is just what I like. Do you understand, or shall I tell you again?—just, *just* what I like!'

'Oh, all right,' returned Flossie, with exasperating good-humour; 'then there's nothing to lose your temper about, darling, is there?'

And this was all that Ella had gained by her loyalty to George so far.

It was the morning after the Chapmans' visit. Ella had seen her mother and Flossie preparing to go out, but, owing to the friction between them, they neither invited her to accompany them, nor did she venture to ask where they were going. At luncheon, however, the unhappy girl divined from the expression of their faces how they had employed the forenoon. They had been inspecting the Campden Hill house! Her mother's handsome face wore a look of frozen contempt. Imagine a strict Quaker's feelings on seeing his son with a pair of black eyes—a Socialist's at finding a peerage under his daughter's pillow—a Positivist's whose children have all joined the Salvation Army, and even then but a faint idea will be reached of Mrs. Hylton's utter dismay and disgust.

Flossie, though angry, took a different view of Ella's share in the business; she knew her better than her mother did, and consequently refused to believe that she was a Philistine at heart. It was her absurd infatuation for George that made her see with his eyes and bow down before the hideous household gods he had chosen to erect. On such weakness Flossie had no mercy.

'Well, Ella, dear,' she began, 'mother and I have seen your house. George has quite surpassed our wildest expectations. Accept my compliments!'

'Flossie,' said her mother severely, 'will you kindly choose some other topic? I really feel too seriously annoyed about all this to bear to hear it spoken of just yet. I think you shall come with me to the Amberleys' garden-party this afternoon, and not Ella, as we are dining out this evening. You had better stay at home and rest, Ella.'

In this, and countless other ways, was Ella made to feel that she was in disgrace.

Nor did Flossie spare her sister when they were alone. 'Poor dear mother!' she said, 'I quite thought that house would have broken her heart—oh, I'm not saying a word against it, Ella, I know *you* like it, and I'm sure it looks very comfortable—everything so sensible and useful, and the kitchen really charming; mother and I liked it best of all the rooms. Such a horrid man let us in; he was at work there, and he would follow us all about, and tell mother his entire history. I don't think he *could* have been quite sober, he would insist on turning all the taps on everywhere. I suppose, Ella, it's ever so much *cheaper* to furnish as you and George have done; that's the worst of pretty things, they do cost such a lot! I'd no idea you were so practical, though,' and so on.

On Sunday George came to luncheon. He was delighted to hear from Flossie that they had been to the house, and gave a boisterously high-spirited account of his labours. 'It *was* a grind,' he informed them, ' and, as for those painter-fellows, I began to think they'd stay out the entire lease.'

' Art is long, George,' observed Flossie, wickedly.

' Oh yes, I know; but they promised faithfully to be out in ten days, and they were over three weeks!'

' But look at the result! George, how *did* you find out that Ella liked grained doors ?'

' Well, to tell you the truth, Flossie, that was a bit of a fluke. The man told me that graining was

coming in again, and I said, " Grain 'em, then "—*I*
didn't know ! '

In short, he was more provokingly dense than ever
to-day, and Ella found herself growing more and
more captious and irritable that afternoon ; he could
not understand why she was so disinclined to talk ; even
the dear little house of which she was so soon to be
the mistress failed to interest her.

' You have told me twice already that you got the
drawing-room carpet a great bargain, and only paid
four pounds ten for the table in the dining-room,'
she broke out. ' Can't we take that for granted in
future ? '

' I forgot I'd told you ; I thought it was the mater,'
he said ; ' and I say, Ella, how about pictures ?
Jessie's promised to do us some water-colours—she's
been taking lessons lately, you know—but we shall
want one or two prints for the dining-room, shan't
we? You can pick them up second-hand very cheap.'

' Oh yes, yes; anything you please, George ! . . .
No, no; I'm not cross, I'm only tired, especially of
talking about the house. It is quite finished, you
know, so what *is* there to discuss ? '

During the days that followed, Flossie devised an
ingenious method of tormenting Ella; she laid out
her pocket-money, of which she had a good deal, on
the most preposterous ornaments—a pair of dangling
cut-glass lustres, bead mats, a trophy of wax fruit
under a glass shade, gaudy fire-screens and flower-

pots, all of which she solemnly presented to her
suffering sister. This was not pure mischief or un-
kindness on Flossie's side, but part of a treatment
she had hit upon for curing Ella of her folly. And
at last the worm turned. Flossie came in one day
with a cheap plush and terra-cotta panel of appalling
ugliness.

'For the drawing-room, dear,' she observed blandly,
and Ella suddenly burst into a flood of tears.

'You are very, very unkind to me, Flossie!' she
sobbed.

'I!' exclaimed Flossie, in a tone of the most innocent surprise. 'Why, Ella, I thought you would be
charmed with it. I'm sure *George* will. And, you
know, it will go beautifully with the rest of your
things!'

'You might understand . . . you might see——'

'I might see what?'

'How *frightfully* miserable I am!' said Ella, which
was the very admission Miss Flossie had been seeking
to provoke.

'Suppose I *do* see,' she said; 'suppose I've been
trying to get you to act sensibly, Ella?'

'Then it's cruel of you!'

'No it's not. It's kind. How am I to help you
unless you speak out? I'm younger than you, Ella,
but I know this—*I* would never mope and make
myself miserable when a word would put everything
right!'

'But it wouldn't, Flossie; it is too late to speak now. I can't tell him how I really feel—I can't!'

'Ah, then you own there is something to tell?'

'What have I said? Flossie, forget what I said; it slipped out. I meant nothing.'

'And you are perfectly happy and satisfied, are you? *Now*, I know how people look when they are perfectly happy and satisfied.'

'It's no use!' cried Ella, suddenly. 'I've tried, and tried, and tried to bear it, but I can't. I *must* tell somebody . . . it is making me ill. I am getting cross and wicked, and unlike what I used to be. Flossie, I can't go and live there—I dread the thought of it; I shrink from it more and more every day! It is all odious, impossible—and yet I must, I must!'

'No, you mustn't; and, what's more, you shan't!'

'Flossie, you mean you will tell mother! You must not, do you hear? If you do, it will only make matters worse. Oh, why did I tell you?' cried Ella, in shame at this lapse from all her heroism. 'Promise me you will say nothing to mother—it is too late now —promise!'

'Very well,' said Flossie reluctantly; 'then I promise. But, all the same, Ella, I think you're a great goose!'

'I didn't promise I wouldn't say anything to *George*, though,' she reflected; and so, on the very next occasion that she caught him alone, she availed herself of an innocent allusion of his to Ella's low spirits to give him the benefit of her candid opinion, which was not tempered by any marked consideration for his feelings.

Ella was in the morning-room alone—she had taken to sitting alone lately, brooding over her trials. She was no heroine, after all; her mind, it is to be feared, was far from superior. She was finding out that she had undertaken too heavy a task; she could not console herself for her lost dream of a charmingly appointed house. She might endure to live in such a home as George had made for her; but to be expected to admire it, to let it be understood that it was her handiwork, that she had chosen or approved of it— this was the burden that was crushing her.

Suddenly the door opened and George stood before her. His expression was so altered that she scarcely recognised him; all the cheery buoyancy had vanished, and his stern, set face had a dignity and character in it now that were wanting before.

'I have just had a talk with Flossie,' he began; 'she has shown me what a—what a mistake I've been making.'

Ella could not help feeling a certain relief, though she said, 'It was very wrong of Flossie—she had no right to speak.'

'She had every right,' he said. 'She might have done it more kindly, perhaps, but that's nothing. Why didn't you tell me yourself, Ella? You might have trusted me!'

'I couldn't—it seemed so cruel, so ungrateful, after all you had done. I hoped you would never know.'

'It's well for you, and for me too, that I know this while there's still time. Ella, I've been a blind, blundering fool. I never had a suspicion of this till—till just now, or you don't think I should have gone on with it a single minute. I came to tell you that you need not make yourself miserable any longer. I will put an end to this—whatever it costs me.'

'Oh, George, I am so ashamed. I know it is weak and cowardly of me, but I can't help it. And—and will it cost you so very much?'

'Quite as much as I can bear.'

'No; but tell me—about *how* much? More than a hundred pounds?'

'I haven't worked it out in pounds, shillings, and pence,' he said grimly; 'but I should put it higher myself.'

'Won't they take back some of the things? They ought to,' she suggested timidly.

'The things? Oh, the furniture! Good Heavens, Ella! do you suppose I care a straw about that? All I can think of is how I could have gone on deceiving myself like this, believing I knew your every thought; and all the time—pah, what a fool I've been!'

'I thought I should get used to it,' she pleaded. 'And oh, you don't know how hard I have tried to bear it, not to let anyone see what I felt—you don't know!'

'And I would rather not know,' he replied, 'for it's not exactly flattering, you see, Ella. And at all events, it's over now. This is the last time I shall trouble you; you will see no more of me after to-day.'

Ella could only stare at him incredulously. Had he really taken the matter so seriously to heart as this? Could he not forgive the wound to his vanity? How hard, how utterly unworthy of him!

'Yes,' he continued, 'I see now we were quite unsuited to one another. I should never have made you happy, Ella; it's best to find it out before it's too late. So let us shake hands and say good-bye, my dear.'

She felt powerless to appeal to him, and yet it was not wholly pride that tied her tongue; she was too shaken and stunned to make the least effort at re-monstrance.

'Then, if it must be,' she said at last, very low— 'good-bye, George.'

He crushed her hand in his strong grasp. 'Don't mind about me,' he said roughly. 'You've nothing to blame yourself for. I daresay I shall get over it all right. It's rather sudden at first—that's all!' And with that he was gone.

Flossie, coming in a little later, found her sister sitting by the window, smiling in a strange, vacant way. '*Well?*' said Flossie eagerly, for she had been anxiously waiting to hear the result of the interview.

'It's all over, Flossie; he has broken it off.'

' Oh, Ella, I'm so glad! I *hoped* he would, but I wasn't sure. Well, you may thank me for delivering you, darling. If I hadn't spoken plainly——'

' Tell me what you said.'

' Oh, let me see. Well, I told him anybody else would have seen long ago that your feelings were altered. I said you were perfectly miserable at having to marry him, only you thought it was too late to say so. I told him he didn't understand you in the least, and you hadn't a single thought or taste in common. I said if he cared about you at all, the best way he could prove it was by setting you free, and not spoiling your life and his own too. I put it as pleasantly as I could,' said Flossie naïvely, ' but he is very trying ! '

' You told him all that ! What made you invent such wicked, cruel lies ? Flossie, it is you that have spoilt our lives, and I will never forgive you—never, as long as I live ! '

' Ella ! ' cried the younger sister, utterly astonished at this outburst. ' Why, didn't you tell me the other day how miserable you were, and how you dared not speak about it ? And now, when I——'

' Go away, Flossie; you have done mischief enough ! '

' Oh, very well, I'm going—if this is all I get for helping you. Is it *my* fault if you don't know your own mind, and say what you don't mean ? And if you really want your dearly beloved George back again, there's time yet; he hasn't gone—he's in the drawing-room with mother.'

How infinitely petty her past misery seemed now! for what trifles she had thrown away George's honest heart! If only there was a chance still! at least false pride should not come between them any longer: so thought Ella on her way to the drawing-room. George was still there; as she turned the door-handle she heard her mother's clear resonant tones. 'Not that that is any excuse for Ella,' she was saying.

Ella burst precipitately into the room. She was only just in time, for George had risen and was evidently on the point of leaving. 'George,' she exclaimed, panting after her rapid flight, 'I—I came to tell you——'

'My dear Ella,' interrupted Mrs. Hylton, 'the kindest thing you can do for George now is to let him go without any more explanations.'

Ella stopped; again her mind became a blank. What had she come for; what was it she felt she must say? While she hesitated, George was already at the other door; he seemed anxious to avoid hearing her; in another second he would be gone.

She cried to him piteously. 'George, dear George, don't leave me! . . . I can't bear it!'

'This is too ridiculous!' exclaimed her mother angrily. 'What is it that you *do* want, Ella?'

'I want George,' she said simply. 'It was all a mistake, George. Flossie mistook—— Oh, you don't

really think that I have left off caring for you? I
haven't, dear, indeed I haven't—won't you believe
me?'

'I had better leave you to come to an understanding together,' said Mrs. Hylton, not in the best of
tempers, for she had been more sorry for George than
for the rupture he came to announce, and she swept
out of the room with very perceptible annoyance.

    .   .   .   .   .   .

'I thought it was all up with me, Ella; I did
indeed,' said George, a minute or two later, his face
still pale after all this emotion. 'But tell me—what's
wrong with the furniture I ordered?'

'Nothing, dear, nothing,' she answered, blushing.
'Don't think about it any more.'

'No? But your mother was talking about it too,'
he insisted. 'Come, Ella, dear, for heaven's sake let us
have no more misunderstandings! I see now what
an ass I was not to wait and let you choose for
yourself; these æsthetic things are not in my line.
But I'd no idea you'd care so much!'

'But I don't now—a bit.'

'Well, I do, then. And the house must be done all
over again, and exactly as you would like it; so there's
no more to be said about it,' said George, without a
trace of pique or wounded vanity.

'George, you are too good to me; I don't deserve it. And indeed you must not—think of the
expense!'

His face lengthened slightly; he knew well enough that the change would cost him dear.

'I'll manage it somehow,' he declared stoutly.

Would her mother help them now? thought Ella, and felt more than doubtful. No, in spite of her own wishes, she must not allow George to carry out his intentions.

'But you forget Carrie and Jessie,' she said; 'we shall hurt their feelings so if we change now.'

'By Jove! I forgot that,' he said. 'Yes, they won't like it—they meant well, poor girls, and took a lot of trouble. Still, you're the first person to be considered, Ella. I'll try and smooth it over with them, and if they choose to be offended, why, they must—that's all. And I tell you what. Suppose we go and see the house now, and you shall tell me just what wants doing to make it right?'

She would have liked to decline this rather invidious office, especially as she felt no compromise to be possible; but he was so urgent that she finally agreed to go with him.

As they gained Campden Hill and the road in which their house stood, George stopped. 'Hullo!' he said, 'that can't be the house—what's the matter with it?'

Very soon it was pretty evident what had been the matter—the walls were scorched and streaming, the window sashes were empty, charred and wasted by fire, the door was blistered and blackened, a stalwart fireman in his undress cap, with his helmet slung at his back, was just opening the gate as they came up.

' Can't come in, sir,' he said, civilly enough. ' No one admitted.'

' Hang it ! ' exclaimed George, ' it's my own fire— I'm the tenant.'

' Oh, I beg your pardon, sir—it's been got under some hours now. I was just going off duty.'

'.Much damage done ? ' inquired George laconic- ally.

' Well, you see, sir,' said the man, evidently con- sidering how to prepare George for the worst, ' we didn't get the call till the house was well alight, and there was three steamers and a manual a-playing on it, so—well, you must expect things to be a bit untidy- like inside. But the walls and the roof ain't much damaged.'

' And how did it happen ?—the house isn't even occupied.'

' Workmen,' said the man. ' Someone was in there early this morning and left the gas escaping some- wheres, and as likely as not a light burning near— and here you are. Well, I'll be off, sir ; there's nothing more to be done 'ere. Good-day, sir, and thank ye, I'm sure.'

' Oh, George ! ' said Ella, half crying, ' our poor, poor little house ! It seems like a judgment on me. How *can* you laugh ! Who will build it up for us now ? '

'Who ? Why, the insurance people, to be sure ! You
see, the firm are agents for the " Curfew," and as soon
as I got all the furniture in I insured the whole concern and got a protection note, so we're all right.
Don't worry, little girl. Why, don't you see this gets
us out of our difficulty ? We can start afresh now without offending anybody.   Look there; there's that
idiot of a plumber who's done all the mischief—
a nice funk he'll be in when he sees us ! '   .

But Mr. Peagrum was quite unperturbed ; if anything, his smudgy features wore a look of sombre com-
placency as he came towards them.   'I'm sorry this
should have occurred,' he said, ' but you'll bear me out
that I warned yer as something was bound to 'appen.
In course I couldn't tell what form it might take, and
fire I must say I did *not* expect.   I 'adn't on'y been
in the place not a quarter of a hour, watering the
gaselier in the libery—the libery as *was*, I *should* say
—when it struck me I'd forgot my screw-driver, so,
fortunately, as things turned out, I went 'ome to my
place to get it, and I come back to see the place all in
a blaze.   It's fate, that's what it is—fate's at the
bottom o' this 'ere job ! '

'Much more likely to be a lighted candle,' said
George.

' I was not on the premises at the time, so I can't
say ; but, be that 'ow it may, there's no denying it's
a singler thing the way my words have been fulfilled
almost literal.'

'Confound you!' said George. 'You take good care your prophecies come off. Why, man, you're not going to pretend you don't know that it's your own carelessness that's brought this about! This isn't the only house you've brought bad luck into, Mr. What's-your-name, since you've started in business!'

'You can't make me lose my temper,' replied the plumber with dignity. 'I put it down to ignirance.'

'So do I,' said George. 'And if I know anyone who's anxious for a little typhoid, or wants his house burnt down at a moderate charge, why, I shall know whom to recommend. Good-day.'

He turned on his heel and walked off, but Ella lingered behind. 'I only just wanted to tell you,' she said, addressing the astonished plumber, 'that you have done us a very great service, and I, at least, am very much obliged to you.' And she fluttered away after her *fiancé*.

The plumber—that instrument of Destiny—looked after the retreating couple, and indulged in a mystified whistle.

''*E* comes a bullyragging of me,' he observed to a lamp-post, 'and she's " very much obliged " '! And I'm blowed if I know what for, either way! Cracked, poor young things, cracked, the pair on 'em—and no wonder, with such a calamity so recent. Ah, well, I do 'ope as this is the end on it. I 'ope I shan't be the means of bringing no more trouble into that little 'ouse—that I kin truly say!'

And—human gratitude having its limits—it is highly probable that this pious aspiration will not be disappointed, so long, at least, as Mr. and Mrs. Chapman's tenancy continues.

DON; THE STORY OF A GREEDY DOG

A TALE FOR CHILDREN

'Daisy, dearest,' said Miss Millikin anxiously to her niece one afternoon, ' do you think poor Don is quite the thing ? He has seemed so very languid these last few days, and he is certainly losing his figure ! '

Daisy was absorbed in a rather ambitious attempt to sketch the lake from the open windows of Applethwaite Cottage, and did not look up from her drawing immediately. When she did speak her reply might perhaps have been more sympathetic. ' He *eats* such a lot, auntie ! ' she said. ' Yes, Don, we *are* talking about you. You know you eat too much, and that's the reason you're so disgracefully fat ! '

Don, who was lying on a rug under the verandah, wagged his tail with an uneasy protest, as if he disapproved (as indeed he did) of the very personal turn Daisy had given to the conversation. He had noticed himself that he was not as active as he used to be ; he grew tired so very soon now when he chased birds (he was always possessed by a fixed idea that, if he only gave his whole mind to it, he could catch any

swallow that flew at all fairly) ; he felt the heat considerably.

Still, it was Don's opinion that, so long as he did
not mind being fat himself, it was no business of any
other person's—certainly not of Daisy's.

' But, Daisy,' cried Miss Millikin plaintively, ' you
don't really mean that I overfeed him ? '

' Well,' Daisy admitted, ' I think you give way to
him rather, Aunt Sophy, I really do.   I know that at
home we never let Fop have anything between his
meals. Jack says that unless a small dog is kept on very
simple diet he'll soon get fat, and getting fat,' added
Daisy portentously, ' means having fits sooner or later.'

' Oh, my *dear* ! ' exclaimed her aunt, now seriously
alarmed. ' What do you think I ought to do about it ? '

' I know what I would do if he was *my* dog,' said
Daisy, with great decision—' diet him, and take no
notice when he begs at table ; I would. I'd begin this
very afternoon.'

' *After* tea, Daisy ? ' stipulated Miss Millikin.

' No,' was the inflexible answer, ' *at* tea. · It's all
for his own good.'

' Yes, dear, I'm sure you're right—but he has such
pretty ways—I'm so afraid I shall forget.'

' I'll remind you, Aunt Sophy.   He shan't take
advantage of you while *I'm* here.'

' You're just a tiny bit hard on him, Daisy, aren't
you ? '

' Hard on Don ! ' cried Daisy, catching him up and

holding him out at arm's length. 'Don, I'm *not* hard on you, am I? I love you, only I see your faults, and you know it. You're full of deceitfulness' (here she kissed him between the eyes and set him down). 'Aunt Sophy, you would never have found out his trick about the milk if it hadn't been for me—*would* you now?'

'Perhaps not, my love,' agreed Miss Millikin mildly.

The trick in question was a certain ingenious device of Don's for obtaining a double allowance of afternoon tea—a refreshment for which he had acquired a strong taste. The tea had once been too hot and burnt his tongue, and, as he howled with the pain, milk had been added. Ever since that occasion he had been in the habit of lapping up all but a spoonful or two of the tea in his saucer, and *then* uttering a pathetic little yelp; whereupon innocent Miss Millikin would as regularly fill up the saucer with milk again.

But, unfortunately for Don, his mistress had invited her niece Daisy to spend part of her summer holidays at her pretty cottage in the Lake District, and Daisy's sharper eyes had detected this little stratagem about the milk on the very first evening!

Daisy was fourteen, and I fancy I have noticed that when a girl is about this age, she not unfrequently has a tendency to be rather a severe disciplinarian when others than herself are concerned. At all events Daisy had very decided notions on the proper method of bringing up dogs, and children too; only there did not happen to be any children at Applethwaite Cottage to try experiments upon; and she was quite sure that Aunt Sophy allowed herself to be shamefully imposed upon by Don.

There was perhaps some excuse for Miss Millikin, for Don was a particularly charming specimen of the Yorkshire terrier, with a silken coat of silver-blue, set off by a head and paws of the ruddiest gold. His manners were most insinuating, and his great eyes glowed at times under his long hair, as if a wistful, loving little soul were trying to speak through them. But, though it seems an unkind thing to say, it must be confessed that this same soul in Don's eyes was never quite so apparent as when he was begging for some peculiarly appetising morsel. He was really fond of his mistress, but at meal times I am afraid he 'put it on' a little bit. Of course this was not quite straightforward; but then I am not holding him up as a model animal.

How far he understood the conversation that has been given above is more than I can pretend to say, but from that afternoon he began to be aware of a very unsatisfactory alteration in his treatment.

Don had sometimes felt a little out of temper with his mistress for being slow to understand exactly what he *did* want, and he had barked, almost sharply, to intimate to the best of his powers—'Not bread and butter, stoopid—*cake*!' So you may conceive his disgust when she did not even give him bread and butter; nothing but judicious advice—*without* jam. She was most apologetic, it is true, and explained amply why she could not indulge him as heretofore, but Don wanted sugar, and not sermons. Sometimes she nearly gave way, and then cruel Daisy would intercept the dainty under his very nose, which he thought most unfeeling.

He had a sort of notion that it was all through Daisy that they were just as stingy and selfish in the kitchen, and that his meals were now so absurdly few and plain. It was very ungrateful of her, for he had gone out of his way to be polite and attentive to her. When he thought of her behaviour to him he felt strongly inclined to sulk, but somehow he did not actually go so far as that. He liked Daisy; she was pretty for one thing, and Don always preferred pretty people, and then she stroked him in a very superior and soothing manner. Besides this, he respected her : she had been intrusted with the duty of punishing him on more than one occasion, and *her* slaps really hurt, while it was hopeless to try to soften her heart by trying to lick the chastising hands—a manœuvre which was always effective with poor Miss Millikin. So he contented himself with letting her see that though he did not understand he conduct towards him, he was willing to overlook it for the present.

' What a wonderful improvement in the dear dog ! ' Miss Millikin remarked one morning at breakfast, after Don had been on short commons for a week or two. 'Really, Daisy, I begin to think you were quite right about him.'

'Oh, I'm *sure* I was,' said Daisy, who always had great confidence in her own judgment.

'Yes,' continued her aunt, 'and, now he's so much better—just this one small bit, Daisy?' Don's eyes already had a green glitter in them and his mouth was watering.

'No, Aunt Sophy,' said Daisy, 'I wouldn't—really. He's better without anything.'

'I wish that girl was gone!' reflected poor Don, as he went sulkily back to his basket. 'It's enough to make a dog steal, upon my tail it is! I'm positively starved—no bones, no chicken, only beastly dry dog-biscuits and milk twice a day! I wish I could rummage about in gutters and places as Jock does—but I don't think the things you find in gutters are ever *really* nice. Jock does—but he's just that low sort of dog who *would*!'

Jock was a humble friend of his down in the village, a sort of distant relation to the Dandie Dinmonts; he was a rough, long-backed creature, as grey as a badger, and with a big solemn head like a hammer. Don was civil to him in a patronising way, but he did not tell him of the indignities he was subject to, perhaps because he had been rather given to boast of his influence over his mistress, and the high consideration he enjoyed at Applethwaite Cottage.

Now Daisy used to go up for solitary rambles on the fells sometimes, when she generally took Don as a protector. He was becoming very nearly as active as ever, and now there was a stronger motive than before for pursuing the swallows—for he had a notion that they would be rather good eating. But one morning she missed him on her way back through the village by the lake; she was sure he was with her on the pier, and she had only stopped to ask some question at the ticket-office about the steamboat times; and when she turned round, Don was gone.

However, her aunt was neither angry nor alarmed. Miss Millikin was not able to walk as much as Don wished, she said, so he was accustomed to take a great deal of solitary exercise; he was such a remarkably intelligent dog that he could be trusted to take care of himself—oh, he would come back.

And towards dusk that evening Don did come back. There was a curious air about him—subdued, almost sad; Daisy remembered long afterwards how unusually affectionate he had been, and how quietly he had lain on her lap till bedtime.

The next morning, when her aunt and she prepared to go for a walk along the lake, Don's excitement was more marked than usual; he leaped up and tried to caress their hands: he assured them in a thousand ways of the delight he felt at being allowed to make one of the party.

After this, it was a painful surprise to find that he

gave them the slip the moment they reached the village. But Miss Millikin said he always did prefer mountain scenery, and no doubt it was tiresome for him to have to potter about as they did. And Master Don began to give them less and less of his society in the daytime, and to wander from morn to dewy eve in solitude and independence; though whether he went up mountains to admire the view, or visited ruins and waterfalls, or spent his days hunting rabbits, no one at Applethwaite Cottage could even pretend to guess.

' *One* good thing, Aunt Sophy,' said Daisy complacently one evening, a little later, ' I've quite cured Don of being troublesome at meals ! '

' He couldn't be *troublesome* if he tried, dear,' said Miss Millikin with mild reproof; ' but I must say you have succeeded quite wonderfully—how *did* you do it ? '

' Why,' said Daisy, ' I spoke to him exactly as if he could understand every word, and I made him thoroughly see that he was only wasting his time by sitting up and begging for things. And you got to believe it at last, didn't you, dear ? ' she added to Don, who was lying stretched out on the rug.

Don pricked the ear that was uppermost, and then uttered a heavy sigh, which smote his mistress to the heart.

' Daisy,' she said, ' it's *no* use—I *must* give him something. Poor pet, he deserves it for being so good and patient all this time. One biscuit, Daisy ? '

Even Daisy relented : ' Well—a *very* plain one, then. Let me give it to him, auntie ? '

The biscuit was procured, and Daisy, with an express intimation that this was a very particular indulgence, tendered it to the deserving terrier.

He half raised his head, sniffed at it—and then fell back again with another weary little sigh. Daisy felt rather crushed. ' I'm afraid he's cross with me,' she said; ' you try, Aunt Sophy.' Aunt Sophy tried, but with no better success, though Don wagged his tail feebly to express that he was not actuated by any personal feeling in the matter —he had no appetite, that was all.

' Daisy,' said Miss Millikin, with something more like anger than she generally showed, ' I was very wrong to listen to you about the diet. It's perfectly plain to me that by checking Don's appetite as we have we have done him serious harm. You can see for yourself that he is past eating anything at all now. Cook told me to-day that he had scarcely touched his meals lately. And yet he's stouter than ever—*isn't* he ? '

Daisy was forced to allow that this was so. ' But what can it be ? ' she said.

' It's *disease*,' said her aunt, very solemnly. ' I've read over and over again that corpulence has nothing whatever to do with the amount of food one eats. And, oh! Daisy, I don't want to blame you, dear—but I'm afraid we have been

depriving him of the nourishing things he really
needed to enable him to struggle against the
complaint ! '

Poor Daisy was overcome by remorse as she
knelt over the recumbent Don. 'Oh, darling Don,'
she said, 'I didn't mean it—you know I didn't,
don't you ? You must get well and forgive me !
I tell you what, aunt,' she said as she rose to her
feet, 'you know you said I might drive you over in
the pony cart to that tennis-party at the Netherbys
to-morrow.   Well, young Mr. Netherby is rather
a " doggy " sort of man, and nice too. Suppose we
take Don with us and ask him to tell us plainly
whether he has anything dreadful the matter with
him ? '

Miss Millikin consented, though she did not
pretend to hope much from Mr. Netherby's skill.
'I'm afraid,' she said, with a sigh, 'that only a
very clever veterinary surgeon would find out what
really is the matter with Don. But you can try,
my dear.'

The following afternoon Miss Millikin entrusted
herself and Don to Daisy's driving, not without some
nervous misgivings.

'You're quite sure you can manage him, Daisy ? '
she said. 'If not, we can take John.'

'Why, Aunt Sophy !' exclaimed Daisy, 'I *always*
drive the children at home ; and sometimes when I'm
on the box with Toppin, he gives me the reins in a

straight part of the road, and Paul and Virginia pull
like anything—Toppin says it's all *he* can do to hold
them.'

Daisy was a little hurt at the idea that she might
find Aunt Sophy's pony too much for her—a sleepy
little ' slug of a thing,' as she privately called it, which
pattered along exactly like a clockwork animal in
urgent need of winding up.

Don seemed a little better that day, and was
lifted into the pony-cart, where he lay on the in-
diarubber mat, sniffing the air as if it was doing him
good.

Daisy really could drive well for her age, and
woke the pony up in a manner that astonished her
aunt, who remarked from time to time that she knew
Wildfire wanted to walk now—he never could trot
long at a time—and so they reached the Netherbys'
house, which was five miles away towards the head of
the lake, well under the hour, a most surprising feat
—for Wildfire.

It was a grown-up tennis-party, and Daisy,
although she had brought her racket, was a little
afraid to play ; besides, she wanted to consult young
Mr. Netherby about Don, who had been left with the
cart in the stables.

Mr. Netherby, who was a good-natured, red-faced
young soldier, just about to join his regiment, was
not playing either, so Daisy went up to him on the
first opportunity.

'You know about dogs, Mr. Netherby, don't you?'

'Rath-er!' said Mr. Netherby, who was a trifle slangy. 'Why? Are you thinking of investing in a dog?'

'It's Aunt Sophy's dog,' explained Daisy, 'and he's ill—*very* ill—and we can't make out what's the matter, so I thought you would tell us perhaps?'

'I'll ride over to-morrow and have a look at him.'

'Oh, but you needn't—he's here. Wait—I'll fetch him—don't you come, please.'

And presently Daisy made her appearance on the lawn, carrying Don, who felt quite a weight, in her arms. She set him down before the young man, who examined him in a knowing manner, while Miss Millikin, and some others who were not playing just then, gathered round. Don was languid, but dignified—he rather liked being the subject of so much notice. Daisy waited breathlessly for the verdict.

'Well,' said Mr. Netherby, 'it's easy enough to see what's wrong with *him*. I should knock off his grub.'

'But,' cried Miss Millikin, 'we *have* knocked off his grub, as you call it. The poor dog is starved—literally starved.'

Mr. Netherby said he should scarcely have supposed so from his appearance.

'But I assure you he has eaten nothing—positively nothing—for days and days!'

'Ah,' said Mr. Netherby, ' chameleon, is he ? then he's had too much air—that's all.'

Just then a young lady who had been brought by some friends living close by joined the group : ' Why,' she said at once, ' that's the little steamer dog.   How did he come here ? '

' He is *not* a little steamer dog,' said Miss Millikin in her most dignified manner; ' he is *my* dog.'

' Oh, I didn't know,' said the first speaker ; ' but —but I'm sure I've seen him on the steamer several times lately.'

' I never use the steamers unless I'm absolutely obliged—I disapprove of them : it must have been some other dog.'

The young lady was positive she had made no mistake.   ' You so seldom see a dog with just those markings,' she said, ' and I don't think anybody was with him ; he came on board at Amblemere and went all round the lake with us.'

' At Amblemere ! ' cried Daisy, ' that's where *we* live ; and, Aunt Sophy, you know Don has been away all day lots of times lately.'

' What did this dog do on the steamer ? ' asked Miss Millikin faintly.

' Oh, he was so sweet ! he went round to everybody, and sat up so prettily till they gave him biscuits and things—he was everybody's pet ; we were all jealous of one another for the honour of feeding him.   The second time we brought buns on purpose. But we quite thought he belonged to the steamer.'

Young Mr. Netherby laughed. 'So *that* is how he took the air! I thought I wasn't far wrong,' he said.

'Put him back in the cart, Daisy,' said Miss Millikin severely; 'I can't bear to look at him.'

Don did his best to follow this dialogue, but all he could make out was that it was about himself, and that he was being as usual exceedingly admired. So he sat and looked as good and innocent and interesting as he knew how. Just then he felt that he would almost rather they did *not* offer him anything to eat— at least not anything very sweet and rich, for he was still not at all well. It was a relief to be back in the cart and in peace again, though he wondered why Daisy didn't kiss the top of his head as she had done several times in carrying him to the lawn. This time she held him at a distance, and said nothing but two words, which sounded suspiciously like ' You *pig* ! ' as she put him down.

Miss Millikin was very grave and silent as they drove home. 'I can't trust myself to speak about it, Daisy,' she said; 'if—if it was true, it shows such an utter want of principle—such deceit; and Don used to be so honest and straightforward! What if we make inquiries at the pier? It—it may be all a mistake.'

They stopped for this purpose at Amblemere. 'Ay, Miss Millikin, mum, he cooms ahn boord reglar, does that wee dug,' said the old boatman, ' and a' makes himsel' rare an' frien'ly, a' do—they coddle him oop fine, amang 'em.   Eh, but he's a smart little dug, we quite look for him of a morning coomin' for his constitutionil, fur arl the worl' like a Chreestian ! '

' Like a very *greedy* Christian ! ' said his disgusted mistress.   ' Daisy,' she said, when she returned to the pony-cart, ' it's all true !   I—I never have been so deceived in any one ; and the worst of it is, I don't know how to punish him, or how to make him feel what a disgraceful trick this is.   Nobody else's dog I ever heard of made his mistress publicly absurd in this way.   It's so—so ungrateful ! '

' Aunt Sophy,' said Daisy, ' I've an idea.   Will you leave him to me, and pretend you don't suspect anything ?   I *will* cure him this time ! '

' You—you won't want to whip him ? ' said Miss Millikin, ' because, though it's all his own doing, he really is not well enough for it just now.'

' No,' said Daisy, ' I won't tell you my plan, auntie, but it's better than whipping.'

And all this time the unconscious Don was wearing an expression of uncomplaining suffering, and looking meekly sorry for himself, with no suspicion in the world that he had been found out.

Next day he felt much better, and as the morning was bright he thought that, after all, he might manage another steamer trip ; his appetite had come back, and his breath was not nearly so short as it had

been. He was just making modestly for the gate
when Daisy stopped him. 'Where are you going,
sir?' she inquired.

Don rolled over instantly with all his legs in the
air and a feeble apology in his eye.

'I want you for just one minute first,' said Daisy
politely, and carried him into the morning-room.
Was he going to be whipped?—she couldn't have the
heart—an invalid like him! He tried to protest by
his whimpering.

But Daisy did nothing of the kind; she merely
took something that was flat and broad and white,
and fastened it round his neck with a very orna-
mental bow and ribbon. Then she opened the French
windows, and said in rather a chilly voice, 'Now run
away and get on your nasty steamer and beg, and
see what you get by it!'

That seemed, as far as he could tell, very sensible
advice, and, oddly enough, it was exactly what he had
been intending to do. It did not strike him as particularly strange that Daisy should know, because
Don was a dog that didn't go very deeply into matters
unless he was obliged.

He trotted off at an easy pace down to the village,
getting hungrier every minute, and hoping that the
people on the steamer would have brought nice things
to-day, when, close to the turning that led to the
landing-stage, he met Jock, and was naturally obliged
to stop for a few moments' conversation.

He was not at all pleased to see him notwithstanding, for I am sorry to say that Don's greediness
had so grown upon him of late that he was actually
afraid that his humble friend (who was a little slow
to find out when he wasn't wanted) would accompany
him on to the steamboat, and then of course the good
things would have to be divided.

However, Don was a dog that was always scrupu-
lously polite, even to his fellow-dogs, and he did not
like to be rude now.

'Hullo!' said Jock (in dogs' language of course,
but I have reason to believe that what follows is as
nearly as possible what was actually said). 'What's
the matter with you this morning?'

Don replied that he was rather out of sorts, and
was going down to a certain lane for a dose of dog-
grass.

'A little dog-grass won't do *me* any harm,' said
Jock; 'I'll come too.'

This was awkward, but Don pretended to be glad,
and they went a little way together.

'But what's that thing round your neck?' asked
the Dandie Dinmont.

'Oh,' said Don, 'that? It's a bit of finery they
put on me at the cottage. It pleases *them*, you know.
Think it's becoming?'

'Um,' answered Jock; 'reminds me of a thing a
friend of mine used to wear. But *he* had a blind
man tied to him. I don't see *your* blind man.'

'They would have given me a blind man of course if I'd asked for it,' said Don airily, 'but what's the use of a blind man—isn't he rather a bore?'

'I didn't ask; but my friend said he believed the thing round his neck, which was flat and white just like yours (only he had a tin mug underneath his), made people more inclined to give him things—he didn't know why. Do *you* find that?'

'How stupid of Daisy to forget the mug!' thought Don. 'I could have brought things home to eat quietly then.—I don't know,' he replied to Jock; 'I haven't tried.'

He meant to put it to the test very soon, though —if only he could get rid of Jock.

'By the way,' he said carelessly, 'have you been round by the hotel lately?'

'No,' answered Jock, 'not since the ostler threw a brush at me.'

'Well,' said Don, 'there was a bone outside the porch, which, if I hadn't been feeling so poorly, I should have had a good mind to tackle myself. But perhaps some other dog has got hold of it by this time.'

'I'll soon make him let go if he has!' said Jock, who liked a fight almost as well as a bone. '*Where* was it, did you say?'

'Outside the hotel. Don't let me keep you. It was a beautiful bone. Good-morning,' said Don.

He did not think it worth while to explain that he

had seen it several days ago, for Don, as you will have remarked already, was a very artful dog.

He got rid of his unwelcome friend in this highly unprincipled manner, and strolled on to the pier full of expectation. Steamers ply pretty frequently on this particular lake, so he had not to wait very long. The little *Cygnet* soon came hissing up, and the moment the gangway was placed Don stepped on board, with tail proudly erect.

As usual, he examined the passengers, first to see who had anything to give, then who looked most likely to give it to him. Generally he did best with children. He was not fond of children (Daisy was quite an exception), but he was very fond of cakes, and children, he had observed, generally had the best cakes. Don was so accomplished a courtier that he would contrive to make every child believe that he or she was the only person he loved in the whole world, and he would stay by his victim until the cake was all gone, and even a little longer, just for the look of the thing, and then move on to some one else and begin again.

There were no children with any cakes or buns on board this time, however. There was a stout man up by the bows, dividing his attention between scenery and sandwiches; but Don knew by experience that tourists' sandwiches are always made with mustard, which he hated. There were three merry-looking, round-faced young ladies on a centre bench, eating

Osborne biscuits. He wished they could have made it sponge-cakes, because he was rather tired of Osborne biscuits; but they were better than nothing. So to these young ladies he went, and, placing himself where he could catch all their eyes at once, he sat up in the way he had always found irresistible.

I don't suppose any dog ever found his expectations more cruelly disappointed. It was not merely that they shook their heads, they went into fits of laughter —they were laughing at him! Don was so deeply offended that he took himself off at once, and tried an elderly person who was munching seed-cake; she did not laugh, but she examined him carefully, and then told him with a frown to go away. He began to think that Daisy's collar was not a success; he ought to have had a mug, or a blind man, or both; he did much better when he was left to himself.

Still he persevered, and went about, wagging his tail and sitting up appealingly. By and by he began to have an uncomfortable idea that people were saying things about him which were not complimentary. He was almost sure he heard the word 'greedy,' and he knew what that meant: he had been taught by Daisy. They must be talking of some other dog—not him; they couldn't possibly know what he was!

Now Don was undeniably a very intelligent terrier indeed, but there was just this defect in his education —he could not read: he had no idea what things could be conveyed by innocent-looking little black

marks. 'Of course not,' some of my readers will
probably exclaim, 'he was only a dog!' But it is
not so absurd as it sounds, for one very distinguished
man has succeeded in teaching his dogs to read and
even to spell, though I believe they have not got into
very advanced books as yet. Still, it may happen
some day that all but hopelessly backward or stupid
dogs will be able to read fluently, and then you may
find that your own family dog has taken this book into
his kennel, and firmly declines to give it up until he
has finished it. At present, thank goodness, we have
not come to this, and so there is nothing remarkable
in the mere fact that Don was unable to read. I only
mention it because, if he *had* possessed this accomplishment, he would never have fallen into the trap
Daisy had prepared for him.

For the new collar was, as you perhaps guessed
long ago, a card, and upon it was written, in Daisy's
neatest and plainest round hand :—

I am a very Greedy little Dog, and have Plenty to eat at Home,
So please do not give me anything, or I shall have a Fit and die!

You can easily imagine that, when this unlucky
Don sat up and begged, bearing this inscription written
legibly on his unconscious little chest, the effect was
likely to be too much for the gravity of all but very
stiff and solemn persons.

Nearly everybody on board the steamer was
delighted with him ; they pointed out the joke to one
another, and roared with laughter, until he grew quite

ashamed to sit up any more. Some teased him by
pretending to give him something, and then eating
it themselves; some seemed almost sorry for him and
petted him; and one, an American, said, 'It was
playing it too low down to make the little critter give
himself away in that style!' But nobody quite liked
to disobey Daisy's written appeal.

Poor Don could not understand it in the least;
he only saw that every one was very rude and
disrespectful to him, and he tried to get away under
benches. But it was all in vain; people routed him out
from his hiding-places to be introduced to each new
comer; he could not go anywhere without being stared
at, and followed, and hemmed in, and hearing always
that same hateful whisper of 'Greedy dog—not to be
given anything,' until he felt exactly as if he was being
washed!

Poor disappointed greedy dog, how gladly he would
have given the tail between his legs to be safe at home
in the drawing-room with Miss Millikin and Daisy!
How little he had bargained for such a terrible trip as
this!

I am sure that if Daisy had ever imagined he
would feel his disgrace so deeply she would not have
had the heart to send him out with that tell-tale card
around his neck; but then he would not have received
a very wholesome lesson, and would certainly have
eaten himself into a serious illness before the summer
ended, so perhaps it was all for the best.

This time Don did *not* go the whole round of the lake ; he had had quite enough of it long before the *Cygnet* reached Highwood, but he did not get a chance until they came to Winderside, and then, watching his opportunity, he gave his tormentors the slip at last. .

.   .   .   .   .   .

Two hours later, as Daisy and her aunt sat sketching under the big holm-oak on the lawn, a dusty little guilty dog stole sneakingly in under the garden-gate. It was Don, and he had run all the way from Winderside, which, though he did not appreciate it, had done him a vast amount of good. 'Oh ! ' cried Daisy, dropping her paint-brush to clap her hands gleefully, ' Look, Aunt Sophy, he has had his lesson already ! '

Miss Millikin was inclined to be shocked when she read the ticket. ' It was too bad of you, Daisy ! ' she said ; ' I would never have allowed it if I had known. Come here, Don, and let me take the horrid thing off.'

' Not yet, please, auntie ! ' pleaded Daisy, ' I want him to be quite cured, and it will take at least till bedtime. Then we'll make it up to him.'

But Don had understood at last. It was this detestable thing, then, that had been telling tales of him and spoiling all his fun ! Very well, let him find himself alone with it—just once ! And he went off very soberly into the shrubbery, whence in a few minutes came sounds of ' worrying.'

In half an hour Don came out again ; his collar

was gone, and in his mouth he trailed a long piece of chewed ribbon, which he dropped with the queerest mixture of penitence and reproach at Daisy's feet. After that, of course, it was impossible to do anything but take him into favour at once, and he was generous enough to let Daisy see that he bore her no malice for the trick she had played him.

What became of the card no one ever discovered; perhaps Don had buried it, though Daisy has very strong suspicions that he ate it as his best revenge.

But what is more important is that from that day he became a slim and reformed dog, refusing firmly to go on board a steamer on any pretence whatever, and only consenting to sit up after much coaxing, and as a mark of particular condescension.

So that Daisy's experiment, whatever may be thought of it, was at least a successful one.

TAKEN BY SURPRISE

BEING THE PERSONAL STATEMENT OF BEDELL
GRUNCHER, M.A.

THERE are certain misconceptions which a man who
is prominently before the public is morally bound to
combat—more for the sake of others than his own
—as soon as it becomes probable that the popular
estimate of his character may be shaken, if not
shattered, should he hold his peace. Convinced as
I am of this, and having some ground to anticipate
that the next few days may witness a damaging blow
to my personal dignity and influence for good, I have
thought it expedient to publish the true history of an
episode which, if unexplained, is only too likely to
prejudice me to a serious extent. Any circumstance
that tends to undermine or lessen the world's reverence
for its instructors is a deplorable calamity, to be
averted at all hazards, even when this can only be
effected by disclosures scarcely less painful to a
delicate mind.

For some years I, Bedell Gruncher, have conse-
crated my poor talents to the guidance and education

of public taste in questions of art and literature. To do this effectively I have laboured—at the cost of some personal inconvenience—to acquire a critical style of light and playful badinage. My lash has ever been wreathed in ribbons of rare texture and daintiest hues ; I have thrown cold water in abundance over the nascent flames of young ambition—but such water was systematically tinctured with attar of roses. And in time the articles appearing in various periodicals above the signature of 'Vitriol' became, I may acknowledge without false modesty, so many literary events of the first magnitude. I attribute this to my early recognition of the true function of a critic. It is not for him to set up sign-posts, or even warning-boards, for those who run and read. To attain true distinction he should erect a pillory upon his study table, and start the fun himself with a choice selection of the literary analogues of the superannuated eggs and futile kittens which served as projectiles in the past. The public may be trusted to keep it going, and also to retain a grateful recollection of the original promoter of the sport. My little weekly and monthly pillories became instantly popular, for all my kittens were well aimed, and my eggs broke and stuck in a highly entertaining fashion. We are so constituted that even the worst of us is capable of a kindly feeling towards the benefactor who makes others imperishably ridiculous in our eyes ; and to do this was my *métier à moi*. At first my identity with the lively but terrible 'Vitriol' was kept a profound secret, but gradually, by some means which I do not at present remember, it leaked out, and I immediately became a social, as well as a literary, celebrity.. Physically I have been endowed with a presence which, though not of unusual height and somewhat inclined to central expansion, produces, I find, an invariably imposing effect, especially with members of the more emotional and impressionable sex. Consequently I was not surprised even at the really extraordinary sensation I inspired upon my first introduction to a very charming young lady, Miss Iris Waverley,. as soon as my *nom de guerre* was (I forget just now by whom) incidentally alluded to. However, as it turned out, she had another and a deeper reason for emotion : it seemed she had been engaged to a young poet whose verses, to her untaught and girlish judgment,. seemed inspired by draughts of the true Helicon, and whose rhythmical raptures had stirred her maiden heart to its depths.

Well, that young poet's latest volume of verse came under my notice for review, and in my customary light-hearted fashion I held it up to general derision for a column or two, and then dismissed it, with an ineffaceable epigrammatic kick, to spin for ever (approximately) down the ringing grooves of criticism.

Miss Waverley, it happened, was inclined to correct her own views by the opinions of others, and

was, moreover, exceptionally sensitive to any association of ridicule with the objects of her attachment—
indeed, she once despatched a dog she fondly loved to
the lethal chamber at Battersea, merely because all
the hair had come off the poor animal's tail! My
trenchant sarcasms had depoetised her lover in a
similar fashion; their livid lightning had revealed
the baldness, the glaring absurdity of the very stanzas
which once had filled her eyes with delicious tears;
he was dismissed, and soon disappeared altogether
from the circles which I had (in perfect innocence)
rendered impossible to him.

Notwithstanding this, Miss Waverley's first senti-
ments towards me were scarcely, oddly enough, of un-
mixed gratitude. I represented the rod, and a very
commendable feeling of propriety made her unwilling
to kiss me on a first interview, though, as our intimacy advanced—well, there are subjects on which I
claim the privilege of a manly reticence.

I hasten over, then, the intermediate stages of
antipathy, fear, respect, interest, and adoration. In
me she recognised an intellect naturally superior, too
indifferent and unambitious to give life to its own
imaginings—too honest, too devoted to humanity, to
withhold merited condemnation from those of others.
I was the radiant sun whose scorching beams melted
the wax from the pinions of many a modern Icarus;
or, to put the metaphor less ingeniously, the shining
light in which, by an irresistible impulse of self-

destruction, the poetical and artistic moths flew and incontinently frizzled.

One trait in my character which Iris valued above all others was the caution with which I habitually avoided all associations of a ridiculous nature; for it was my pride to preserve a demeanour of unsullied dignity under circumstances which would have been trying, if not fatal, to an ordinary person. So we became engaged; and if, pecuniarily speaking, the advantage of the union inclined to my side, I cannot consider that I was the party most benefited by the transaction.

It was soon after this happy event that Iris entreated from me, as a gift, a photograph of myself. I could not help being struck by this instance of feminine parsimony with regard to small disbursements, since, for the trifling sum of one shilling, it was perfectly open to her to procure an admirable presentment of me at almost any stationer's; for, in obedience to a widely expressed demand, I had already more than once undergone the ordeal by camera.

But no; she professed to desire a portrait more peculiarly her own—one that should mark the precise epoch of our mutual happiness—a caprice which reminded me of the Salvation Army recruit who was photographed, by desire, 'before and after conversion'; and I demurred a little, until Iris insisted with such captivating pertinacity that—although my personal expenses (always slightly in excess of my income) had

been further swelled since my engagement by the in-
numerable *petits soins* expected by an absurd custom
from every lover—I gave way at length.

It was her desire that my portrait should form a
pendant to one of herself which had been recently
taken by a fashionable photographer, and I promised
to see that this wish should be gratified. It is possible that she expected me to resort to the same artist;
but there were considerations which induced me to
avoid this, if I could. To the extent of a guinea (or
even thirty shillings) I could refuse her nothing; but
every one knows what sums are demanded by a photographer who is at all in vogue. I might, to be sure,
as a public character, have sat without being called
upon for any consideration, beyond the right to dispose
of copies of my photograph; but I felt that Iris would
be a little hurt if I took this course, and none of the
West-end people whom I consulted in the matter
quite saw their way to such an arrangement, just
then. There was a temporary lull, they assured me,
in the demand for likenesses of our leading literary men, and I myself had been photographed within
too recent a period to form any exception to the
rule.

So, keeping my promise constantly in mind, I
never entered a secluded neighbourhood without being
on the look-out for some unpretending photographic
studio which would combine artistic excellence with
moderate charges.

And at last I discovered this photographic phœnix, whose nest, if I may so term it, was in a retired suburb which I do not care to particularise. Upon the street level was a handsome plate-glass window, in which, against a background of dark purple hangings and potted ferns, were displayed cartes, cabinets, and groups, in which not even my trained faculties could detect the least inferiority to the more costly productions of the West-end, while the list of prices that hung by the door was conceived in a spirit of exemplary modesty. After a brief period of hesitation I stepped inside, and, on stating my wish to be photographed at once, was invited by a very civil youth with a slight cast in his eye to walk upstairs, which I accordingly did.

I mounted flight after flight of stairs, till I eventually found myself at the top of the house, in an apartment pervaded by a strong odour of chemicals, and glazed along the roof and the whole of one side with panes of a bluish tint. It was empty at the moment of my entrance, but, after a few minutes, the photographer burst impetuously in—a tall young man, with long hair and pale eyes, whose appearance denoted a nervous and high-strung temperament. Perceiving him to be slightly overawed by a certain unconscious dignity in my bearing, which frequently does produce that effect upon strangers, I hastened to reassure him by discriminating eulogies upon the specimens of his art that I had been inspecting below, and I saw at once that he was readily susceptible to flattery.

'You will find me,' I told him frankly, 'a little more difficult to satisfy than your ordinary *clientèle*; but, on the other hand, I am peculiarly capable of appreciating really good work. Now I was struck at once by the delicacy of tone, the nice discrimination of values, the atmosphere, gradation, feeling, and surface of the examples displayed in your window.'

He bowed almost to the ground; but, having taken careful note of his prices, I felt secure in commending him, even to the verge of extravagance; and, besides, does not the artistic nature demand the stimulus of praise to enable it to put forth its full powers?

He inquired in what style I wished to be taken, whether full-length, half-length, or vignette. 'I will answer you as concisely as possible,' I said. 'I have been pressed, by one whose least preference is a law to me, to have a photograph of myself executed which shall form a counterpart or pendant, as it were, to her own. I have, therefore, taken the precaution to bring her portrait with me for your guidance. You will observe it is the work of a firm in my opinion greatly overrated—Messrs. Lenz, Kamerer, & Co.; and, while you will follow it in style and the disposition of the accessories, you will, I make no doubt, produce, if you take ordinary pains, a picture vastly superior in artistic merit.'

This, as will be perceived, was skilfully designed

to put him on his mettle, and rouse a useful spirit of emulation. He took the portrait of Iris from my hands and carried it to the light, where he examined it gravely in silence.

'I presume,' he said at length, 'that I need hardly tell you I cannot pledge myself to produce a result as pleasing as this—under the circumstances?'

'That,' I replied, 'rests entirely with you. If you overcome your natural diffidence, and do yourself full justice, *I* see no reason why you should not obtain something even more satisfactory.'

My encouragement almost unmanned him. He turned abruptly away and blew his nose violently with a coloured silk handkerchief.

'Come, come,' I said, smiling kindly, 'you see I have every confidence in you—let us begin. I don't know, by the way,' I added, with a sudden after-thought, 'whether in your leisure moments you take any interest in contemporary literature?'

'I—I have done so in my time,' he admitted; 'not very lately.'

'Then,' I continued, watching his countenance with secret amusement for the spasm I find this announcement invariably produces upon persons of any education, 'it may possibly call up some associations in your mind if I tell you that I am perhaps better known by my self-conferred *sobriquet* of "Vitriol."'

Evidently I had to do with a man of some intelligence—I obtained an even more electrical effect than usual. ' " *Vitriol!* " ' he cried, ' *not* surely Vitriol, the great critic ? '

' The same,' I said carelessly. ' I thought I had better mention it.'

' You did well,' he rejoined, ' very well ! Pardon my emotion—may I wring that hand ? '

It is not my practice to shake hands with a photographer, but I was touched and gratified by his boyish enthusiasm, and he seemed a gentlemanly young fellow too, so I made an exception in his favour ; and he did wring my hand—hard.

' So you are Vitriol ? ' he repeated in a kind of daze, ' and you have sought me out—*me*, of all people in the world—to have the honour of taking your photograph ! '

' That is so,' I said, ' but pardon me if I warn you that you must not allow your head to be turned by what is, in truth, due to the merest accident.'

' But what an accident ! ' he cried ; ' after what I have learnt I really could not think of making any charge for this privilege ! '

That was a creditable and not unnatural impulse, and I did not check it. ' You shall take me as often as you please,' I said, ' and for nothing.'

' And may I,' he said, a little timidly—' would you give me permission to exhibit the results ? '

' If I followed my own inclinations,' I replied, ' I should answer " certainly not." But perhaps I have no right to deprive you of the advertisement, and still less to withhold my unworthy features from public comment. I may, for private reasons,' I added, thinking of Iris, 'find it advisable to make some show of displeasure, but you need not fear my taking any proceedings to restrain you.'

'We struggling photographers must be so careful,' he sighed. 'Suppose the case of your lamented demise—it would be a protection if I had some written authority under your hand to show your legal representatives.'

'*Actio personalis moritur cum personâ,*' I replied ; 'if my executors brought an action, they would find themselves non-suited.' (I had studied for the Bar at one period of my life.)

'Quite so,' he said, 'but they might drag me into court, nevertheless. I should really prefer to be on the safe side.'

It did not seem unreasonable, particularly as I had not the remotest intention either of bringing an action or dying; so I wrote him a hasty memorandum to the effect that, in consideration of his photographing me free of charge (I took care to put *that* in), I undertook to hold him free from all molestation or hindrance whatever in respect of the sale and circulation of all copies resulting from such photographing as aforesaid.

'Will that do ? ' I said as I handed it to him.

His eyes gleamed as he took the document. 'It

is just what I wanted,' he said gratefully ; 'and now, if you will excuse me, I will go and bring in a few accessories, and then we will get to work.'

He withdrew in a state of positive exultation, leaving me to congratulate myself upon the happy chance which had led me to his door. One does not discover a true artist every day, capable of approaching his task in a proper spirit of reverence and enthusiasm ; and I had hardly expected, after my previous failures, to be spared all personal outlay. My sole regret, indeed, was that I had not stipulated for a share in the profits arising from the sale—which would be doubtless a large one ; but meanness is not one of my vices, and I decided not to press this point.

Presently he returned with something which bulged inside his velvet jacket, and a heap of things which he threw down in a corner behind a screen.

'A few little properties,' he said ; 'we may be able to introduce them by-and-by.'

Then he went to the door and, with a rapid action, turned the key and placed it in his pocket.

'You will hardly believe,' he explained, 'how nervous I am on occasions of importance like this ; the bare possibility of interruption would render me quite incapable of doing myself justice.'

I had never met any photographer quite so sensitive as that before, and I began to be uneasy about his success ; but I know what the artistic temperament is, and, as he said, this was not like an ordinary occasion.

'Before I proceed to business,' he said, in a voice that positively trembled, 'I must tell you what an exceptional claim you have to my undying gratitude. Amongst the many productions which you have visited with your salutary satire you may possibly recall a little volume of poems entitled " Pants of Passion " ? '

I shook my head good-humouredly. 'My good friend,' I told him, 'if I burdened my memory with all the stuff I have to pronounce sentence upon, do you suppose my brain would be what it is ? '

He looked crestfallen. 'No,' he said slowly, 'I ought to have known—you would not remember, of course. But *I* do. I brought out those Pants. Your mordant pen tore them to tatters. You convinced me that I had mistaken my career, and, thanks to your monitions, I ceased to practise as a Poet, and became the Photographer you now behold ! '

'And I have known poets,' I said encouragingly, ' who have ended far less creditably. For even an indifferent photographer is in closer harmony with nature than a mediocre poet.'

'And I *was* mediocre, wasn't I ? ' he inquired humbly.

'So far as I recollect,' I replied (for I did begin to remember him now), ' to attribute mediocrity to you would have been beyond the audacity of the grossest sycophant.'

'Thank you,' he said; 'you little know how you encourage me in my present undertaking—for you will admit that I can *photograph*?'

'That,' I replied, 'is intelligible enough, photography being a pursuit demanding less mental ability in its votaries than that of metrical composition, however halting.'

'There is something very soothing about your conversation,' he remarked; 'it heals my self-love—which really was wounded by the things you wrote.'

'Pooh, pooh!' I said indulgently, 'we must all of us go through that in our time—at least all of *you* must go through it.'

'Yes,' he admitted sadly, 'but it ain't pleasant, is it?'

'Of that I have never been in a position to judge,' said I; 'but you must remember that your sufferings, though doubtless painful to yourself, are the cause, under capable treatment, of infinite pleasure and amusement to others. Try to look at the thing without egotism. Shall I seat myself on that chair I see over there?'

He was eyeing me in a curious manner. 'Allow me,' he said; 'I always pose my sitters myself.' With that he seized me by the neck and elsewhere without the slightest warning, and, carrying me to the further end of the studio, flung me carelessly, face downwards, over the cane-bottomed chair to which I had referred. He was a strong athletic young man, in spite of his long hair—or might that have been, as in Samson's case, a contributory cause? I was like an infant in his hands, and lay across the chair, in an exceedingly uncomfortable position, gasping for breath.'

'Try to keep as limp as you can, please,' he said, 'the mouth wide open, as you have it now, the legs careless—in fact, trailing. Beautiful! don't move.'

And he went to the camera. I succeeded in partly twisting my head round. 'Are you *mad*?' I cried indignantly; 'do you really suppose I shall consent to go down to posterity in such a position as this?'

I heard a click, and, to my unspeakable horror, saw that he was deliberately covering me from behind the camera with a revolver—*that* was what I had seen bulging inside his pocket.

'I should be sorry to slay any sitter in cold blood,' he said, 'but I must tell you solemnly, that unless you instantly resume your original pose—which was charming—you are a dead man!·'

Not till then did I realise the awful truth—I was locked up alone, at the top of a house, in a quiet neighbourhood, with a mad photographer! Summoning to my aid all my presence of mind, I resumed the original pose for the space of forty-five hours—

they were seconds really, but they *seemed* hours ; it
was not needful for him to exhort me to be limp
again—I was limper than the dampest towel !

'Thank you very much,' he said gravely as he
covered the lens; 'I think that will come out very
well indeed. You may move now.'

I rose, puffing, but perfectly collected. 'Ha-ha,'
I laughed in a sickly manner (for I *felt* sick), 'I—I
perceive, sir, that you are a humorist.'

'Since I have abandoned poetry,' he said as he
carefully removed the negative to a dark place, 'I
have developed a considerable sense of quiet humour.
You will find a large Gainsborough hat in that corner
—might I trouble you to put it on for the next
sitting ?'

'Never ! ' I cried, thoroughly revolted. 'Surely,
with your rare artistic perception, you must be aware
that such a headdress as that (which is no longer
worn even by females) is out of all keeping with my
physiognomy. I will *not* sit for my photograph in
such a preposterous thing ! '

'I shall count ten very slowly,' he replied pen-
sively, 'and if by the time I have finished you are
not seated on the back of that chair, your feet crossed
so as to overlap, your right thumb in the corner of
your mouth, a pleasant smile on your countenance,
and the Gainsborough hat on your head, you will
need no more hats on this sorrowful earth. One—
two——'

I was perched on that chair in the prescribed attitude long before he had got to seven ! How can I describe what it cost me to smile, as I sat there under the dry blue light, the perspiration rolling in beads down my cheeks, exposed to the gleaming muzzle of the revolver, and the steady Gorgon glare of that infernal camera ?

'That will be extremely popular,' he said, lowering the weapon as he concluded. 'Your smile, perhaps, was a *little* too broad, but the pose was very fresh and unstudied.'

I have always read of the controlling power of the human eye upon wild beasts and dangerous maniacs, and I fixed mine firmly upon him now as I said sternly, 'Let me out at once—I wish to go.'

Perhaps I did not fix them quite long enough ; perhaps the power of the human eye has been exaggerated : I only know that for all the effect mine had on him they might have been oysters.

'Not yet,' he said persuasively, 'not when we're getting on so nicely. I may never be able to take you under such favourable conditions again.'

That, I thought, I could undertake to answer for ; but who, alas ! could say whether I should ever leave that studio alive ? For all I knew, he might spend the whole day in photographing me, and then, with a madman's caprice, shoot me as soon as it became too dark to go on any longer ! The proper course to take, I knew, was to humour him, to keep him in a good temper, fool him to the top of his bent—it was my only chance.

'Well,' I said, 'perhaps you're right. I—I'm in no great hurry. Were you thinking of taking me in some different style ? I am quite at your disposition.'

He brought out a small but stout property-mast, and arranged it against a canvas background of coast scenery. 'I generally use it for children in sailor costume,' he said, 'but I *think* it will bear your weight long enough for the purpose.'

I wiped my brow. 'You are not going to ask me to climb that thing ? ' I faltered.

'Well,' he suggested, 'if you will just arrange yourself upon the cross-trees in a negligent attitude, upside down, with your tongue protruded as if for medical inspection, I shall be perfectly satisfied.'

I tried argument. 'I should have no objection in the world,' I said ; 'it's an excellent idea—only, *do* sailors ever climb masts in that way ? Wouldn't it be better to have the thing correct while we're about it ?'

'I was not aware that you were a sailor,' he said ; '*are* you ? '

I was afraid to say I was, because I apprehended that, if I did, it might occur to him to put me through some still more frightful performance.

'Come,' he said, 'you won't compel me to shed blood so early in the afternoon, will you ? Up with you.'

I got up, but, as I hung there, I tried to obtain a modification of some of the details. 'I don't think,' I said artfully, 'that I'll put out my tongue—it's rather overdone, eh? *Everybody* is taken with his tongue out nowadays.'

'It is true,' he said, 'but I am not well enough known in the profession yet to depart entirely from the conventional. Your tongue out as far as it will go, please.'

'I shall have a rush of blood to the head, I know I shall,' I protested.

'Look here,' he said; 'am I taking this photograph, or are you?'

There was no possible doubt, unfortunately, as to who was taking the photograph. I made one last remonstrance. 'I put it to you as a sensible man,' I began; but it is a waste of time to put anything to a raving lunatic as a sensible man. It is enough to say that he carried his point.

'I wish you could see the negative!' he said as he came back from his laboratory. 'You were a little red in the face, but it will come out black, so it's all right. That carte will be quite a novelty, I flatter myself.'

I groaned. However, this was the end; I would get away now at all hazards, and tell the police that there was a dangerous maniac at large. I got down from the mast with affected briskness. 'Well,' I said, 'I mustn't take advantage of your good nature any longer. I'm exceedingly obliged to you for the—the pains you have taken. You will send *all* the photographs to this address, please ? '

' Don't go yet,' he said. ' Are you an equestrian, by the way ? '

If I could only engage him in conversation I felt comparatively secure.

' Oh, I put in an appearance in the Row sometimes, in the season,' I replied ; ' and, while I think of it,' I added, with what I thought at the time was an inspiration, ' if you will come with me now, I'll show you my horse—you might take me on horseback, eh ? ' I did not possess any such animal, but I wanted to have that door unlocked.

' Take you on horseback ? ' he repeated. ' That's a good idea—I had rather thought of that myself.'

' Then come along and bring your instrument,' I said, ' and you can take me at the stables ; they're close by.'

' No need for that,' he replied cheerfully. ' I'll find you a mount here.'

And the wretched lunatic went behind the screen and wheeled out a small wooden quadruped covered with large round spots !

' She's a strawberry roan,' he said ; ' observe the strawberries. So, my beauty, quiet, then ! Now settle yourself easily in the saddle, as if you were in the Row, with your face to the tail.'

' Listen to me for one moment,' I entreated tremulously. ' I assure you that I am not in the habit of appearing in Rotten Row on a spotted wooden horse, nor does any one, I assure you—*any* one mount a horse of any description with his face towards the crupper ! If you take me like that, you will betray your ignorance—you will be laughed at ! '

When people tell you it is possible to hoodwink the insane by any specious show of argument, don't believe them; my own experience is that demented persons can be quite perversely logical when it suits their purpose.

' Pardon me,' he said, ' *you* will be laughed at possibly—not I. I cannot be held responsible for the caprices of my clients. Mount, please ;, she'll carry you perfectly.'

' I will,' I said, ' if you'll give me the revolver to hold. I—I should like to be done with a revolver.'

' I shall be delighted to do you with a revolver,' he said grimly, ' but not yet; and if I lent you the weapon now, I could not answer for your being able to hold the horse as well—she has never been broken in to firearms. *I'll* hold the revolver. One—two— three.'

I mounted ; why had I not disregarded the expense and gone to Lenz and Kamerer ? Lenz does not pose his customers by the aid of a revolver. Kamerer, I was sure, would not put his patrons through these degrading tomfooleries.

He took more trouble over this than any of the

others ; I was photographed from the back, in front, and in profile ; and if I escaped being made to appear abjectly ridiculous, it can only be owing to the tragic earnestness which the consciousness of my awful situation lent to my expression.

As he took the last I rolled off the horse, completely prostrated. 'I think,' I gasped faintly, 'I would rather be shot at once—*without* waiting to be taken in any other positions. I really am not equal to any more of this ! ' (He was quite capable, I felt, of photographing me in a perambulator, if it once occurred to him !)

'Compose yourself,' he said soothingly, 'I have obtained all I wanted. I shall not detain you much longer. Your life, I may remark, was never in any imminent danger, as this revolver is unloaded. I have now only to thank you for the readiness with which you have afforded me your co-operation, and to assure you that early copies of each of the photographs shall be forwarded for Miss Waverley's inspection.'

'Miss Waverley ! ' I exclaimed ; 'stay, how do *you* know that name ?'

'If I mistake not, it was her photograph that you kindly brought for my guidance. I ought to have mentioned, perhaps, that I once had the honour of being engaged to her—until you (no doubt from the highest motives) invested my little gift of song with a flavour of unromantic ridicule. That ridicule I am now enabled to repay, with interest calculated up to the present date.'

'So you are Iris's poet!' I burst out, for, somehow, I had not completely identified him till that moment. 'You scoundrel! do you think I shall allow you to circulate those atrocious caricatures with impunity? No, by heavens! my solicitor shall——'

'I rely upon the document you were kind enough to furnish,' he said quietly. 'I fear that any legal proceedings you may resort to will hardly avert the publicity you seem to fear. Allow me to unfasten the door. Good-bye ; mind the step on the first landing. Might I beg you to recommend me amongst your friends?'

I went out without another word ; he was mad, of course, or he would not have devised so outrageous a revenge for a fancied injury, but he was cunning enough to be my match. I knew too well that if I took any legal measures, he would contrive to shift the whole burden of lunacy upon *me*. I dared not court an inquiry for many reasons, and so I was compelled to pass over this unparalleled outrage in silence.

Iris made frequent inquiries after the promised photograph, and I had to parry them as well as I could—which was a mistake in judgment on my part, for one afternoon while I was actually sitting with her, a packet arrived addressed to Miss Waverley.

I did not suspect what it might contain until it

was too late. She recognised that photographs were inside the wrappings, which she tore open with a cry of rapture—and then!

She had a short fainting fit when she saw the Gainsborough hat, and as soon as she revived, the extraordinary appearance I presented upside down on the mast sent her into violent hysterics. By the time she was in a condition to look at the equestrian portraits she had grown cold and hard as marble. 'Go,' she said, indicating the door, 'I see I have been wasting my affection upon a vulgar and heartless buffoon!'

I went—for she would listen to no explanations; and indeed I doubt whether, even were she to come upon this statement, it would serve to restore my tarnished ideal in her estimation. But, though I have lost her, I am naturally anxious (as I said when I began) that the public should not be misled into drawing harsh conclusions from what, if left unexplained, may doubtless have a singular appearance.

It is true that, up to the present, I have not been able to learn that any of those fatal portraits have absolutely been exposed for sale, though I direct my trembling steps almost every day to Regent Street, and search the windows of the Stereoscopic Company with furtive and foreboding eyes, dreading to be confronted with presentments of myself — Bedell Gruncher, 'Vitriol,' the great critic!—lying across a chair in a state of collapse, sucking my thumb in a Gainsborough hat, or bestriding a ridiculous wooden horse with my face towards its tail!

But they cannot be long in coming out now; and my one hope is that these lines may appear in print in time to forestall the prejudice and scandal which are otherwise inevitable. At all events, now that the world is in possession of the real facts, I am entitled to hope that the treatment to which I have been subjected will excite the indignation and sympathy it deserves.

PALEFACE AND REDSKIN

A COMEDY-STORY FOR GIRLS AND BOYS

ACT THE FIRST

WHERE IS THE ENEMY?

IT was a very hot afternoon, and Hazel, Hilary, and Cecily Jolliffe were sitting under the big cedar on the lawn at The Gables. Each had her racket by her side, and the tennis-court lay, smooth and inviting, close by; but they did not seem inclined to play just then, and there was something in the expression of all three which indicated a common grievance.

'Well,' said Hazel, the eldest, who was nearly fourteen, 'we need not have excited ourselves about the boys' holidays, if we had only known. They don't give us much of their society—why, we haven't had one single game of cricket together yet!'

'And then to have the impudence to tell us that they didn't care much about *our* sort of cricket!' said Hilary, 'when I can throw up every bit as far as Jack, and it takes Guy three overs to bowl me! It's beastly cheek of them.'

'*Hilary!*' cried Cecily, 'what would mother say if she heard you talk like that?'

'Oh, it's the holidays!' said Hilary, lazily. 'Besides, it is a shame! They would have played with us just as they used to, if it hadn't been for that Clarence Tinling.'

'Yes,' Hazel agreed, 'he hates cricket. I do believe that's the reason why he invented this silly army, and talked Jack and Guy into giving up everything for it.'

'They haven't any will of their own, poor things!' said Hilary.

'You forget, Hilary,' put in Cecily, 'Tinling is the guest. They ought to give way to him.'

'Well,' said Hilary, 'it's ridiculous for great boys who have been two terms at school to go marching about with swords and guns. Big babies!'

Perhaps there was a little personal feeling at the bottom of this, for she had offered herself for enlistment, and had been sternly rejected on the ground of her sex.

'I wish he would go, I know that,' said Hazel, making a rather vicious little chop at her shoe with her racket; 'those boys talk about nothing but their stupid army from morning to night. Uncle Lambert says they make him feel quite gunpowdery at lunch. And what do you think is the last thing they've done? —put up a great fence all round their tent, and shut themselves up there all day!'

N

'Except when they're sentries and hide,' put in Hilary; 'they're always jumping up somewhere and wanting you to give the countersign. It isn't like home, these holidays!'

'Perhaps,' suggested Cecily, 'it makes things safer, you know.'

'Duffer, Cis!' cried Hilary, contemptuously, for Cecily had appointed herself professional peacemaker to the family, and her efforts were about as successful as such domestic offices ever are.

'Look out!' cried Hilary, presently; 'they're coming. Don't let's take the least notice of them. They hate that more than anything.'

From the shrubbery filed three boys, the first and tallest of whom wore an imposing dragoon's helmet with a crimson plume, and carried a sabre-tache and a drawn sword; the other two had knapsacks and crossbelts, and wore red caps like those of the French army; they carried guns on their shoulders.

'Halt! 'Tention! Dis-miss!' shouted the commanding officer, and the army broke off with admirable precision.

'Don't be alarmed,' said the General considerately to the three girls; 'the army is only out on fatigue duty.'

'Then wouldn't the army like to sit down?' suggested Hilary, forgetting all about her recent proposal.

'Ah, you don't understand,' said General Tinlin
with some pity. 'It's a military term.'

He was a pale, puffy boy, with reddish hair and
freckles, who was evidently fully alive to the dignity
of his position.

'Suppose we let military things alone for a little
while,' said Hazel. 'We want the army to come and
play tennis. You will, won't you, Jack and Guy? and
Cis will umpire—she likes it.'

'I don't mind a game,' said Jack.

'I'll play, if you like,' added Guy; but he
had forgotten that the General was a bit of a
martinet.

'That's nice discipline,' he said. 'I don't know
whether you know it; but in some armies you'd be
court-martialled for less than that.'

'Well, may we, then?' asked Guy a little impatiently.

'No salute now!' cried his superior. 'I shall
never make you fellows smart. Why, at the Haver-
sacks, last Easter, there were half a dozen of us, and
we drilled like machines. Of course you mayn't play
tennis—this is only a bivouac; and it's over now.
Attention! The left wing of the force will occupy the
shrubbery; the right will push on and blow up the
gate.

'Which of us is the left wing?' inquired Guy.

'You are, of course.'

'Oh, all right; only you said Jack was just now,'

grumbled Guy, who was evidently a little disposed to
rebel at being deprived of his tennis.

'Look here,' said the General; 'either let's do the
thing thoroughly, or not do it at all.   It's no pleasure
to *me* to be General, I can tell you; and if I can't
have perfect discipline in the ranks—why, we might
as well drop the army altogether!'

'Oh, all right,' said Jack, who was a sweet-tempered
boy, 'we won't do it again.'

And they went off to carry out their separate
instructions, Clarence Tinling remaining by the
cedar.

'I have to be a little sharp now and then,' he
explained.   'Why, if I didn't keep an iron rule over
them, they'd be getting insubordinate in no time.
You mustn't think I've any objection to their playing
tennis, or anything of that sort; only discipline must
be kept up; though it seems severe, perhaps, to you.'

'It doesn't seem to be half bad fun for *you*, at all
events,' said Hazel.

'Of course,' added Hilary, whose cheeks were
flushed and eyes suspiciously bright as she plucked
all the blades of grass that were within her reach,
'we're glad if you're enjoying being here; but it's a
little slow for us girls.   You might give the army a
half-holiday now and then.'

'An army, especially a small army, like ours,' said
Clarence, grandly, 'ought to be constantly prepared
for action; else it's no use.   Then, look at the pro-

tection it is. Why, we've just built a fortified place close to the kitchen garden, where you could all retire to if we were attacked; and, properly provisioned, we could hold out for almost any time.'

'Thank you,' said Hilary. 'I should feel a good deal safer in the box-room. And then, who's going to attack us?'

'Well, you never know,' replied Clarence; 'but, if they did come, it's something to feel we should be able to defend ourselves.'

'Yes, Hilary,' Cecily remarked, 'an army would certainly be a great convenience then.'

'That would depend on what it did,' said her sister. 'It wouldn't be much of a convenience if it ran away.'

'I don't think Jack and Guy would ever do that,' observed Hazel.

'I suppose that means that you think I should?' inquired Clarence, who was quick at discovering personal allusions.

'I wasn't thinking about you at all,' said Hazel, with supreme indifference; 'we don't know you well enough to say whether you're brave or not—we do know our brothers.'

'There wouldn't be much sense in my being the General if I wasn't the bravest, would there?' he demanded.

'Well, as to that, you see,' retorted Hilary, 'we don't see much sense in any of it.'

'Girls can't be expected to see sense in anything,' he said sulkily.

'At all events, no one can be expected to see bravery till there's some danger,' said Hazel; 'and there isn't the least!'

'That's all you know about it; but I've something more important to do than stay here squabbling. I'm off to see what the army's up to.' And he marched off with great pomp.

When he had disappeared, Hilary remarked frankly, 'Isn't he a pig?'

'I don't think it's nice to call our visitors "pigs," Hilary!' remonstrated Cecily, 'and he's not really more greedy than most boys.'

'Don't lecture, Cis. I didn't mean he was that kind of pig—I said he was a pig. And he is!' said Hilary, not over lucidly. 'I wonder what Jack and Guy can see in him. I thought that when they wrote asking him to be invited, that he'd be sure to be such a jolly boy!'

'He may be a jolly boy—at school,' was all that even the tolerant Cecily could find to urge in his favour.

'I believe,' said Hazel, 'that they're not nearly so mad about him as they were—didn't you notice about the tennis just now?'

'He bullies them—that's what it is,' explained Hilary; 'only with talking, I mean, of course, but he talks such a lot, and he will have his own way, and, if they say anything, he reminds them he's a visitor, and ought to be humoured. I wish it was any use getting Uncle Lambert to speak to him—but he's so stupid!'

'Is he, though?' said a lazy voice from behind the cedar.

'Oh, Uncle Lambkin!' cried Hilary, 'I didn't know you were there!'

'Don't apologise,' was the answer. 'I know it must be a trial to have an uncle on the verge of imbecility—but bear with me. I am at least harmless.'

'Of course we know you're really rather clever,' said Hazel, 'but you *are* stupid about some things—you never interfere, whatever people do!'

'Don't I, really?' said their uncle, as he disposed himself on his back, and tilted his hat over his nose; 'you do surprise me! What a mistake for a man to make, who has come down for perfect quiet! Whom shall I begin to interfere with?'

'Well, you might snub that horrid Tinling boy, instead of encouraging him, as you always do!'

'.Encourage him! He's got a fine flow of martial enthusiasm, and a good supply of military terms, and I listen when he gives me long accounts of thrilling engagements, when he came out uncommonly strong—and the enemy, so far as I can gather, never came out at all. I'm passive, because I can't help myself; and then he amuses me in his way—that's all.'

'Do you believe he's brave, uncle?'

'I only know that I saw him kill two wasps with his teaspoon,' was the reply. 'They don't award the Victoria Cross for it—but it's a thing I couldn't have done myself.'

'I should hope not!' exclaimed Hilary; 'but everybody knows you're a coward,' she added (she did not intend this remark to be taken seriously), 'and you're awfully lazy. Still, there are some things you might do!'

'If that means fielding long-leg till tea-time, I respectfully disagree. Irreverent girls, have you never been taught that a digesting uncle is a very solemn and sacred thing?'

'Now you are going to be idiotic again! But as to cricket—why, you must know that we never get a game now! And next summer I shall be too old to play!'

'I *never* mean to be too old for cricket,' said Hilary, with conviction; 'but we've had none for weeks, uncle, positive weeks!'

'Quite right, too!' observed Uncle Lambert, sleepily. 'Not a game for girls—only spoil your hands—do you think I want a set of nieces with paws like so many glovers' signs?'

'That's utter nonsense,' said Hazel, calmly, 'because we always play in gloves. Mother makes us. At least, when we did play. Now the boys will only play soldiers, and, if they do happen to be inclined for a set at tennis, Clarence comes up and orders them off as pickets or outposts, or something ! '

' But he's not Bismarck or Boulanger, is he ? I always understood this was a free country.'

' You know what Guy and Jack are—they can't bear their visitor to think he isn't welcome.'

' Well, they seem to have made him feel very much at home—but it isn't my business ; if they choose to declare the house in a state of siege, and turn the garden into a seat of war, I can't help it— I'd rather they wouldn't, but it's your mother's affair, not mine ! '

And he closed the discussion by lighting a cigarette, and relapsing into a contented silence.

Uncle Lambert was short and stout, with a round red face, a heavy auburn moustache, and little green eyes which never seemed to notice anything. His nieces were fond of him, though they often wished he would pay them the occasional compliment of talking sensibly ; but he never did, and he spent all his time at The Gables in elaborately doing nothing at all.

Clarence Tinling had gone off in a decided huff— so much so indeed that he left his devoted army to carry out their rather misty manœuvres without any help from him. He was beginning to find a falling-off in their docility of late, which was no doubt owing to their sisters ; it was excessively annoying to him that those girls should be so difficult to convince of the protective value of a fortress, and especially that they should decline to take his own superior nerve and courage for granted. And the worst of it was, nothing but some imminent danger was ever likely to convince them, such were their prejudice and narrow-mindedness.

Later that afternoon the family assembled for tea in the cool, shady dining-room ; Mrs. Jolliffe, with a gentle anxiety on her usually placid face, sat at the head (Colonel Jolliffe was away shooting in the North just then). 'Where are all the boys?' she said, looking round the table. 'Why don't they come in?'

'It's no use asking us, mother,' said Hilary, 'we see so very little of them ever.'

'Very likely they are washing their hands,' said her mother.

'So *like* them!' murmured Uncle Lambert in confidence to his tea-cake. 'But here's the noble General, at all events. Well, Field Marshal, what have you done with the Standing Army?'

Tinling addressed himself to his hostess. 'Oh, Mrs. Jolliffe, I'm so sorry I was late, but I had just to run round to the stables for a minute. Oh, the other two? They're on duty—they're guarding the camp. In fact, I can't stay here very long myself.'

'But the poor dear boys must have their tea!' cried Mrs. Jolliffe.

'Well, you know,' said their veteran officer, as he helped himself to the marmalade, 'I don't think

a little roughing it is at all a bad thing for them—
teaches them that a soldier's life is not all jam.'

'No,' said Hazel, 'the General seems to get most
of that.'

All Clarence said was: 'I'll trouble one of you
girls for the tea-cake.'

'I don't think it's fair that the poor army should
"rough," as you call it, while you stuff, Clarence,' said
Hazel, indignantly. 'Mustn't they come in to tea,
mother? It is such nonsense!'

'Yes, dear, run and call them in,' said Mrs.
Jolliffe. 'I can't let my boys go without their meals,
Clarence, it's so bad for them.'

'It's not discipline,' said the chief; 'still, if they
must come, you had better take them this permit
from me.' And he scribbled a line on a scrap of
paper, which he handed to Hazel, who received it with
the utmost disdain.

Hazel crossed the lawn and over a little rustic
bridge to the kitchen garden and hothouses, beyond
which was the paddock, where the fortress had been
erected. It was a very imposing construction, built,
with some help from the village carpenter, of
portions of some disused fencing. The stockade had
loopholes in it, and above the top she could see
a fluttering flag and the point of a tent. Jack was
perched up on a kind of look-out, and Guy was pacing
solemnly before the covered entrance with a musket
of very mild aspect over his shoulder.

'Who goes there?' he called out, some time after recognising her.

Hazel vouchsafed no direct reply to this challenge. 'You're to come in to tea *directly*,' she announced in her most peremptory tone.

'Advance, and give the countersign,' said the sentinel.

'Don't be a donkey!' returned Hazel, tossing back her long brown hair impatiently.

Guy levelled his firearm. It is exasperating when a sister can't enter into the spirit of the thing better than that. Who ever heard of a sentry being told, on challenging, 'not to be a donkey'? 'My orders are to fire on all suspicious persons,' he informed her.

Hazel stopped both her ears. 'No, Guy, please— it makes me jump so.'

'There's no cap on,' said he.

'Then there's a ramrod, or a pea, or something horrid,' she objected; 'do turn it the other way.'

'Hazel's all right, Guy,' said Jack, in rebuke of this excessive zeal; 'we can let her pass.'

'As if I wanted to pass!' exclaimed Hazel. 'I only came to bring you back to tea; and if you're afraid to go without leave, there's a permission from Clarence for you.'

'Oh! come in and have a look now you're here,' said the garrison more hospitably. 'You can't think how jolly the inside is.'

'Well, if I must,' she said; though, as a matter of fact, she was exceedingly curious to see the interior of the stronghold.

'It's like the ones in "Masterman Ready" and "Treasure Island," you see,' explained Jack, proudly. 'And it's pierced for musketry, too; we could open a withering fire on besiegers before they could come near us.'

'They would have to be rather stupid to want to besiege this, wouldn't they?' said Hazel.

'I don't see that—besiegers must besiege something. And it is snug, isn't it, now?'

Hazel was secretly much impressed. In the centre of the enclosure was the commander's tent, with a lantern fixed at the pole for night watches; and rugs and carpets were strewn about; at one of the angles of the palisading was the look-out—an elaborate erection of old wine-cases and egg-boxes—on the top of which was fixed a seven-and-sixpenny telescope that commanded the surrounding country for quite a hundred yards.

She was not the person, however, to go into raptures; she merely smiled a rather teasing little smile, and said, 'Mar-vellous!' but somehow, whatever sarcasm underlay this was accepted by both boys as a tribute.

'You can see now,' said Guy, in a reasonable tone, ' that there wouldn't have been room here for all you girls—now, would there?'

'Girls are always in the way—everywhere,' said Hazel, with a reproachful inflection which was quite lost upon her brothers.

'I knew you'd be sensible about it,' said Jack; 'you can't think what fun we have in here—especially at night, when the lantern's lit. Hallo! there's some one calling.'

A shrill whistle sounded from the kitchen garden, and, a moment after, a stone came flying over the stockade, and was stopped by the canvas of the tent.

'That's cool cheek!' said Jack; 'get up and reconnoitre, Guy—quick!'

Guy mounted the scaffold, and brought the telescope to bear upon the immediate neighbourhood with admirable coolness and science—but no particular result.

'We shall have to scour the bush and see if we can find any traces of the enemy,' said he with infinite relish.

'Was that the stone?' said Hazel, pointing to one that lay at the foot of the fence; 'because there seems to be some paper wrapped round it.'

'So there is!' said Jack, proceeding to unfold it. Presently he exclaimed, 'I *say*!'

'What is it now?' asked Hazel.

'Nothing for you—it's private!' said Jack, mysteriously. 'Here, Guy, come down and look at this.'

Guy read it and whistled. 'We must report this to the General at once,' he said gravely.

Both boys were very solemn, and yet had a certain novel air of satisfied importance.

'Shall we tell her?' asked Guy.

'She must know it some time,' returned Jack; 'we'll break it by degrees.—We've just had notice that we're going to be attacked by Red Indians, Hazel; don't be alarmed.'

'I'll try not to be,' she said, conquering a very strong inclination to laugh. She saw that they took it quite seriously; and, though she had at once suspected that some one in the village was playing them a trick, she did not choose to enlighten them. Hazel had a malicious desire to see what the General would do. 'I don't believe he will like the idea at all,' she said to herself. 'What fun it will be!'

Hazel's expectations seemed about to be fulfilled; for already she could hear steps on the plank of the little bridge, and in another minute the General himself entered the fortress.

'I say, you fellows,' he began, 'this is too bad— no one on guard, and a girl inside! Why, she might be a spy for anything you could tell!'

'Thank you, Clarence!' said Hazel; for this insinuation was rather trying to a person of her dignity.

'I say, General,' began Jack, 'never mind about

rowing us now; we've some queer news to report. This has just fallen into our hands.'

Hazel watched Tinling closely as he read the paper. It was grimy, and printed in lead pencil, and contained these words:—'BE ON THE LUKOUT. RED INGIANS ON THE WORPATH. I HERD THEM SAYING THEY MENT TO ATACK YURE FORT AT NITEFAL. FROM A FREND.'

She was soon compelled to own that she had done him a great injustice. He was certainly as far as possible from betraying the slightest fear; on the contrary, his eye seemed actually to brighten with satisfaction. He behaved exactly as all heroes in books of adventure do on such occasions—he went through it twice carefully, and then inquired at what time the warning had arrived.

'About five minutes ago. Round a stone,' answered Guy, with true military conciseness.

'This will be a bad business,' observed the General, his face brightening with the joy of battle. 'We have no time to spare—we must give these demons a lesson they will not forget!' (this was out of the books). 'Look to your arms, my men, and see that we are provisioned for a siege (you might get the cook to give us some of that shortbread, and the rest of the cake we had at tea, Private Jack). We cannot tell to what straits we may be reduced.'

'Then,' inquired Hazel, demurely, 'you mean to stay here and fight them?'

'To the last gasp!' said the General.

Hazel liked him better then than she had done since his first arrival.

'He really is a plucky boy after all,' she thought. 'I wonder if it will last?'

ACT THE SECOND

WHERE IS THE ARMY?

THE General's self-possession and resource were indeed remarkable.

'We ought to have a cannon,' he said; 'there's a big roll of matting somewhere in the house. If we got that, and widened a loophole, and shoved it through, it would look just like the muzzle of a cannon in the dark.'

'Would that frighten a Red Indian much?' asked Hazel.

'Not if he knew what it was, perhaps; but who's going to tell him? Jack, just run up to the house, like a good fellow, and see if you can find it, will you? You can go with him, Guy.'

'You seem rather to like the idea of being attacked,' said Hazel, when she and Clarence were alone together. He was gratified to notice the new friendliness in her voice.

'Well, you see,' he explained loftily, 'I don't

O

suppose I'm pluckier than most people, but it just
happens that I'm not afraid of Red Indians, that's
all; when I saw all those at Buffalo Bill's I wasn't
even excited: it's constitutional, I fancy.' He always
modelled his talk a good deal upon books, and a crisis
like this naturally brought out his largest language.

'I'd better see you safe back to the house, I think,'
he added; 'I don't expect them for an hour yet, but
you can never depend on savages—they might be
lurking about the grounds already, for what we know.'

And, although Hazel had her own private ideas
about the reality of the danger, she was struck by his
coolness and courage, for which, whether justified or
not by the occasion, she was quite fair-minded enough
to give him due credit.

Meanwhile, the other two boys, bursting with
excitement, had rushed up to the verandah, under
which their mother and uncle were sitting.

'Mother! Uncle Lambert! What do you think?
Our camp is going to be attacked this very night by
Indians!'

'Yes, dears,' said Mrs. Jolliffe, serenely; 'but have
you had your teas yet?'

Trifles such as these harrow the martial soul
more than conflicts.

'But, mother, did you hear what we said? The
fort is to be stormed by Red Indians!'

'Very well, dears, so long as you don't make too
much noise,' was the sole comment of this most

provokingly placid lady. What she ought to have done was, of course, to throw down her work, raise her eyes to the clouds, clasp her hands, and observe, in an agitated tone, 'Heaven protect us! We are lost!' But few mothers are capable of really rising to emergencies of this kind.

Hilary and Cecily had been playing tennis, and, overhearing the alarming news, came up to the steps of the verandah. 'Did you say Red Indians were coming here?'

Uncle Lambert shook his head lugubriously. 'I always warned your father,' he remarked; 'but he *would* come to live in Berkshire.'

'Why?' inquired Cecily. 'Is Berkshire a bad place for Red Indians, uncle?'

'I should say it was one of the worst places in all Europe!' he said solemnly.

Both Hilary and Cecily had heard and read a good deal about Red Indians lately, and had also, with their brothers, visited the American Exhibition, so that it did not strike either of them as unlikely just then that there should be a few scattered about in England, just as gipsies are.

'But what are you going to do about it?' they asked their brother.

'Lick 'em, of course!' said Guy. 'Now you see that an army is some use, after all.'

'Don't be taken alive, there's good boys,' advised their frivolous uncle, who seemed still unable to realise

the extreme gravity of the occasion.   'Sell your lives
as dearly as possible.'

'What is the use of telling them that, uncle?' exclaimed Cecily.   'They wouldn't get the money; and
do you think any of *us* would touch it?   How can
you talk in that horrid way?   Jack and Guy, don't
go to that camp.   Let the Indians have it, if they
want to; you can soon build another.'

'You don't understand,' said Jack, impatiently.
'We can't have a lot of Red Indians in our camp—it
wouldn't be safe for you.'

'Oh, I shall go and speak to Clarence,' she cried.
'I'm sure he won't want to fight them.'   And she ran
down to the end of the lawn, where he could be seen
returning with Hazel.

'I want to speak to you quite alone,' she said.
'No, Hazel, it's a secret,' and she drew him aside.

'Clarence,' she said, and her blue eyes were
dark with fear, 'tell me—are the Indians really
coming?'

'You can judge for yourself,' he said, and gave
her the paper.   'We've just had this thrown over the
stockade.   It seems to have been written by somebody
who is in their secrets.'

'How badly Red Indians do spell!' said Cecily,
shuddering as she read.

'It may be a white man's writing,' he said; 'perhaps a prisoner, or a confederate who repents.'

'But, Clarence, dear,' entreated Cecily (ten minutes

ago she would not have added the epithet), 'you won't stay out and sit up for them, will you?'

'Do you think we're a set of cowards?' he demanded grandly.

'Not you, Clarence; but—but Jack and Guy are not very big boys, are they? I mean, they're a little too young to fight full-sized Indians.'

'There will be all sorts of sized Indians, I expect,' said Clarence. 'Of course, I don't say they'll come. They may think discretion's the better part of valour when they find we're prepared; but I must say I anticipate an attack myself.'

'I wish you would do without Jack and Guy. Couldn't you?' suggested Cecily.

His eyes gleamed. 'Cecily,' he said, 'tell me the worst—the army are getting in a funk?'

'No,' she cried; and then she resolved to sacrifice their reputation for their safety. 'At least, they haven't said anything; but I'm sure they'd feel more comfortable in the drawing-room. Can't you order them to stay and guard us? You're General.'

'And I am to face the foe alone?' he cried. 'Well, I am older than them' (I must decline to be responsible for the grammar of the characters of this story). 'I have lived my life—I shall be the less missed. . . . Let it be as you say.'

All this was strictly according to the books, and he enjoyed himself immensely.

'Thank you, dear, dear Clarence. I'd no idea

you were so noble and brave. Try not to let those
Indians hit you.'

'I cannot answer for the future,' he said ; 'but
since you wish it I will do my best.'

After all there was some good in girls. Here was
one who said exactly the right things, without needing
any prompting whatever.

Cecily hunted up Jack and Guy, who were poking
about in the house. 'You're not to guard the stockade,' she announced, with ill-concealed triumph.

'Oh, aren't we, though ?' said Guy ; 'who says so ?
Not mother !'

'No—Clarence ; he said I was to tell you to go on
duty in the drawing-room.'

'What bosh !' said Guy. 'As if any Indians
would come there ! I don't care what Clarence says,
I shall go in the stockade !'

'So shall I !' said Jack. 'Now let's get that piece
of matting, and go down sharp—the evening star's
out already.'

Poor Cecily was in despair ; what was to be done
when they were so obstinate as this ?

'I know where there's some beautiful matting,'
she said.

'Where ? Tell us, quick !'

'Come with me, and I'll show you.' She led the
way along a corridor to the wing where the billiard-
room was. 'Wait till I see if it's there still,' she said,

and went into the billiard-room and looked around. ' Yes, it *is* there,' she told them as she came out.

' I don't see it, Cecily; where? ' they cried from within.

Cecily shut the door softly, and turned the key (which she had managed to abstract on entering) in the outer lock.

' It's on the floor,' she cried through the keyhole; ' I didn't tell a story—and don't be angry, boys, dear, it's all for your good! '

Then, without waiting to hear their indignant outcry, she scudded along the corridor and down the staircase, with the sounds of muffled shouts and kicks growing fainter behind her.

' I don't mind so much now,' she thought; 'they'll be awfully angry when they come out — but the Indians will have gone by that time! '

Clarence had already retreated to his stronghold when she entered the drawing-room.

Everything seemed as usual; Uncle Lambert, in evening dress, was playing desultory snatches from *Ruddigore*. Mrs. Jolliffe came down presently, and he took her in to dinner with one of his tiresome jokes. No one seemed at all anxious about poor Tinling, fighting all alone down in the paddock.

She curled herself up on a settee by one of the open windows, and listened, trying to catch the sound of Indian yells. ' Hazel,' she said anxiously, ' do you think the Indians will hurt Tinling? '

Hazel gave a little laugh. 'I don't think the army's in any very great danger, Cis,' she replied.

'Hazel doesn't believe there are any Indians at all,' explained Hilary.

'Well,' said Cecily, softly, 'I've kept the army out of danger, whether there are or not!'

But she felt relieved by her sisters' evident tranquillity, and by-and-by, when Mrs. Jolliffe came in from the dining-room and settled down with her embroidery as if there were not the least chance of a savage coming whooping in the open window, Cecily almost forgot her fears.

They came back in full force, however, as, a little later on, she heard a quick, light step on the gravel outside, and started with a little scream of terror. 'Don't tell them where the army are!' she cried; and then she saw that her alarm was needless, for it was the gallant General who stepped into the room. Hazel looked up from the album which she was making for a children's hospital, Hilary threw away her book, Mrs. Jolliffe had ceased to embroider, but that was because she was peacefully dozing.

'Victory!' said Clarence, waving his sword.

'Then they did come?' cried Cecily, triumphantly.

'Rather!' he replied. 'I couldn't tell how many there were, but they were overcome with panic at the first discharge. I fancy *these* Indians had never heard firearms before.'

'How funny that we shouldn't have heard any now!' remarked Hazel, resting her chin on her palms, while her grey eyes had a rather mocking sparkle in them.

'Not funny at all,' he said, 'considering the wind was the other way. I let them come on, and then poured a volley into the thickest part of their ranks—that made them waver, and then I made a sortie, and you should have just seen them scuttle!'

'I wish I had,' said Hazel, as she pasted another Christmas card into her album. 'And weren't you wounded at all?'

'A mere scratch,' he said lightly (which is what book-heroes always say).

'It looks as if you had been amongst the gooseberry-bushes,' said Hilary, examining his arm as he pulled up his sleeve.

'Does it? Well, I only know it's lucky for me there were no poisoned arrows.'

'Oughtn't you to have it burnt, though, Clarence, just in case?' suggested Cecily, in all good faith; 'there's sure to be a red-hot poker in the kitchen.'

But Clarence was very decidedly of opinion that such a precaution was not necessary.

'And you're quite sure the Indians are all gone?' she asked.

'There isn't one of 'em within miles,' he said confidently, 'I'll answer for that.'

'Then come upstairs with me, and we'll let the army out. They'll be in such a temper!'

They found the two boys, who had tired of kicking and shouting by that time, sitting gloomily on the long seats in the dark.

'Guy, dear—Jack,' said Cecily, timidly, 'you can come out now. Clarence has beaten the Indians.'

'Without us?' groaned Guy. 'Cecily, I'll never speak to you again! Tinling, I—we—you don't think we funked, do you? She locked us up here!'

All the General's native magnanimity came out now.

'We won't say any more about it,' he said. 'It was rather a close shave, with only one man to do it all. But, there, I managed somehow, and perhaps it was just as well you weren't there. The first rush was no joke, I can tell you.'

Jack punched his own head with both hands.

'Oh, it's too bad!' he said—he was almost in tears. 'They'll all think we deserted you! Did you kill many of them, Tinling?'

'I didn't see any corpses,' he replied; 'but I shouldn't be surprised if some of them died when they got home.'

'They may come again to-morrow night,' said Jack, more cheerfully.

'Not much fear of that—they've had their lesson. They were seized with utter panic.'

'Which way did they go?' asked Guy, evidently bent on pursuing them.

'Oh, in all directions. But you wouldn't catch them up now; they ran too fast for me even!'

'Then I shall go to bed,' said the entire army, in great depression. 'It is a shame we couldn't be there. Good-night, General.' And, pointedly ignoring poor Cecily, they marched off to their quarters. She looked wistfully after them.

'They'll never forgive me—I know they won't!' she said to Tinling.

'Don't you mind,' he said, 'you acted very wisely. And, after all, these raw young troops can never be depended on under fire, you know—I mean, under arrows.'

Cecily drew herself up a little haughtily.

'I locked them in because I didn't want them to get hurt,' she said, 'not because I thought they'd be afraid.'

Uncle Lambert did not hear about the result of the engagement until the following day, but then, to make up for any delay, he heard a good deal about it. Even Clarence was not quite prepared for the enthusiasm he showed.

'Splendid, my boy, splendid!' he kept repeating, while he hit him rather hard on the back; 'you're a hero. A grateful country ought to give you the Bath for it. I shall take care this affair is generally known.'

And the poor army looked on with hot cheeks and envious eyes. But for Cecily, they might have been heroes, too!

Even Hazel seemed to have understood that a really brilliant victory had been achieved; she brought Tinling a magnificent flag of pink glazed calico, on which she had painted in crimson letters: 'Indians' Terror.'

'I did not think of making the motto "Seven at one blow,"' she said, with a mischievous dimple.

'I like the other best,' said the General, unsuspectingly.

Jack and Guy went down to the camp as usual, but for some time they were in very low spirits, in spite of their commander's well-meant efforts to raise them.

'You'll do better next time,' he said kindly.

'But we've told you over and over again how it was!' they would exclaim.

'Yes, I know, I know. It's all right. I'm not complaining: I never expected you to be as cool as I was, your first time.' But even this did not seem to console the army to any large extent; they hunched their shoulders and kicked pebbles about with great apparent interest.

The fact was, they could not help seeing that they had lost their prestige. It was true that their mother and elder sister at least (in spite of the flag) did not seem to treat the past danger with all the seriousness

it deserved. It even struck Jack and Guy sometimes
that they were under the delusion that the whole
thing had been only a new development of the game.
But as the General said : 'Even if that were so, it
was kinder not to undeceive them. He certainly was
contented to leave them in their error ; he knew well
enough what he had had to go through—he did not
like even now to think of his despair when he found
he would have to face the danger all alone.'

He was always making the army writhe by little
unintentional reminders of this kind, and they had
cruel misgivings that Uncle Lambert, though he was
always quite kind and encouraging, did not in his
heart believe that their unfortunate absence in the
hour of peril was quite an accident on their part.

How they longed for an opportunity of wiping out
their disgrace, and how their hearts sank when Tinling, from the depths of his experience, declared it
very improbable that the attack would ever again be
renewed. In the school-stories, the good boy who
refuses to fight when he is kicked, and is sent to
Coventry as a coward, always gets a speedy chance
to clear his character. Someone (generally the very
boy who kicked him) falls into a mill-stream, or a
convenient horse runs away, or else a mad but considerate bull comes into the playground—and the
good boy is always at hand to dive, or hang on to the
bridle and be dragged several yards in the dust, or
slowly retreat backwards, throwing down first his hat

and then his coat to amuse and detain the infuriated
bull.

But out of stories, unfortunately, as even Jack
and Guy dimly perceived, things are not always
arranged so satisfactorily. They might have to wait
for weeks, perhaps months or years, before Uncle
Lambert fell into the fish-pond—and, even if he did,
he could probably swim better than they could. Then
they were neither of them sure that they could suc-
cessfully stop a runaway horse, or a maniac bull,
without a little more practice than they had had
as yet. ·

However, Fortune was kind, and took pity on
them in a most unexpected manner. For one morning, soon after breakfast, when Hazel was practising
in the music-room, and Hilary and Cecily feeding
their rabbits, Jack came up in a highly-excited state
of mind to the verandah where his officer was seated
doing nothing in particular. 'General,' he said, with
a very creditable salute, 'do come down to the camp
at once.'

'Oh, bother!' said the veteran warrior, who had,
by the way, shown rather a tendency to rest on his
laurels of late.

'No, but it isn't humbug, really,' protested Jack ;
'it's something you'll like awfully.'

The General marched down in a very stately manner ; it would have been undignified to run, eager as
he was to get down to the stockade, thinking it not

unlikely that Lintoft, the carpenter, really had found time to make a cannon for them after all, or, at the very least, that there would be some change in the internal arrangements of the stronghold which it would be his duty as superior officer to criticise, if not condemn.

Now it must be explained here that, during the last two or three days, the outside wall of the fort had been placarded with various bills, all glorying in the recent repulse of the enemy by a single-handed defender, and containing most insulting reflections on the courage of Red Indians as a race; while, in case they might not have enough knowledge of English to understand these taunts, they were accompanied by sketches which were certainly scathing enough to infuriate the least susceptible savage.

To do Clarence justice, they were not due to any elation on his part, but had all been executed by the army in the wild hope that they might thus stir up the foe to a fresh demonstration, when they themselves might recover their lost spurs.

These placards, as Clarence found on reaching the stockade, had been scrawled over with a kind of red and yellow paint so as to be quite illegible.

'Ochre,' said Guy; 'but that's not the best of it, for we found this pinned with an arrow to one of the posts.' And he produced a thin strip of white bark, on which were writing and drawings in crimson. 'They must have done it with their own blood,'

commented Jack, with great gusto; 'but read it—do
read it.'

Clarence did not need a second invitation to read
the document, which was as follows :—

'WAH NA SA PASH BOO (YELLOW VULTURE),

*Chief of Black Bogallala Tribe, to the Great White Chief,
Tin Lin,* DEFIANCE.

'The wigwam of Yellow Vulture wants but one
ornament—the scalp of the white chief.   Yellow Vulture has seen the taunts calling the red warriors
"women with the hearts of deer."   He will show the
Paleface that the anger of the dusky ones is a big
heap-lot terrible.   When the sun has set behind the
hills, and the stars light their watch-fires, then will
Yellow Vulture and his braves be at hand.   The scalp
of the Paleface shall adorn the tepee of the Red Man.

'WAH-WAH !'

In order that there should be no possible mistake
about the intention, the message was supplemented by
a rude representation of the process of scalping, evidently the work of a practised hand.

'Didn't I tell you we had something jolly to show
you !' exclaimed Jack.

But joy, or some equally powerful emotion, rendered the General incapable of speaking for several
moments.

ACT THE THIRD

WHERE IS THE GENERAL?

IT was some little time before Clarence Tinling gave any opinion upon this bloodthirsty document. He turned exceedingly red, and examined it suspiciously on both sides. It seemed as if he did not altogether welcome this second opportunity for distinguishing himself. When he spoke it was with a sort of angry anxiety.

'You think yourselves very clever, I dare say,' he said; 'but you needn't fancy you'll take me in! Come, you had better say so at once—you did this yourselves? It is not half bad—I will say that for it.'

'That we didn't,' cried Guy. 'Why, just look at it, Tinling. Any one could see that it's an Indian's doing. No, it's all right; they really are coming.'

'It's all skittles, I tell you,' said Clarence, still more angrily, though he was paler again now. 'What should Indians come here for?'

'Well, he says why, there,' said Jack, 'and they came the other evening.'

Clarence's colour rose again. 'That's different,' he said; 'I mean, it's not the same tribe.'

'No, these are Black Bogallalas,' said Jack. 'What were the first ones, Tinling?'

'I didn't ask them,' said the General shortly.

'How many braves should you think Wah Na

P

What's-his-name will bring?' asked Guy. 'As many as came the other evening? How many did come the first time?'

'Do you think I had nothing better to do than count?' he retorted. 'Is there anything else you would like to know?'

'Well, we'll hang out the lantern to-night, and watch how many come inside its rays,' said Jack, with a briskness which displeased his chief.

'You wouldn't be quite so jolly cheerful over it if you knew what it was like!' he grumbled.

'Why not?' said Guy. 'You beat the others easily enough by yourself, and we shall be three this time.'

'Oh, it's all very fine to talk,' retorted the General; 'but we shall see what your mother and uncle say about it. They—they may think we ought not to take any notice of it.'

Jack's eyes opened wide at this. 'Not take any notice of an attack by Black Bogallalas! I don't see how we can very well help noticing it!'

'It all depends on what Mrs. Jolliffe says,' replied the conscientious General. 'I'm only a visitor here, and it wouldn't be the right thing for me to lead you into danger without leave.'

'Well, you weren't so particular the first time the Indians came!' remarked Guy.

'Will you shut up about that first time!' the Commander burst out, in exasperation; 'it's the

second time now—that is, if it isn't all humbug.
That's what I mean to find out first—you stay here
till I come back, will you ? '

Taking the strip of bark with him, he went slowly
up to the house. He had an uneasy feeling that the
Indian's challenge was genuine enough, but he still
hoped to have it pronounced a forgery. This may
seem strange indeed to some, considering the courage
of which he had already given proof, but I do not
wish to make any further mystery, particularly as
most of my readers will probably have already guessed
the secret of this apparent contrast.

The fact is, then, that Clarence Tinling had the
best of reasons for being cool and courageous on the
previous occasion. Those Indians were entirely
imaginary ; he had written the warning himself, and
instructed the coachman's boy to throw it over the
stockade ; the attack on the fort and the brilliant
victory were an afterthought.

What had he done it for ? That is rather difficult
to explain—perhaps he hardly knew himself ; he had
a vague idea of proving to those disrespectful girls
that enemies did exist, and that the protection of an
Army was not to be despised.

Then when he found himself alone in the camp,
the temptation to carry his invention further was too
much for him ; and after Jack and Guy and Cecily,
and even Uncle Lambert himself, accepted his story
without hesitation, and treated him as a hero—why,

it would have looked so silly to explain then, and so he went through with it.

Lying is lying, whatever explanations and excuses may be made respecting it, and I am afraid it must be admitted that Tinling, if he began by a mere harmless device for giving a new turn to the game, ended by telling some very unmistakable lies.

Now he found himself in a most delicate position: what if an attack by Red Indians should really be quite possible? Mr. Lambert Jolliffe had certainly not seemed to see anything incredible in the former visit, and, though Clarence had not a very high opinion of his abilities, he was grown up, and was not likely to be misinformed on such a point as that—at all events, he was the best person to consult just then. As he expected, he found him under the big ilex on his back, with his after-breakfast pipe, no longer alight, between his lips.

'Mr. Jolliffe; I say, Mr. Jolliffe,' began Clarence.

Lambert Jolliffe sat up, and fixed his glass in one drowsy eye. 'Hullo, Sir Garnet—I beg your pardon, Lord Wolseley, I mean. You ought to hear what they're saying at the War Office, I can tell you!'

Praise is sweet, even when we do not deserve it, and Clarence felt a thrill of satisfaction at this somewhat vague tribute.

'I wanted to ask you,' he said, 'should you say that Red Indians were—well, common in England?'

'You have asked me a straightforward question,

and I'll give you a straightforward answer,' was
the reply. ' Till quite lately I should say they were
absolutely unknown in this country.'

Clarence's face brightened; he felt quite fond of
Uncle Lambert, and began to think him a particularly
well-informed and entertaining person.

' Yes,' continued Uncle Lambert, thoughtfully, ' I
must confess I thought it a little unlikely at first that
you should have been annoyed by Red Indians; but,
of course, when I remembered the Earl's Court Show,
I saw at once that it was quite possible.' Clarence
felt a cold qualm. He had, as we already know, seen
Buffalo Bill's wonderful show, which, indeed, was responsible for much of his recent military enthusiasm.
But till that moment, curiously enough, it had not
occurred to him to connect the mysterious Wah Na
Sa Pash Boo with the denizens of the Wild West
whom he had seen careering about the immense
arena at Earl's Court.

' Do you mean,' he said, with an effort, ' that you
thought some of Buffalo Bill's Indians had managed
to *escape* ? '

' Well, I don't know any other way to account for
such a thing. Do you ? '

Clarence did not answer this question directly :
' But,' he objected desperately, ' those were *converted*
Indians. They went to church, and the Lyceum, and
all that ! '

Uncle Lambert shrugged his shoulders : ' Once an

Indian always an Indian ! ' he said. 'They must have their fling now and then, I suppose, and then the old Adam crops up. And you see,' he added, 'it cropped up in that attack on you the other night. Fortunately for us, and indeed for the whole country, you were prepared for them—otherwise no one can tell what horrors we might not have seen.'

'We may—we may see them yet ! ' said the hero, gloomily. 'Just look at this, Mr. Jolliffe.'

Lambert took the bark from him, and read it with a thoughtful frown. At last he said :

'Well, I rather expected something of this sort when I saw you posting up all those insulting notices —Indians are so confoundedly touchy, you know.'

'You might have said that at the time, then ! ' exclaimed the General reproachfully.

Lambert lifted his eyebrows.

'My dear chap, I thought you knew. Wasn't that what you were all driving at ? '

'Not me,' said Clarence. 'I was against it from the first. I told them it was caddish to insult a fallen foe, but they would go and stick up those *beastly* notices.'

'All's well that ends well, eh ? You've got a rise out of 'em this time. I congratulate you, my boy, on getting the chance of a second brush with the Indians. And this time you'll have the army with you.'

'A lot of good they are ! ' said Clarence, in a muffled voice.

'Come, it's not good form for a General to run down his troops ; but you heroes are always so modest. I'll be bound, now, you've determined not to mention this in the house till the danger is passed ? '

'No, I haven't, though. I shall mention it, most likely. Why not ? '

'To save them useless anxiety. Because, unless I am wrong, you see cause to apprehend (I must ask you not to conceal anything from me)—to apprehend that this will be a more serious affair than the last ? '

'Yes, I do,' replied the General, promptly, 'a good deal.'

'I feared as much,' said Uncle Lambert, with a very grave face. 'But in that case, isn't it as well not to terrify my sister and those poor girls unnecessarily ? '

'I don't see that. Mrs. Jolliffe might think we ought to be guarding the inside of the house.'

'Oh,' said Uncle Lambert, 'but I should object to that strongly. You see it's very plain that it's *you* the Yellow Vulture's after. He won't think of coming near the house unless you're in it, and then what will become of us all ? '

'You'll take care you don't get mixed up in it, I can see,' said Tinling, savagely.

'I shall take very good care indeed. Oh, but you must make allowances for me, my boy. Remember, I've not been in military training for days and days, as you have.'

'If that's all, I could get you up in the drill in half-an-hour,' proposed Tinling, eagerly.

'Thanks, but I have a better reason still. Tastes differ so much. You like to spend your evenings in beating off wild Indians from a stockade. Now, I prefer a plain, comfortable dinner, and a quiet cigar. I'm not sure that your way isn't the manlier of the two—but it's not nearly so much in my line.'

'Why don't you say you're a funk, and have done with it ? ' Tinling said rudely.

'My dear young friend,' was the placid answer, 'if Providence has endowed you with a meed of personal courage beyond that of others, it is ungraceful to taunt those who are less fortunate. While I am by no means prepared to admit that I am what you so pleasingly term " a funk," I readily allow that——'

But Tinling did not stay to hear any more ; he turned on his heel with an anger that had a spice of envy in it. Why, why had not he been content with an ordinary reputation, instead of one that he must sustain now at all hazards ? He could deceive himself no longer ; his foolish vanity, which had allowed the army to post those rash defiances, had brought down some real Red Indians upon him, and he was horribly afraid.

As he walked restlessly down the path, a veil seemed drawn across the brilliant sky, the dahlias and 'red-hot pokers' and gladioli in the beds burnt with a sinister glow, the smell of the sweet peas and mignonette seemed oppressive, the bees droning about the lavender patches had a note of warning in their buzz, he felt chilly in the shade and sick in the sun.

He saw nothing for it but fighting, but the idea of facing a horde of howling savages with only two boys younger than himself was too appalling; he must engage recruits, grown-up ones, and with this intention he went to the stable-yard, where he found Chinnock, the coachman, sluicing the carriage-wheels.

'Chinnock,' he began, with an attempt to seem casual and careless, 'we're going to be attacked by Red Indians again to-night.'

Chinnock touched a sandy forelock, as he raised his red grinning face.

'Lor', sir, be you indeed? Well, you young genl'men du have rare goings on down in the paddock, that you du.'

'It's—it's real Red Indians this time, Chinnock— B—black Bogallalas!'

Chinnock had deliberately moved to the harness-room, and Tinling had to repeat his information.

'Ah, indeed, sir! Red Injians? Well, to think o' that!' he said cheerfully, as if he was humouring some rather childish remark.

'But we shall want every available man; do you think you can spare time to come and help?'

''Bout what time, sir?' said Chinnock.

'About nine—half-past eight, say. Do try.'

'Can't come as late as that, nohow, sir. That's

my supper-hour, that is. If the mistress don't want the carriage to-day, I dessay I could step down 'bout five for half-an-hour or so, if that would suit.'

'That wouldn't be any use at all, Chinnock; we shan't begin till dark.'

'Then I'm afraid I can't be of no sarvice to 'ee, sir.'

The poor General turned away: evidently the coachman had no intention of risking his life. He remembered Joe, the gardener's boy and stable-help —he was better than no one. Joe was rolling the tennis-court, and grinned sheepishly on being pressed to join.

'Noa, sur,' he said, 'it doan't lay in my work fur to fight no Injins. I see one onst at Reading Vair, I did, a nippin' about he wur, and a roarin'! I bain't goin' to hev naught to do with the likes o' he!'

Tinling saw only one hope left. If he could see Mrs. Jolliffe and tell her of the danger which threatened him, she might refuse permission to fight at all, or, at the very least, she would see that he had proper assistance. So into the house he went, and the first person he found was Hazel, who was knitting her pretty forehead over the Latin exercise which had been given her as a holiday task.

'I say, Hazel,' he said, with a trembling voice; but she interrupted him:

'Oh, perhaps you can help me. What's the Latin for "Balbus says it is all over with the General"?'

He shivered; it sounded so like an omen. 'No, but Hazel, listen,' he said; 'the Indians are coming again to-night.'

'If you're not going to talk sensibly,' said Hazel, 'go out this instant.'

He saw she was utterly unsympathetic, and he wandered on to the hall, which was used as a morning-room, where Hilary sat painting a pansy, and he broke the news to her in much the same words. She actually laughed, and she had been almost as frightened as Cecily when he had told her of the other Indians.

'You are too killing over those Red Indians!' she said. Privately, he thought that the Red Indians would do all the killing.

'You needn't laugh; it's true!' he said solemnly.

'Oh, of course!' said Hilary; 'but don't come so near, or you'll upset my glass of water.' Hilary, too, was hopeless; he was reduced to his last cards now, and came in upon Mrs. Jolliffe as she sat at her writing-table. She looked up with a sweet, vague smile.

'What is it now, dear boy?' she asked. 'I hope you are managing to amuse yourself.'

'I think I ought to tell you,' he said thickly, 'that a tribe of Bogallala Indians are going to storm our encampment this evening.'

Perhaps Mrs. Jolliffe was getting a little bored with military topics. 'Yes, yes,' she said absently, 'that will be very nice, I'm sure. Don't be too late in coming in, there's good boys.'

'You don't *mind* our being there ?—there will be danger !' he said with meaning.

'Mind? Not in the very least, so long as you are enjoying yourself,' she said kindly.

There went one card: he had but one more. 'Could you let Corklett and George' (they were the butler and page respectively) 'come down to the camp about half-past eight? We should be so much safer if we had them with us.'

'What are you thinking of, Clarence? We dine at eight, remember ; how can I send either of them down then? You really must be reasonable.'

Clarence was by no means an ill-mannered boy in general, but fear made him insolent at this.

'Of course, if you think your dinner is more important than us !' he burst out hotly.

'Clarence, I can't allow you to speak to me in that way. It is ridiculous for you to expect me to alter my arrangements to suit your convenience,' said Mrs. Jolliffe ; 'leave the room, or I shall be really angry with you. I don't wish to hear any more—go.'

He went with a swelling heart, and in the garden he met Cecily. If he could only induce her to beg him not to risk his life again ! He disclosed the situation as impressively as he could ; but, alas ! Cecily seemed perfectly tranquil.

'I'm not a bit afraid this time,' she said, ' because you beat them so easily before; there's only one thing, Clarence. You know I daren't lock the army in again—they've made it up; but they *were* so cross over it! So I want you to promise to look after them.'

'I shall have enough to do to look after myself, I expect,' he answered roughly; ' you don't know what these Indians are.'

'Oh, but I do, Clarence; I saw them at the " Wild West." I thought they looked rather nice then. And you know you frightened them so before. You are so awfully brave—aren't you ? '

'I—I don't think I feel quite so awfully brave as I did then,' he admitted.

'Ah, but you will. Jack and Guy will be quite safe with you. Good-bye; I'm going to get some mulberry-leaves for my silkworms.' And she ran off cheerfully.

It was his hard fate that everybody persisted in treating the affair in one of two ways—either they looked upon it as part of the army game, or else considered him such a champion, on the strength of his past exploits, that there was practically no danger even if a whole tribe of Redskins came to attack him.

Luncheon that day was a terrible meal for him. Uncle Lambert (though he was too great a coward to go near the fight himself) seemed very anxious that the defenders should be in good condition. 'Give yourself a chance, General,' he would say; 'another slice of this roly-poly pudding may just turn the scale between you and Yellow Vulture. Look at the army —they're victualling for a regular siege!'

But Clarence was quite unable to follow their example; he was annoyed with them for what he considered was 'showing off'—though he might have reflected that to consume three helpings of jam-and-suet in rapid succession was an almost impossible form of bravado.

The rest of the afternoon he spent in trying to lower the army's confidence by telling all the gruesome stories of Indian warfare he could think of; but he frightened himself a great deal more than them, and at last had to abandon the attempt in despair.

For Jack and Guy had no nerves to speak of; they were eager to clear their tarnished reputation, and the possibility of harm coming to them did not seem to present itself. They had formed rather a poor opinion of Buffalo Bill's Indians, whose yell turned out to be very little more than short yelps, and who ran away directly a Cowboy showed his nose. Hadn't Clarence defeated them with ease already? What Clarence had done alone they surely could do together, and then they had an unbounded belief in the impregnable character of their stockade.

Tinling found that he could not undeceive them without exposing himself, which he would still rather die than do, and he roamed about the grounds, making a little mental calculation whenever a clock struck in the heavy afternoon stillness : ' In so many hours from this I shall be fighting hand-to-hand with real Indians ! '

Then at tea-time he thought (for the first time) the smell of cake quite detestable, and he hardly knew how he forced himself to sit quietly on his chair.

' General Tinling,' said Uncle Lambert, ' before you, so to speak, " go to the front " and occupy the post of danger, will you oblige me by drawing up the troops before the verandah ? I should like, though unable to accompany you myself, to say a few words of farewell.'

Clarence sulkily acquiesced, and Lambert Jolliffe addressed the army : ' Soldiers,' he said, ' a great responsibility rests upon you this day. You are expected solemnly and earnestly to strive your utmost *not* to

> Let the red man dance
> By *our* red cedar tree,

to quote (with a trifling variation) from Tennyson's " Maud." For myself, I have no fears of the result. Under the leadership of your veteran General, victory must infallibly crown your arms. We peaceful civilians shall rest secure in the absolute confidence such protection inspires, and be the first to welcome your triumphant return. Should your hearts fail you at any moment, I have already instructed you how to act.

To the Commander himself I should consider the mere suggestion an impertinence. Go, then, devoted spirits, where Glory leads, and endeavour to avoid the indignity of scalping—if only for the sake of appearances. Soldiers, I have done. May the God of Battles (I need hardly explain to scholars that I refer to Mars) keep his eye on you!'

Hazel and Hilary were also on the verandah, and used their handkerchiefs freely—but principally to conceal their mouths. 'They'll be sorry they laughed by-and-by;' thought Clarence; 'they'll wish they had cried just a little, perhaps!'—a reflection the pathos of which very nearly made him cry himself, as he marched down to the stockade, feeling distinctly unwell.

Before he entered the fort he tore down the fatal notices. 'What's the good of that?' asked Guy.

'Well, the Indians have seen 'em,' said the General.

'But they'll think we want to back out of it,' objected Jack.

'Let them think!' was the bold retort.

Inside the fort Jack and Guy set to work in the highest spirits to barricade the entrance with wheel-barrows and an old mowing-machine; then they lit the lantern, and polished their guns, sharpened their swords, and looked to the springs of their pistols for about the hundredth time.

'I say, this would jolly well pepper a Red Indian, wouldn't it!' cried Guy, showing a pistol, the tiny barrel of which was constructed to discharge swanshot with a steel watch-spring.

'I tell you what,' said Jack, with the air of a trapper, 'I shall reserve my peas till I've fired away all the corks, and take a deliberate aim each time.'

It was impossible to persuade them that these missiles would not be accepted as deadly by savages, who of course would know no better; and again, had not the first victory been won by these simple means?

So General Tinling held his peace, and the western sky slowly changed from crocus to green, and from green to deep violet, and the evening star lighted its steady golden fire, the grasshoppers set up a louder chirp, a bat executed complicated figures overhead, and the boys unconsciously began to speak in whispers.

'It's getting too dark to see much with this telescope,' said Jack, 'I wish we had a night-glass. The Indians ought to be here by this time—they said "sunset," didn't they? If I *was* a Red Indian I would be punctual! When do you suppose they'll come, Clarence—soon?'

'How on earth do I know?' snapped the General from within the tent.

'Well, you needn't get in a bait over it. How did they come on the first time—did they crawl along like snakes till they were quite near, and then give a yell and rush at the stockade?'

'I forget what they did—don't bother me!'

Q

' I suppose they'll all have tomahawks,' said Guy.
' Clarence, does scalping hurt ? '

There was a slight convulsion inside the tent, but
no answer.

' I wonder if the Bogallala torture prisoners,' Jack
observed ; ' I don't think I could stand *that.*'

The General came to the tent-door at this : ' Can't
you fellows shut up ? ' he said fiercely. ' They'll hear
you ! '

' They're not here yet—we shall know when they
come, by the signalling—let's all keep quite quiet for a
minute or two.'

There was a breathless interval of silence. At last
Jack said : ' I hear something—a sort of low grunting
noise, like pigs.'

' Perhaps it is the pigs at the farm,' suggested
Guy.

' Indians can imitate all kinds of birds, I know,'
reasoned Jack, not directly to the point, perhaps, but
he was getting excited.

Tinling felt a dull rage against the other two.
How dared they pretend not to be afraid ? It was all
swagger—he knew that very well. Various unpleasant
recollections began to rise in his mind. He remembered how that Indian spy had stalked the settler's
cabin at Earl's Court. He could see him now, stealing
over the sand, then listening with his ear to the ground,
and turning to beckon on the ambushed warriors.
He even remembered the way the yellow and red

striped blinds of the log hut flapped in the wind, and
how the horse that was hobbled outside raised his
head from his hay, and pricked his ears uneasily, as
the foe came gliding nearer and nearer. Then their
way of fighting—he had thought it rather comic *then*
—they hopped and pranced about like so many lively
frogs, but the butchery would not be rendered any
more agreeable by being accompanied by laughable
gestures! And there was an almost naked light-yellow
savage, whom he recalled dancing the war dance—he
tried not to think of all this, but it came vividly before
him.

'S-s-h—*Cave*!' cried Guy, suddenly, as he looked
through the loophole; 'I can see just the top of one's
head and feathers among the currant bushes. I'll
touch him up in a second.'

He raised his tiny spring pistol, and was just
aiming, when Tinling, almost beside himself, darted
on him, and struck it out of his hand. 'What are
you doing now?' he said, through his teeth. 'What
is the good of *irritating* them?'

'Why, they *are* irritated,' said Guy, 'or they
wouldn't come.'

'If they are,' retorted Clarence, raising his voice,
'whose doing was it? You can't say I had anything
to do with putting up those defiances! Haven't I
always said I respected Red men? They've got feelings
like us. When you go and insult them, of course
they get annoyed—who wouldn't, I should like to

know ?   I honour a chief like Yellow Vulture myself,
and I don't care if he hears me say so. I say I honour
him ! '

His voice rose almost to a scream as he concluded.

' I say, Tinling, I do believe you're in a funk ! '
said Guy, after a moment of wondering silence.

' If you are, say so, and we shall know what to
do,' added Jack, feeling in his pocket.   ' Are you ? '

' Feel his hands,' suggested Guy.

' Look here,' said Clarence, dashing aside the
obstacles before the door, ' I'm not going to stay here
to be treated in this way.   If it hadn't been for your
foolery in sticking up the notices we should have been
friends with the Indians now.   I don't want to
quarrel with any Bogallala.   And you have the
cheek to ask me if I'm in a funk, and to want to feel
my hands.   Well, it just serves you right—I'm going.'

' Well, go then ; who wants you ? ' said Guy.

But softer-hearted Jack said, ' Clarence, you
mustn't.   You'll be safe in here ; but out there—— '

But the General had already vanished.   He was
crouching outside in the shadow of the stockade.   He
could not bear being penned up any longer ; he must
at least have a run for his life.

Had the enemy heard him declare his innocence ?
If so, it did not seem to have softened them.   They
were still crouching—silent, hidden, relentless—
behind the currant bushes, their scouts signalling to
one another, for no *real* grasshopper ever made so much

noise as that. He must make a bolt for it, and take his chance of their arrows missing him. Over the open space of grey-green grass he scuttled, and actually succeeded in reaching the friendly shadow of the holly hedge unharmed; but that was probably because they felt so certain of cutting him off at their pleasure.

On tiptoe and trembling went the General along the narrow paths, green with damp, and latticed by the shadows which branches cast in the sickly moonlight, until—just when he was almost clear of the gloom—his knees bent under him; for there, at the end of the walk, against the starry sky, stood a towering figure, with bristling feather head-dress, and tomahawk poised.

'Oh, please, sir, don't!' he faltered, and shut his eyes, expecting the Indian to bound upon him. But when he opened his eyes again, the savage was gone! He must have slipped behind a ragged old yew which had once been clipped and trimmed to look like a chess-king.

Clarence Tinling tottered on through the shrubbery, which was full of terrors. Warriors, stealthy and cruel, lurked behind every rustling laurel; far away on the lawn he saw their spears through the tall pampas grass; he heard them chirping, clucking, and grunting in every direction as they lay in wait for him, until at last he gained the broad gravel path, at the end of which—oh, how far away they seemed!

—were the three lighted windows of the drawing-room. He could see the interior quite plainly, and the group round the piano where the shaded lamp made a spot of brilliant colour. What were they all doing? Were they huddled together, waiting, watching in an agony of suspense? Nothing of the kind: it will be scarcely credited, perhaps, but this heartless domestic circle were positively passing the time with music, as if nothing were happening!

If only he could reach that bright drawing-room before the rush came! He felt that there were lithe forms stealing along behind the flower-beds. He dared not run, but dragged his heavy feet along the gravel; and then, all at once, from the rhododendron bushes rose a wild, unearthly yell. He could bear it no longer; he would make one last effort, even if they tomahawked him on the very verandah.

Somehow—he never knew how—he found himself in the midst of that quiet musical party, wild with terror, scarcely able to speak.

'The Red Indians!' he gasped. 'Don't let them get me! Save me—hide me somewhere!' and he remembered afterwards that he made a mad endeavour to get inside the piano.

He was instantly surrounded by the astonished family. 'My dear Clarence,' said Mrs. Jolliffe, 'you're perfectly safe—you've been frightening yourself with your own game. There are no Indians here.'

Another howl from the shrubbery seemed to con-
tradict her. 'There, didn't you hear that?' he cried.
'Oh, you won't believe me till it's too late! There
are hundreds of them round the stockade. They may
have scalped Jack and Guy by this time!'

'And why ain't you being scalped too?' inquired
Uncle Lambert.

'I'm sure you needn't talk!' he retorted; 'you
weren't any more anxious to fight than I am.'

'But isn't that different? I thought you had
fought them before, and conquered?'

'Then you thought wrong! Those—those weren't
real Indians—I made them up, then!'

'Now we've got it!' said Uncle Lambert. 'Well,
Master Clarence, you've made your little confes-
sion, and now it's my turn—*I* made Yellow Vulture
up!'

'Are you sure—really sure—on your honour?'
he asked eagerly.

'Honest Injun!' said Lambert. 'You see, I
began to think the military business was getting
rather overdone; the army, like Wordsworth's world,
was "too much with us," and it occurred to me to
see whether the General's courage would stand an
outside test—so I composed that little challenge.
Yes, you see before you the only Wah Na Sa Pash
Boo—no others are genuine!'

Tinling felt that those girls were laughing at him;
they had probably been in the secret for some time;

but he could not care much just then—the relief was
so delicious!

'It was too bad of you, Lambert,' said Mrs.
Jolliffe. 'He was really horribly frightened, and
there are those other two down in the stockade all
alone—you might have thought of that—they will be
half out of their minds by this time!'

'My dear Cecilia,' was the reply, 'don't be uneasy,
I *did* think of it. The moment they begin to feel at
all uncomfortable they have directions to open a
certain packet which explains the whole thing. If
the gallant General had not been in quite such a
hurry, he would have spared himself this unpleasant
experience.'

'Let's all go down, and see how they're getting
on,' said Hazel.

'I know this,' said the General sullenly, 'they
were in quite as big a funk as I was!'

'Then why didn't they run in, and ask to be
hidden too?' inquired Hilary.

'Why? Because they didn't dare!' retorted
Tinling, boldly.

'You know,' he remarked to Cecily, as they were
going down together through the warm darkness,
'it's not fair of your uncle to play these tricks on
fellows.'

'Perhaps it isn't quite,' said Cecily, impartially;
'but then he didn't *begin*, did he?'

'Ahoy!' shouted Uncle Lambert, as they neared

the stockade, and he was answered by a ringing cheer from the fortress.

'Come on—we ain't afraid of you! Don't skulk there—see what you'll get!' And a volley of peas, corks, and small shot flew about their ears.

Lambert Jolliffe ran forward: 'Hi, stop that! spare our lives!' he cried, laughing. 'Jack, you young rascal, put down that confounded popgun—can't you see we're not Red Indians?'

'What, is it you, uncle?' said Guy, in a rather crestfallen tone. 'Where are the Red Indians then?'

'They had to go up to town to see their dentist. But do you mean to say you haven't opened my envelope after all?'

'I thought you told us it was only in case we got frightened?' said Jack.

'What does the General say to *that*?' cried Lambert—but Clarence Tinling was nowhere to be found. He had slipped off to his bedroom, and the next morning he announced at breakfast that he 'thought his people would be wanting him at home.'

So the army was disbanded, for there was a general disarmament, and on the afternoon after Tinling's departure the entire Jolliffe family engaged in a grand cricket match, when lazy Uncle Lambert came out unexpectedly strong as an overhand bowler.

SHUT OUT

I⊤ is towards the end of an afternoon in December, and Wilfred Rolleston is walking along a crowded London street with his face turned westward. A few moments ago and he was scarcely conscious of where he was or where he meant to go: he was walking on mechanically in a heavy stupor, through which there stole a haunting sense of degradation and despair that tortured him dully. And suddenly, as if by magic, this has vanished: he seems to himself to have waked from a miserable day dream to the buoyant consciousness of youth and hope. Temperaments which are subject to fits of heavy and causeless depression have their compensations sometimes in the reaction which follows ; the infesting cares, as in Longfellow's poem, 'fold their tents, like the Arabs, and as silently steal away,' and with their retreat comes an exquisite exhilaration which more equable dispositions can never experience.

Is this so with Rolleston now ? He only knows that the cloud has lifted from his brain, and that in the clear sunshine which bursts upon him now he can ook his sorrows in the face and know that there is nothing so terrible in them after all.

It is true that he is not happy at the big City day school which he has just left. How should he be ? He is dull and crabbed and uncouth, and knows too well that he is an object of general dislike ; no one there cares to associate with him, and he makes no attempt to overcome their prejudices, being perfectly aware that they are different from him, and hating them for it, but hating himself, perhaps, the most.

And though all his evenings are spent at home there is little rest for him even there, for the work for the next day must be prepared ; and he sits over it till late, sometimes with desperate efforts to master the difficulties, but more often staring at the page before him with eyes that are almost wilfully vacant.

All this has been and is enough in itself to account for the gloomy state into which he had sunk. But— and how could he have forgotten it ?—it is over for the present.

To-night he will not have to sit up struggling with the tasks which will only cover him with fresh disgrace on the morrow; for a whole month he need not think of them, nor of the classes in which the hand of everyone is against him. For the holidays have begun ; to-day has been the last of the term. Is there no reason for joy and thankfulness in that ? What a fool he has been to let those black thoughts gain such a hold over him !

Slowly, more as if it had all happened a long time ago instead of quite recently, the incidents of the morning come back to him, vivid and clear once more —morning chapel and the Doctor's sermon, and afterwards the pretence of work and relaxed discipline in the class rooms, when the results of the examinations had been read out, with the names of the boys who had gained prizes and their remove to the form above. He had come out last of course, but no one expected anything else from him; a laugh had gone round the desks when his humble total closed the list, and he had joined in it to show them he didn't care. And then the class had been dismissed, and there had been friendly good-byes, arrangements for walking home in company or for meeting during the holidays—for all but him; he had gone out alone—and the dull blankness had come over him from which he has only just recovered.

But, for the present at all events, he has got rid of it completely; he is going home, where at least he is not despised, where he will find a sanctuary from gibes and jostlings and impositions; and the longer he thinks of this the higher his spirits rise, and he steps briskly, with a kind of exultation, until the people he passes in the streets turn and look at him, struck by his expression. 'They can see how jolly I'm feeling,' he thinks with a smile.

The dusk is falling, and the shops he passes are brilliant with lights and decorations, but he does not

stop to look at any of them ; his mind is busy with
settling how he shall employ himself on this the first
evening of his liberty, the first for so long on which
he could feel his own master.

At first he decides to read. Is there not some
book he had begun and meant to finish, so many days
ago now that he has even forgotten what it was all
about, and only remembers that it was exciting ?

And yet, he thinks, he won't read to-night—not on
the very first night of the holidays. Quite lately—
yesterday or the day before—his mother had spoken to
him, gently but very seriously, about what she called
the morose and savage fits which would bring misery
upon him if he did not set himself earnestly to overcome them.

And there were times, he knew, when it seemed
as if a demon possessed him and drove him to
wound even those who loved him and whom he
loved—times when their affection only roused
in him some hideous spirit of sullen contradiction.

He feels softened now somehow, and has a new
longing for the love he has so often harshly repulsed.
He *will* overcome this sulkiness of his ; he will begin
this very evening ; as soon as he gets home he will
tell his mother that he is sorry, that he does love
her really, only that when these fits come on him he
hardly knows what he says or does.

And she will forgive him, only too gladly ; and his
mind will be quite at ease again. No, not quite ;

there is still something he must do before that: he has a vague recollection of a long-standing coolness between himself and his younger brother, Lionel. They never have got on very well together; Lionel is so different—much cleverer even already, for one thing; better looking too, and better tempered. Whatever they quarrelled about Wilfred is very sure that he was the offender; Lionel never begins that kind of thing. But he will put himself in the right at once, and ask Lionel to make friends again; he will consent readily enough—he always does.

And then he has a bright idea: he will take his brother some little present to prove that he really wishes to behave decently for the future. What shall he buy?

He finds himself near a large toy shop at the time, and in the window are displayed several regiments of brightly coloured tin warriors—the very thing! Lionel is still young enough to delight in them.

Feeling in his pockets, Rolleston discovers more loose silver than he had thought he possessed, and so he goes into the shop and asks for one of the boxes of soldiers. He is served by one of two neatly dressed female assistants, who stare and giggle at one another at his first words, finding it odd, perhaps, that a fellow of his age should buy toys—as if, he thinks indignantly, they couldn't see that it was not for *himself* he wanted the things.

But he goes on, feeling happier after his purchase.

They will see now that he is not so bad after all. It
is long since he has felt such a craving to be thought
well of by somebody.

A little farther on he comes to a row of people,
mostly women and tradesmen's boys, standing on the
curb stone opposite a man who is seated in a little
wooden box on wheels drawn up close to the pavement. He is paralytic and blind, with a pinched
white face framed in an old-fashioned fur cap with
big ear lappets ; he seems to be preaching or
reading, and Rolleston stops idly enough to listen
for a few moments, the women making room for him
with alacrity, and the boys staring curiously round
at the new arrival with a grin.

He hardly pays much attention to this ; he is
listening to the poem which the man in the box
is reciting with a nasal and metallic snuffle in his
voice :

> There's a harp *and* a crown,
> For you and *for* me,
> Hanging on the boughs
> Of that Christmas tree !

He hears, and then hurries on again, repeating the
stanza mechanically to himself, without seeing
anything particularly ludicrous about it. The words
have reminded him of that Christmas party at the
Gordons', next door. Did not Ethel Gordon ask him
particularly to come, and did he not refuse her
sullenly ? What a brute he was to treat her like that !

If she were to ask him again, he thinks he would not say no, though he does hate parties.

Ethel is a dear girl, and never seems to think him good-for-nothing, as most people do. Perhaps it is sham though—no, he can't think that when he remembers how patiently and kindly she has borne with his senseless fits of temper and tried to laugh away his gloom.

Not every girl as pretty as Ethel is would care to notice him, and persist in it in spite of everything; yet he has sulked with her of late. Was it because she had favoured Lionel? He is ashamed to think that this may have been the reason.

Never mind, that is all over now; he will start clear with everybody. He will ask Ethel, too, to forgive him. Is there nothing he can do to please her? Yes some time ago she had asked him to draw something for her. (He detests drawing lessons, but he has rather a taste for drawing things out of his own head.) He had told her, not too civilly, that he had work enough without doing drawings for girls. He will paint her something to-night as a surprise; he will begin as soon as tea is cleared away; it will be more sociable than reading a book.

And then already he sees a vision of the warm little panelled room, and himself getting out his colour-box and sitting down to paint by lamp-light— for any light does for his kind of colouring—while his mother sits opposite and Lionel watches the picture growing under his hand.

What shall he draw? He gets quite absorbed in thinking over this; his own tastes run in a gory direction, but perhaps Ethel, being a girl, may not care for battles or desperate duels. A compromise strikes him; he will draw a pirate ship: that will be first rate, with the black flag flying on the main-mast, and the pirate captain on the poop scouring the ocean with a big glass in search of merchantmen; all about the deck and rigging he can put the crew, with red caps, and belts stuck full of pistols and daggers.

And on the right there shall be a bit of the pirate island, with a mast and another black flag—he knows he will enjoy picking out the skull and cross-bones in thick Chinese white—and then, if there is room, he will add a cannon, and perhaps a palm tree. A pirate island always has palm trees.

He is so full of this projected picture of his that he is quite surprised to find that he is very near the square where he lives; but here, just in front of him, at the end of the narrow lane, is the public-house with the coach and four engraved on the ground glass of the lower part of the window, and above it the bottles full of coloured water.

And here is the greengrocer's. How long is it since it was a barber's?—surely a very little time. And there is the bootmaker's, with its outside display of dangling shoes, and the row of naked gas jets blown to pale blue specks and whistling red tongues by turns as a gust sweeps across them.

This is his home, this little dingy, old-fashioned red-brick house at an angle of the square, with a small paved space railed in before it. He pushes open the old gate with the iron arch above, where an oil-lamp used to hang, and hurries up to the door with the heavy shell-shaped porch, impatient to get to the warmth and light which await him within.

The bell has got out of order, for only a faint jangle comes from below as he rings; he waits a little and then pulls the handle again, more sharply this time, and still no one comes.

When Betty does think proper to come up and open the door he will tell her that it is too bad keeping a fellow standing out here, in the fog and cold, all this time. . . . She is coming at last—no, it was fancy; it seems as if Betty had slipped out for something, and perhaps the cook is upstairs, and his mother may be dozing by the fire, as she has begun to do of late.

Losing all patience, he gropes for the knocker, and, groping in vain, begins to hammer with bare fists on the door, louder and louder, until he is interrupted by a rough voice from the railings behind him.

'Now then, what are you up to there, eh?' says

the voice, which belongs to a burly policeman who
has stopped suspiciously on the pavement.

'Why,' says Rolleston, 'I want to get in, and I
can't make them hear me. I wish you'd try what
you can do, will you?'

The policeman comes slowly in to the gate. 'I
dessay,' he says jocularly. 'Is there anythink else?
Come, suppose you move on.'

A curious kind of dread of he knows not what
begins to creep over Wilfred at this.

'Move on?' he cries, '*why* should I move on?
This is my house; don't you see? I live here.'

'Now look 'ere, my joker, I don't want a job
over this,' says the constable, stolidly. 'You'll bring
a crowd round in another minute if you keep on that
'ammering.'

'Mind your own business,' says the other with
growing excitement.

'That's what you'll make me do if you don't look
out,' is the retort. 'Will you move on before I make
you?'

'But, I say,' protests Rolleston, 'I'm not joking;
I give you my word I'm not. I do live here. Why,
I've just come back from school, and I can't get in.'

'Pretty school *you* come from!' growls the policeman; ''andles on to *your* lesson books, if *I* knows
anything. 'Ere, out you go!'

Rolleston's fear increases. 'I won't! I won't!'
he cries frantically, and rushing back to the door

beats upon it wildly. On the other side of it are love and shelter, and it will not open to him. He is cold and hungry and tired after his walk; why do they keep him out like this?

'Mother!' he calls hoarsely. 'Can't you hear me, mother? It's Wilfred; let me in!'

The other takes him, not roughly, by the shoulder. 'Now you take my advice,' he says. 'You ain't quite yourself; you're making a mistake. I don't want to get you in trouble if you don't force me to it. Drop this 'ere tomfool game and go home quiet to wherever it is you *do* live.'

'I tell you I live here, you fool!' shrieks Wilfred, in deadly terror lest he should be forced away before the door is opened.

'And I tell you you don't do nothing of the sort,' says the policeman, beginning to lose his temper. 'No one don't live 'ere, nor ain't done not since I've bin on the beat. Use your eyes if you're not too far gone.'

For the first time Rolleston seems to see things plainly as they are; he glances round the square—that is just as it always is on foggy winter evenings, with its central enclosure a shadowy black patch against a reddish glimmer, beyond which the lighted windows of the houses make yellow bars of varying length and tint.

But this house, his own—why, it is all shuttered and dark; some of the window panes are broken;

there is a pale grey patch in one that looks like a dingy bill; the knocker has been unscrewed from the door, and on its scraped panels someone has scribbled words and rough caricatures that were surely not there when he left that morning.

Can anything—any frightful disaster—have come in that short time? No, he will not think of it; he will not let himself be terrified, all for nothing.

'Now, are you goin'?' says the policeman after a pause.

Rolleston puts his back against the door and clings to the sides. 'No!' he shouts. 'I don't care what you say; I don't believe you: they are all in there—they are, I tell you, they are—they *are*!'

In a second he is in the constable's strong grasp and being dragged, struggling violently, to the gate, when a soft voice, a woman's, intercedes for him.

'What is the matter? Oh, don't—don't be so rough with him, poor creature!' it cries pitifully.

'I'm only exercisin' my duty, mum,' says the officer; 'he wants to create a disturbance 'ere.'

'No,' cries Wilfred, 'he lies! I only want to get into my own house, and no one seems to hear me. *You* don't think anything is the matter, do you?'

It is a lady who has been pleading for him; as he wrests himself from his captor and comes forward she sees his face, and her own grows white and startled.

'Wilfred!' she exclaims.

'Why, you know my name!' he says. 'Then you can tell him it's all right. Do I know you? You speak like—is it—*Ethel*?'

'Yes,' she says, and her voice is low and trembling, 'I am Ethel.'

He is silent for an instant; then he says slowly, 'You are not the same—nothing is the same: it is all changed—changed—and oh, my God, what am *I*?'

Slowly the truth is borne in upon his brain, muddled and disordered by long excess, and the last shred of the illusion which had possessed him drifts away.

He knows now that his boyhood, with such possibilities of happiness as it had ever held, has gone for ever. He has been knocking at a door which will open for him never again, and the mother by whose side his evening was to have been passed died long long years ago.

The past, blotted out completely for an hour by some freak of the memory, comes back to him, and he sees his sullen, morbid boyhood changing into something worse still, until by slow degrees he became what he is now—dissipated, degraded, lost.

At first the shock, the awful loneliness he awakes to, and the shame of being found thus by the woman for whom he had felt the only pure love he had known, overwhelm him utterly, and he leans his head upon his arms as he clutches the railings, and sobs with a grief that is terrible in its utter abandonment.

The very policeman is silent and awed by what he feels to be a scene from the human tragedy, though he may not be able to describe it to himself by any more suitable phrase than ' a rum start.'

' You can go now, policeman,' says the lady, putting money in his hand. ' You see I know this—this gentleman. Leave him to me; he will give you no trouble now.'

And the constable goes, taking care, however, to keep an eye occasionally on the corner where this has taken place. He has not gone long before Rolleston raises his head with a husky laugh: his manner has changed now; he is no longer the boy in thought and expression that he was a short time before, and speaks as might be expected from his appearance.

' I remember it all now,' he says. ' You are Ethel Gordon, of course you are, and you wouldn't have anything to do with me—and quite right too—and then you married my brother Lionel. You see I'm as clear as a bell again now. So you came up and found me battering at the old door, eh? Do you know, I got the fancy I was a boy again and coming home to—bah, what does all that matter? Odd sort of fancy though, wasn't it? Drink is always playing me some cursed trick now. A pretty fool I must have made of myself!'

She says nothing, and he thrusts his hands deep in his ragged pockets. ' Hallo! what's this I've got?' he says, as he feels something at the bottom of one of

them, and, bringing out the box of soldiers he had
bought half an hour before, he holds it up with a harsh
laugh which has the ring of despair in it.

'Do you see this?' he says to her. 'You'll laugh
when I tell you it's a toy I bought just now for—guess
whom—for your dear husband! Must have been
pretty bad, mustn't I? Shall I give it to you to take
to him—no? Well, perhaps he has outgrown such
things now, so here goes!' and he pitches the box
over the railings, and it falls with a shiver of broken
glass as the pieces of painted tin rattle out upon the
flag-stones.

'And now I'll wish you good evening,' he says,
sweeping off his battered hat with mock courtesy.

She tries to keep him back. 'No, Wilfred, no;
you must not go like that. We live here still, Lionel
and I, in the same old house,' and she indicates the
house next door; 'he will be home very soon. Will
you' (she cannot help a little shudder at the thought
of such a guest)—'will you come in and wait for
him?'

'Throw myself into his arms, eh?' he says.
'How delighted he would be! I'm just the sort of
brother to be a credit to a highly respectable young
barrister like him. You really think he'd like it?
No; it's all right, Ethel; don't be alarmed: I was
only joking. I shall never come in your way,
I promise you. I'm just going to take myself off.'

'Don't say that,' she says (in spite of herself she

feels relieved) ; ' tell me—is there nothing we can do— no help we can give you ? '

'Nothing,' he answers fiercely; 'I don't want your pity. Do you think I can't see that you wouldn't touch me with the tongs if you could help it ? It's too late to snivel over me now, and I'm well enough as I am. You leave me alone to go to the devil my own way; it's all I ask of you. Good-bye. It's Christmas, isn't it ? I haven't dreamed *that* at all events. Well, I wish you and Lionel as merry a Christmas as I mean to have. I can't say more than that in the way of enjoyment.'

He turns on his heel at the last words and slouches off down the narrow lane by which he had come. Ethel Rolleston stands for a while, looking after his receding form till the fog closes round it and she can see it no more. She feels as if she had seen a ghost ; and for her at least the enclosure before the deserted house next door will be haunted evermore— haunted by a forlorn and homeless figure sobbing there by the railings.

As for the man, he goes on his way until he finds a door which—alas !—is not closed against him.

TOMMY'S HERO

A STORY FOR SMALL BOYS

It was the night after Tommy had been taken to his first pantomime, and he had been lying asleep in his little bedroom (for now that he was nine he slept in the night nursery no longer); he had been asleep, when he was suddenly awakened by a brilliant red glare. At first he was afraid the house was on fire, but when the red turned to a dazzling green, he gave a great gasp of delight, for he thought the transformation scene was still going on. 'And there's all the best part still to come,' he said to himself.

But as he became wider awake, he saw that it was out of the question to expect his bedroom to hold all those wonders, and he was almost surprised to see that there was even so much as a single fairy in it. A fairy there was, nevertheless; she stood there with a star in her hair, and her dress shimmering out all around her, just as he had seen her a few hours before, when she rose up, with little jerks, inside a great gilded shell, and spoke some poetry, which he didn't quite catch.

She spoke audibly enough now, nor was her voice so squeaky as it had sounded before. 'Little boy,' she began, 'I am the ruling genius of Pantomime Fairyland. You entered my kingdom for the first time last night—how did you enjoy yourself?'

'Oh,' said Tommy, '*so* much; it was splendid, thank you!'

She smiled and seemed well pleased. 'I always call to inquire on a new acquaintance,' she said. 'And so you liked our realms, as every sensible boy does? Well, Tommy, it is in my power to reward you; every night for a certain time you shall see again the things you liked best. What *did* you like best?'

'The clown part,' said Tommy, promptly.

For it ought to be said here that he was a boy who had always had a leaning to the kind of practical fun which he saw carried out by the clown to a pitch of perfection which at once enchanted and humbled him. Till that harlequinade, he had thought himself a funny boy in his way, and it had surprised him that his family had not found him more amusing than they did; but now he felt all at once that he was only a very humble beginner, and had never understood what real fun was.

For he had not soared much above hiding behind doors, and popping out suddenly on a passing servant, causing her to 'jump' delightfully; once, indeed, he used to be able to 'sell' his family by pretending all manner of calamities, but they had grown so stupid lately that they never believed a single word he said.

No, the clown would not own him as a follower: he would despise his little attempts at practical jokes. 'Still,' thought Tommy, 'I can try to be more like him; perhaps he will come to hear of me some day!'

For he had never met anyone he admired half so much as that clown, who was always in a good temper (to be sure he had everything his own way—but then he deserved to), always quick and ready with his excuses; and if he did run away in times of danger, it was not because he was really afraid! Then how deliciously impudent he was to shopkeepers! Who but he would have dared to cheapen a large fish by making a door mat of it, or to ask the prices of cheeses on purpose to throw mud at them? Not that he couldn't be serious when he chose—for once he unfurled a Union Jack and said something quite noble, which made everybody clap their hands for two minutes; and he told people the best shops to go to for a quantity of things, and he could not have been joking *then*, for they were the same names that were to be seen on all the hoardings.

This will explain how it was natural that Tommy, on being asked which part of the pantomime he preferred, should say, without the slightest hesitation, 'Oh, the *clown* part!'

The fairy seemed less pleased. 'The clown part!' she repeated. 'What, those shop scenes tacked on right at the end without rhyme or reason?'

'Yes,' said Tommy, 'those ones!'

'And the great wood with the shifting green and violet lights, and the white bands of fairies dancing in circles—didn't you like them?'

'Oh yes,' said the candid Tommy; 'pretty well. I didn't care much for them.'

'Well,' she said, 'but you liked the grand processions, with all their gorgeous dresses and monstrous figures, surely you liked *them*?'

'There was such a lot of it,' said Tommy. 'The clown was the best.'

'And if you could, you'd rather see those last scenes again than all the rest?' she said, frowning a little.

'Oh, wouldn't I just!' said Tommy; 'but may I—really and truly?'

'I see you are not one of *my* boys,' said the Genius of Pantomime, rather sadly. 'It so happens that those closing scenes are the very ones I have least control over—they are a part of my kingdom which has fallen into sad decay and rebellion. But one thing, O Tommy, I *can* do for you. I will give you the clown for a friend and companion—and much good may he do you!'

'But would he *come*?' he asked, hardly daring to believe in such condescension.

'He must, if *I* bid him; it is for you to make
him feel comfortable and at home with you;—the
longer you can keep him the better I shall be
pleased.'

'Oh, *how* kind of you!' he cried; 'he shall stay
all the holidays. I'd rather have him than anybody
else. What fun we shall have—what fun!'

The green fire faded out and the fairy with it.
He must have fallen asleep again, for, when he opened
his eyes, there was the clown at the foot of his bed
making a face.

''Ullo!' said the clown; 'I say, are you the nice
little boy I was told to come and stay with?'

'Yes, yes,' said Tommy; 'I am so glad to see you.
I'm just going to get up.'

'I know you are,' said the clown, and upset him
out of bed into the cold bath.

This he could not help thinking a little bit unkind
of the clown on such a cold morning, particularly as
he followed it up by throwing a hair-brush, two pieces
of soap, and a pair of shoes at him before he could
get out again.

But it woke him, at all events, and he ventured
(with great respect) to throw one of the shoes back;
it just grazed the clown's top-knot.

To Tommy's alarm, the clown set up a hullaballoo
as if he was mortally injured.

'You cruel, unkind little boy,' he sobbed, 'to play
so rough with a poor clown!'

'But you threw them at me first,' pleaded Tommy, 'and much harder, too ! '

'I'm the oldest,' said the clown, 'and you've got to make me feel at home, or I shall go away again.'

'I won't do it again, and I'm very sorry,' pleaded Tommy; but the clown wouldn't be friends with him for ever so long, and was only appeased at last by being allowed to put Tommy upside down in a tall wicker basket which stood in a corner.

Then he helped Tommy to dress by buttoning all his clothes the wrong way, and hiding his stockings and necktie. While he was doing this, Sarah, the under-nurse, came in, and he strutted up to her and began to dance quietly. 'Go away, imperence,' said Sarah.

'Beautiful gal,' said the clown (though Sarah was extremely plain), 'I love yer ! ' and he put out his tongue and wagged his head at her until she ran out of the room in terror.

He looked so absurd that Tommy was delighted with him again, and yet, when the bell rang for breakfast, he felt · obliged to give his new friend a hint.

'I say,' he said, 'you don't mind my telling you— but mother's very particular about manners at table ; ' but the clown relieved him instantly by saying that so was he—*very* particular ; and he slid down the banisters and turned somersaults in the hall until Tommy joined him.

'I do hope father and mother won't be unkind to him,' he thought, as he went in, 'because he does seem to feel things so.'

But nothing could be more polite than the welcome Tommy's parents gave the stranger, as he came in, bowing very low, and making a queer little skipping step. Tommy's mother said she was always glad to see any friend of her boy's, while his father begged the clown to make himself quite at home. All *he* said was, 'I'm disgusted to make your acquaintance;' but he certainly made himself at home—in fact, he was not quite so particular.about his manners as he had led Tommy to expect.

He volunteered to divide the sausages and bacon himself, and did so in such a way that everybody else got very little and he himself got a great deal. If it had been anybody else, Tommy would certainly have called this ' piggish '; as it was, he tried to think it was all fun, and that he himself had no particular appetite.

His cousin Barbara, a little girl of about his own age, was staying with them just then, and came down presently to breakfast. 'Oh, my!' said the clown, laying a great red hand on his heart, 'what a nice little gal you are, ain't yer? Come and sit by me, my dear!'

'No, thank you; I'm going to sit by Aunt Mary,' she replied, looking rather shy and surprised.

'Allow me, missy,' he persisted, 'to pass you the strawberry-jam and the muffins ! '

'I'll have some jam, thank you,' she replied.

He looked round and chuckled. 'Oh, I say; that little gal said "thank you" before she got it ! ' he exclaimed. 'There ain't no muffins, and I've eaten all the jam ! ' which made Tommy choke with laughter.

Barbara flushed. 'That's a very stupid joke,' she pronounced severely, 'and rude, too ; it's a pity you weren't taught to behave better when you were young.'

'So I was ! ' said the clown, with his mouth full.

'Then you've forgotten it,' she said; 'you're nothing but a big baby, that you are ! '

'Yah ! ' retorted the clown; 'so are *you* a big baby ! ' which, as even Tommy saw, was not a very brilliant reply. It was a singular fact about the clown that the slightest check seemed to take away all his brilliancy.

'You know you're not telling the truth now,' said Barbara, so contemptuously, that the clown began to weep bitterly. 'She says I don't speak the truth ! ' he complained, 'and she *knows* it will be my aunt's birthday last Toosday ! '

'You great silly thing, what has that to do with it ? ' cried Barbara, indignantly. 'What *is* there to cry about ? ' which very nearly made Tommy quarrel with her, for why couldn't she be polite to *his* friend ?

S

However, the clown soon dried his eyes on the tablecloth, and recovered his cheerfulness ; and presently he noticed the *Times* lying folded by Tommy's papa's plate.

' Oh, I say, mister,' he said, ' shall I air the newspaper for yer ? '

' Thank you, if you will,' was the polite reply.

He shook it all out in one great sheet and wrapped it round him, and waddled about in it until Tommy nearly rolled off his seat with delight.

' When you've *quite* done with it——' his father was saying mildly, as the clown made a great hole in the middle and thrust his head out of it with a bland smile.

' I'm only just looking through it,' he explained ; ' you can have it now,' and he rolled it up in a tight ball and threw it at his host's head.

Breakfast was certainly not such a dull meal as usual that morning, Tommy thought ; but he wished his people would show a little more appreciation, instead of sitting there all stiff and surprised ; he was afraid the clown would feel discouraged.

When his papa undid the ball, the paper was found to be torn into long strips, which delighted Tommy ; but his father, on the other hand, seemed annoyed, possibly because it was not so easy to read in that form. Meanwhile, the clown busied himself in emptying the butter-dish into his pockets, and this did shock the boy a little, for he knew it was not polite to pocket things at meals, and wondered how he could be so nasty.

Breakfast was over at last, and the clown took Tommy's arm and walked upstairs to the first floor with him.

'Who's in there?' he asked, as they passed the spare bedroom.

'Granny,' said the boy; 'she's staying with us; only she always has breakfast in her room, you know.'

'Why, you don't mean to say you've got a granny!' cried the clown, with joy; 'you are a nice little boy; now we'll have some fun with her.' Tommy felt doubtful whether she could be induced to join them so early in the morning, and said so. 'You knock, and say you've got a present for her if she'll come out,' suggested the clown.

'But I haven't,' objected Tommy; 'wouldn't that be a story?' He had unaccountably forgotten his old fondness for 'sells.'

'Of course it would,' said the clown; 'I'm always a tellin' of 'em, I am.'

Tommy was shocked once more, as he realised that his friend was not a *truthful* clown. But he knocked at the door, nevertheless, and asked his grandmother to come out and see a friend of his.

'Wait one minute, my boy,' she answered, 'and I'll come out.'

Tommy was surprised to see his companion

preparing to lie, face downwards, on the mat just outside the door.

'Get up,' he said; 'you'll trip grandma up if you stay there.'

'That's what I'm doing it for, stoopid,' said the clown.

'But it will hurt her,' he cried.

'Nothing hurts old women,' said the clown; 'I've tripped up 'undreds of 'em, and I ought to know.'

'Well, you shan't trip up my granny, anyhow,' said Tommy, stoutly; for he was not a bad-hearted boy, and his grandmother had given him a splendid box of soldiers on Christmas Day. 'Don't come out, granny; it's a mistake,' he shouted.

The clown rose with a look of disgust.

'Do you call this actin' like a friend to me?' he demanded.

'Well,' said Tommy, apologetically, 'she's my granny, you see.'

'She ain't *my* granny, and, if she was, I'd let you trip her up, I would; *I* ain't selfish. I shan't stop with you any longer.'

'Oh, do,' said Tommy; 'we'll go and play somewhere else.'

'Well,' said the clown, relenting, 'if you're a good boy you shall see me make a butter-slide in the hall.'

Then Tommy saw how he had wronged him in thinking he had pocketed the butter out of mere greediness, and he felt ashamed and penitent; the clown made a beautiful slide, though Tommy wished he would not insist upon putting all the butter that was left down his back.

'There's a ring at the bell,' said the clown; 'I'll open the door, and you hide and see the fun.'

So Tommy hid himself round a corner as the door opened.

'Walk in, sir,' said the clown, politely.

'Master Tommy in?' said a jolly, hearty voice. It was dear old Uncle John, who had taken him to the pantomime the night before. 'I thought I'd look in and see if he would care to come with me to the Crystal——oh!' And there was a scuffling noise and a heavy bump.

Tommy ran out, full of remorse. Uncle John was sitting on the tiles rubbing his head, and, oddly enough, did not look at all funny.

'Oh, uncle,' cried the boy, 'you're not hurt? I didn't know it was you!'

'I'm a bit shaken, my boy, that's all,' said his uncle; 'one doesn't come down like a feather at my age.' And he picked himself slowly up. 'Well, I must get home again,' he said; 'no Crystal Palace to-day, Tommy, after this. Good-bye.'

And he went slowly out, leaving Tommy with the feeling that he had had enough of slides. He even wiped the flooring clean again with a waterproof and the clothes-brush, though the clown (who had been hiding) tried to prevent him.

' We ain't 'ad 'arf the fun out of it yet ! ' he complained (he always spoke in rather a common way, as
Tommy began to notice with pain).

' I've had enough,' said Tommy. ' It was my
Uncle John who slipped down that time, and he's
hurt, and he'd come to take me to the Crystal
Palace ! '

' Well, he hadn't come to take *me*,' said the clown ;
' you are stingy about your relations, you are ; you
ain't 'arf a boy for a bit o' fun.'

Tommy felt this rebuke very much, he had hoped
so to gain the clown's esteem ; but he would not give
in, he only suggested humbly that they should go up
into the play-room.

The play-room was at the top of the house, and
Barbara and two little sisters of Tommy's were playing there when they came in, the clown turning in
his toes and making awful faces.

The two little girls ran into a corner, and seemed
considerably frightened by the stranger's appearance,
but Barbara reassured them.

' Don't take any notice,' she said, ' it's only a
horrid friend of Tommy's. He won't interfere with
us.'

' Oh, Barbara,' the boy protested, ' he's awfully nice
if you only knew him. He can make you laugh. Do
let us play with you. He wants to, and he won't be
rough.'

' Do,' pleaded the clown, ' I'll behave so pretty ! '

'Well,' said Barbara, 'mind you do, then, or you shan't stop.'

And for a little while he did behave himself. Tommy showed him his new soldiers, and he seemed quite interested; and then he had a ride on the rocking horse, and was sorry when it broke down under him ; and after that he came suddenly upon a beautiful doll which belonged to the youngest sister.

'Do let me nurse it,' he said, and the little girl gave it up timidly. Of course he nursed it the wrong way up, and at last he forgot, and sat down on it, the head, which was wax, being crushed to pieces !

Tommy was in fits of laughter at the droll face he made as he held out the crushed doll at arm's length, and looked at it with one eye shut, exclaiming, ' Poor thing ! what a pity ! I do 'ope I 'aven't made its 'ead ache ! '

But the two little girls were crying bitterly in one another's arms, and Barbara turned on the clown with tremendous indignation.

'You did it on purpose, you know you did ! ' she said.

'Go away, little girl ; don't talk to me ! ' said the clown, putting Tommy in front of him.

'Tommy,' she said, 'what did you bring your friend up here for ? He only spoils everything he's allowed to touch. Take him away ! '

'Barbara,' pleaded Tommy, 'he's a *visitor*, you know ! '

'I don't care,' she replied. 'Mr. Clown, you shan't stay here; this is our room, and we don't want you. Go away!' She walked towards him looking so fierce that he backed hastily. 'Go downstairs,' she said, pointing to the door. 'You, too, Tommy, for you encouraged him!'

'Nyah, nyah, nyah!' said the clown, a sound by which he intended to imitate her anger. 'Oh, please, I'm going; remember me to your mother.' And he left the room, followed rather sadly by Tommy, who felt that Barbara was angry with him. 'That's a very disagribble little girl,' remarked the clown, confidentially, when they were safe outside, and Tommy thought it wiser to agree.

'What have you got in your pockets?' he asked, presently, seeing a hard bulge in his friend's white trunks.

'Only some o' your nice soldiers,' said the clown, and walked into the schoolroom, where there was a fire burning. 'Are they brave?' he asked.

'Very,' said Tommy, who had quite persuaded himself that this was so. 'Look here, we'll have a battle.' He thought a battle would keep the clown quiet. 'Here's two cannon and peas, and you shall be the French and I'll be English.'

'All right,' said the clown, and took his share of the soldiers and calmly put them all in the middle of the red-hot coals. 'I want to be quite sure they can stand fire first,' he explained; and then, as they melted, he said, 'There, you see, they're all running away. I never see such cowards.'

Tommy was in a great rage, and could almost have cried, if it had not been babyish, for they were his best regiments which he could see dropping down in great glittering stars on the ashes below. 'That's a caddish thing to do,' he said, with difficulty; 'I didn't give them to you to put in the fire!'

'Oh, I thought you did,' said the clown, 'I beg your pardon;' and he threw the rest after them as he spoke.

'You're a beast!' cried Tommy, indignantly; 'I've done with you, after this.'

'Oh, no, yer ain't,' he returned.

'I have, though,' said Tommy; 'we're not friends any longer.'

'All right,' said the clown; 'when I'm not friends with any one, I take and use the red-'ot poker to 'em,' and he put it in the fire to heat as he spoke.

This terrified the boy. It was no use trying to argue with the clown, and he had seen how he used a red-hot poker. 'Well, I'll forgive you this time,' he said hastily; 'let's come away from here.'

'I tell you what,' said the clown, 'you and me'll go down in the kitchen and make a pie.'

Tommy forgot his injuries at this delightful idea; he knew what the clown's notion of pie-making would be. 'Yes,' he said eagerly, 'that will be jolly; only

I don't know,' he added doubtfully, 'if cook will let us.'

However, the clown soon managed to secure the kitchen to himself; he had merely to attempt to kiss the cook once or twice and throw the best dinner service at the other servants, and they were left quite alone to do as they pleased.

What fun it was, to begin with! The clown brought out a large deep dish, and began by putting a whole turkey and an unskinned hare in it out of the larder; after that he put in sausages, jam, pickled walnuts, and lemons, and, in short, the first thing that came to hand.

'It ain't 'arf full yet,' he said at last, as he looked gravely into the pie.

'No,' said Tommy, sympathetically, 'can't we get anything else to put in?'

'The very thing,' cried the clown, 'you're just about the right size to fill up—my! what a pie it's going to be, eh?' And he caught up his young friend, just as he was, rammed him into the pie, and poured sauce on him.

But he kicked and howled until the clown grew seriously displeased. 'Why carn't you lay quiet,' he said angrily, 'like the turkey does? you don't deserve to be put into such a nice pie!'

'If you make a pie of me,' said Tommy, artfully, 'there'll be nobody to look on and laugh at you, you know!'

'No more there won't,' said the clown, and allowed him to crawl out, all over sauce. 'It was a pity,' he declared, 'because he fitted so nicely, and now they would have to look about for something else;' but he contrived to make a shift with the contents of the cook's work-basket, which he poured in—reels, pin-cushions, wax, and all. He had tried to put the kitchen cat in too, but she scratched his hands and could not be induced to form the finishing touch to the pie.

How the clown got the paste and rolled it, and made Tommy in a mess with it, and how the pie was finished at last, would take too long to tell here; but somehow it was not quite such capital fun as he had expected—it seemed to want the pantomime music or something; and then Tommy was always dreading lest the clown should change his mind at the last minute, and put him in the pie after all.

Even when it was safely in the oven he had another fear lest he should be made to stay and eat it, for it had such very peculiar things in it that it could not be at all nice. Fortunately, as soon as it was put away the clown seemed to weary of it him-self.

'Let me and you go and take a walk,' he sug-gested.

Tommy caught at the proposal, for he was fast becoming afraid of the clown, and felt really glad to get him out of the house; so he got his cap, and the clown put on a brown overcoat and a tall hat, under which his white and red face looked stranger than ever, and they sallied forth together.

Once Tommy would have thought it a high privilege to be allowed to go out shopping with a clown; but, if the plain truth must be told, he did not enjoy himself so very much after all. People seemed to stare at them so, for one thing, and he felt almost ashamed of his companion, whose behaviour was outrageously ridiculous. They went to all the family tradesmen, to whom Tommy was, of course, well known, and the clown *would* order the most impossible things, and say they were for Tommy! Once he even pushed him into a large draper's shop, full of pretty and contemptuous young ladies, and basely left him to explain his presence as he could.

But it was worse when they happened to meet an Italian boy with a tray of plaster images on his head.

'Here's a lark!' said the clown, and elbowed Tommy against him in such a way that the tray slipped and all the images fell to the ground with a crash.

It was certainly amusing to see all the pieces rolling about; but, while Tommy was still laughing, the boy began to howl and denounce him to the crowd which gathered round them. The crowd declared that it was a shame, and that Tommy ought to be made to pay for it; and no one said so more loudly and indignantly than the clown!

Before he could escape he had to give his father's name and address, and promise that he would pay for the damage, after which he joined the clown (who had strolled on) with a heavy heart, for he knew that that business would stop all his pocket-money for years after he was grown up! He even ventured to reproach his friend : 'I shan't sneak of you, of course, he said, 'but you know *you* did it ! ' The clown's only answer to this was a reproof for telling wicked stories.

At last they passed a confectioner's, and the clown suddenly remembered that he was hungry, so they went in, and he borrowed sixpence from Tommy, which he spent in buns.

He ate them all himself slowly, and was so very quiet and well-behaved all the time that Tommy hoped he was sobering down. They had gone a little way from the shop when he found that the clown was eating tarts.

' You might give me one,' said Tommy ; and the clown, after looking over his shoulder, actually gave him all he had left, filling his pocket with them, in fact.

' I never saw you buy them,' he said wonderingly, which the clown said was very peculiar ; and just then an attendant came up breathlessly.

' You forgot to pay for those tarts,' she said.

The clown replied that he never took pastry. She

insisted that they were gone, and he must have taken them.

'It wasn't me, please,' said the clown; 'it was this little boy done it. Why, he's got a jam tart in his pocket now. Where's a policeman?'

Tommy was so thunderstruck by this treachery that he could say nothing. It was only what he might have expected, for had not the clown served the pantaloon exactly the same the night before? But that did not make the situation any the funnier now, particularly as the clown made such a noise that two real policemen came hurrying up.

Tommy did not wait for them. No one held him, and he ran away at the top of his speed. What a nightmare sort of run it was!—the policemen chasing him, and the clown urging them on at the top of his voice. Everybody he passed turned round and ran after him too.

Still he kept ahead. He was surprised to find how fast he could run, and all at once he remembered that he was running the opposite way from home. Quick as thought he turned up the first street he came to, hoping to throw them off the scent and get home by a back way.

For the moment he thought he had got rid of them; but just as he stopped to take breath, they all came whooping and hallooing round the corner after him; and he had to scamper on, panting, and sobbing, and staggering, and almost out of his mind with fright. If he could only get home first, and tell his mother! But they were gaining on him, and the clown was leading and roaring with delight as he drew closer and closer. He came to a point where two roads met. It was round another corner, and they could not see him. He ran down one, and, to his immense relief, found they had taken the other. He was saved, for his house was quite near now.

He tried to hasten, but the pavement was all slushy and slippery, and his boots felt heavier and heavier, and, to add to his misery, the pursuers had found out their mistake. As he looked back, he could see the clown galloping round the corner and hear his yell of discovery.

'Oh, fairy, dear fairy,' he gasped, 'save me this time. I *do* like your part best, now!'

She must have heard him and taken pity, for in a second he had reached his door, and it flew open before him. He was not safe even yet, so he rushed upstairs to his bedroom, and bounced, just as he was, into his bed.

'If they come up I'll pretend I'm ill,' he thought, as he covered his head with the bedclothes.

They *were* coming up, all of them. There was a great trampling on the stairs. He heard the clown officiously shouting: 'This way, Mr. Policeman, sir!' and then a tremendous battering at his door.

He lay there shivering under the blankets.

'Perhaps they'll think the door's locked, and go

away,' he tried to hope, and the battering went on not quite so violently.

. 'Master Tommy! Master Tommy!' It was Sarah's voice. They had got her to come up and tempt him out. Well, she *wouldn't*, then!

And then—oh! horror!—the door was thrown open. He sprang out of bed in an agony.

'Sarah! Sarah! keep them out,' he gasped. 'Don't let them take me away!'

'Lor', Master Tommy! keep who out?' said Sarah, wonderingly.

'The—the clown—and the policemen,' he said. 'I know they're behind the door.'

'There, there!' said Sarah; 'why, you ain't done dreaming yet. That's what comes of going out to these late pantomimes. Rub your eyes; it's nearly eight o'clock.'

Tommy could have hugged her. It was only a dream after all, then. As he stood there, shivering in his nightgown, the nightmare clown began to melt away, though even yet some of the adventures he had gone through seemed too vivid to be quite imaginary.

. . . .

Singularly enough, his Uncle John actually did call that morning, and to take him to the Crystal Palace, too; and as there was no butter-slide for him to fall down on, they were able to go. On the way Tommy told him all about his unpleasant dream.

'I shall always hate a clown after this, uncle,' he said, as he concluded.

'My good Tommy,' said his uncle, 'when you are fortunate enough to dream a dream with a moral in it, don't go and apply it the wrong way up. The real clown, like a sensible man, keeps his fun for the place where it is harmless and appreciated, and away from the pantomime conducts himself like any other respectable person. Now, your *dream* clown, Tommy——'

'I know,' said Tommy, meekly. 'Should you think the pantomime was good here, Uncle John?'

A CANINE ISHMAEL

(FROM THE NOTES OF A DINER-OUT)

'Tell me,' she said suddenly, with a pretty imperiousness that seemed to belong to her, 'are you fond of dogs?' How we arrived at the subject I forget now, but I know she had just been describing how a collie at a dog-show she had visited lately had suddenly thrown his forepaws round her neck in a burst of affection—a proceeding which, in my own mind (although I prudently kept this to myself), I considered less astonishing than she appeared to do.

For I had had the privilege of taking her in to dinner, and the meal had not reached a very advanced stage before I had come to the conclusion that she was the most charming, if not the loveliest, person I had ever met.

It was fortunate for me that I was honestly able to answer her question in a satisfactory manner, for, had it been otherwise, I doubt whether she would have deigned to bestow much more of her conversation upon me.

'Then I wonder,' she said next, meditatively, 'if

you would care to hear about a dog that belonged
to—to someone I know very well? Or would it bore
you?'

I am very certain that if she had volunteered to
relate the adventures of Telemachus, or the history
of the Thirty Years' War, I should have accepted the
proposal with a quite genuine gratitude. As it was,
I made it sufficiently plain that I should care very
much indeed to hear about that dog.

She paused for a moment to reject an unfortunate
entrée (which I confess to doing my best to console),
and then she began her story. I shall try to set it
down as nearly as possible in her own words, although
I cannot hope to convey the peculiar charm and
interest that she gave it for me. It was not, I need
hardly say, told all at once, but was subject to the
inevitable interruptions which render a dinner-table
intimacy so piquantly precarious.

' This dog,' she began quietly, without any air of
beginning a story, ' this dog was called Pepper. He
was not much to look at—rather a rough, mongrelly
kind of animal; and he and a young man had kept
house together for a long time, for the young man
was a bachelor and lived in chambers by himself.
He always used to say that he didn't like to get
engaged to anyone, because he was sure it would put
Pepper out so fearfully. However, he met somebody
at last who made him forget about Pepper, and he
proposed and was accepted—and then, you know,'

she added, as a little dimple came in her cheek, ' he had to go home and break the news to the dog.'

She had just got to this point, when, taking advantage of a pause she made, the man on her other side (who was, I daresay, strictly within his rights, although I remember at the time considering him a pushing beast) struck in with some remark which she turned to answer, leaving me leisure to reflect.

I was feeling vaguely uncomfortable about this story ; something, it would be hard to say what, in her way of mentioning Pepper's owner made me suspect that he was more than a mere acquaintance of hers.

Was it *she*, then, who was responsible for——? It was no business of mine, of course ; I had never met her in my life till that evening—but I began to be impatient to hear the rest.

And at last she turned to me again : ' I hope you haven't forgotten that I was in the middle of a story. You haven't ? And you would really like me to go on ? Well, then—oh yes, when Pepper was told, he was naturally a little annoyed at first. I daresay he considered he ought to have been consulted previously. But, as soon as he had seen the lady, he withdrew all opposition—which his master declared was a tremendous load off his mind, for Pepper was rather a difficult dog, and slow as a rule to take strangers into his affections, a little snappy and surly, and very easily hurt or offended. Don't you know dogs who are sensitive like that? *I* do, and I'm always so sorry for them—they feel little things so much, and one never can find out what's the matter, and have it out with them! Sometimes it's shyness; once I had a dog who was quite painfully shy—self-consciousness it was really, I suppose, for he always fancied everybody was looking at him, and often when people were calling he would come and hide his face in the folds of my dress till they had gone—it was too ridiculous! But about Pepper. He was devoted to his new mistress from the very first. I am not sure that she was quite so struck with him, for he was not at all a lady's dog, and his manners had been very much neglected. Still, she came quite to like him in time; and when they were married, Pepper went with them for the honeymoon.'

'*When they were married!*' I glanced at the card which lay half-hidden by her plate. Surely *Miss* So-and-so was written on it?—yes, it was certainly 'Miss.' It was odd that such a circumstance should have increased my enjoyment of the story, perhaps—but it undoubtedly did.

'After the honeymoon,' my neighbour continued, 'they came to live in the new house, which was quite a tiny one, and Pepper was a very important personage in it indeed. He had his mistress all to himself for the greater part of most days, as his master had to be away in town; so she used to talk to him intimately, and tell him more than she would have thought of confiding to most people. Sometimes, when she thought there was no fear of callers coming, she would make him play, and this was quite a new sensation for Pepper, who was a serious-minded animal, and took very solemn views of life. At first he hadn't the faintest idea what was expected of him ; it must have been rather like trying to romp with a parish beadle, he was so intensely respectable ! But as soon as he once grasped the notion and understood that no liberty was intended, he lent himself to it readily enough and learnt to gambol quite creditably. Then he was made much of in all sorts of ways ; she washed him twice a week with her very own hands—which his master would never have dreamt of doing—and she was always trying new ribbons on his complexion. That rather bored him at first, but it ended by making him a little conceited about his appearance. Altogether he was dearly fond of her, and I don't believe he had ever been happier in all his life than he was in those days. Only, unfortunately, it was all too good to last.'

Here I had to pass olives or something to somebody, and the other man, seeing his chance, and, to do him justice, with no idea that he was interrupting a story, struck in once more, so that the history of Pepper had to remain in abeyance for several minutes.

My uneasiness returned. Could there be a mistake about that name-card after all ? Cards *do* get re-arranged sometimes, and she seemed to know that young couple so very intimately. I tried to remember whether I had been introduced to her as a Miss or Mrs. So-and-so, but without success. There is some fatality which generally distracts one's attention at the critical moment of introduction, and in this case it was perhaps easily accounted for. My turn came again, and she took up her tale once more. 'I think when I left off I was saying that Pepper's happiness was too good to last. And so it was. For his mistress was ill, and, though he snuffed and scratched and whined at the door of her room for ever so long, they wouldn't let him in. But he managed to slip in one day somehow, and jumped up on her lap and licked her hands and face, and almost went out of his mind with joy at seeing her again. Only (I told you he was a sensitive dog) it gradually struck him that she was not *quite* so pleased to see him as usual—and presently he found out the reason. There was another animal there, a new pet, which seemed to take up a good deal of her attention. Of course you guess what that was—but Pepper had never seen a baby before, and he took it as a personal slight and was dreadfully offended. He simply walked straight out of the room and downstairs to the kitchen, where he stayed for days.

'I don't think he enjoyed his sulk much, poor doggie; perhaps he had an idea that when they saw how much he took it to heart they would send the baby away. But as time went on and this didn't seem to occur to them, he decided to come out of the sulks and look over the matter, and he came back quite prepared to resume the old footing. Only everything was different. No one seemed to notice that he was in the room now, and his mistress never invited him to have a game; she even forgot to have him washed—and one of his peculiarities was that he had no objection to soap and warm water. The worst of it was, too, that before very long the baby followed him into the sitting-room, and, do what he could, he couldn't make the stupid little thing understand that it had no business there. If you think of it, a baby must strike a dog as a very inferior little animal: it can't bark (well, yes, it *can* howl), but it's no good whatever with rats, and yet everybody makes a tremendous fuss about it! The baby got all poor Pepper's bows now; and his mistress played games with it, though Pepper felt he could have done it ever so much better, but he was never allowed to join in. So he used to lie on a rug and pretend he didn't mind, though, really, I'm certain he felt it horribly. I always believe, you know, that people never give dogs half credit enough for feeling things, don't you?

'Well, at last came the worst indignity of all : Pepper was driven from his rug—his own particular rug—to make room for the baby; and when he had got away into a corner to cry quietly, all by himself, that wretched baby came and crawled after him and pulled his tail!

'He always *had* been particular about his tail, and never allowed anybody to touch it but very intimate friends, and even then under protest, so you can imagine how insulted he felt.

It was too much for him, and he lost the last scrap of temper he had. They said he bit the baby, and I'm afraid he did—though not enough really to hurt it; still, it howled fearfully, of course, and from that moment it was all over with poor Pepper—he was a ruined dog!

'When his master came home that evening he was told the whole story. Pepper's mistress said she would be ever so sorry to part with him, but, after his misbehaviour, she should never know a moment's peace until he was out of the house—it really wasn't safe for baby!

'And his master was sorry, naturally; but I suppose he was beginning rather to like the baby himself, and so the end of it was that Pepper had to go. They did all they could for him; found him a comfortable home, with a friend who was looking out for a good house-dog, and wasn't particular about breed, and, after that, they heard nothing of him for a long while. And, when they did hear, it was rather a bad report: the friend could do nothing with Pepper at all; he had to tie him up in the stable, and then he snapped at everyone who came near, and howled all night—they were really almost afraid of him.

'So when Pepper's mistress heard that, she felt

more thankful than ever that the dog had been sent away, and tried to think no more about him. She had quite forgotten all about it, when, one day, a new nursemaid, who had taken the baby out for an airing, came back with a terrible account of a savage dog which had attacked them, and leaped up at the perambulator so persistently that it was as much as she could do to drive it away. And even then Pepper's mistress did not associate the dog with him ; she thought he had been destroyed long ago.

'But the next time the nurse went out with the baby she took a thick stick with her, in case the dog should come again. And no sooner had she lifted the perambulator over the step, than the dog *did* come again, exactly as if he had been lying in wait for them ever since outside the gate.

'The nurse was a strong country girl, with plenty of pluck, and as the dog came leaping and barking about in a very alarming way, she hit him as hard as she could on his head. The wonder is she did not kill him on the spot, and, as it was, the blow turned him perfectly giddy and silly for a time, and he ran round and round in a dazed sort of way—do you think you could lower that candle-shade just a little ? Thanks ! ' she broke off suddenly, as I obeyed. ' Well, she was going to strike again, when her mistress rushed out, just in time to stop her. For, you see, she had been watching at the window, and although the poor beast was miserably thin, and rough, and neglected-looking, she knew at once that it must be Pepper, and that he was not in the least mad or dangerous, but only trying his best to make his peace with the baby. Very likely his dignity or his conscience or something wouldn't let him come back quite at once, you know; and perhaps he thought he had better get the baby on his side first. And then all at once, his mistress—I heard all this through her, of course—his mistress suddenly remembered how devoted Pepper had been to her, and how fond she had once been of him, and when she saw him standing, stupid and shivering, there, her heart softened to him, and she went to make it up with him, and tell him that he was forgiven and should come back and be her dog again, just as in the old days !——'

Here she broke off for a moment. I did not venture to look at her, but I thought her voice trembled a little when she spoke again. ' I don't quite know *why* I tell you all this. There was a time when I never could bear the end of it myself,' she said; ' but I have begun, and I will finish now. Well, Pepper's mistress went towards him, and called him; but— whether he was still too dizzy to quite understand who she was, or whether his pride came uppermost again, poor dear! I don't know—but he gave her just one look (she says she will never forget it—never; it went straight to her heart), and then he walked very slowly and deliberately away.

' She couldn't bear it; she followed; she felt she

simply *must* make him understand how very, very sorry she was for him; but the moment he heard her he began to run faster and faster, until he was out of reach and out of sight, and she had to come back. I know she was crying bitterly by that time.'

'And he never came back again?' I asked, after a silence.

'Never again!' she said softly; 'that was the very last they ever saw or heard of him. And—and I've always loved every dog since for Pepper's sake!'

'I'm almost glad he did decline to come back,' I declared; 'it served his mistress right—she didn't deserve anything else!'

'Ah, I didn't want you to say that!' she protested; 'she never meant to be so unkind—it was all for the baby's sake!'

I was distinctly astonished, for all her sympathy in telling the story had seemed to lie in the other direction.

'You don't mean to say,' I cried involuntarily, 'that you can find any excuses for her? I did not expect *you* would take the baby's part!'

'But I did,' she confessed, with lowered eyes—'I *did* take the baby's part—it was all my doing that Pepper was sent away—I have been sorry enough for it since!'

It was her own story she had been telling at second-hand after all—and she was not Miss So-and-so! I had entirely forgotten the existence of any other members of the party but our two selves, but at the moment of this discovery—which was doubly painful—I was recalled by a general rustle to the fact that we were at a dinner-party, and that our hostess had just given the signal.

As I rose and drew back my chair to allow my neighbour to pass, she raised her eyes for a moment and said almost meekly:

'I *was* the baby, you see!'

MARJORY

INTRODUCTION

I HAVE thought myself justified in printing the following narrative, found among the papers of my dead friend, Douglas Cameron, who left me discretion to deal with them as I saw fit. It was written indeed, as its opening words imply, rather for his own solace and relief than with the expectation that it would be read by any other. But, painful and intimate as it is in parts, I cannot think that any harm will be done by printing it now, with some necessary alterations in the names of the characters chiefly concerned.

Before, however, leaving the story to speak for itself, I should like to state, in justice to my friend, that during the whole of my acquaintance with him, which began in our college days, I never saw anything to indicate the morbid timidity and weakness of character that seem to have marked him as a boy. Reserved he undoubtedly was, with a taste for solitude that made him shrink from the society of all but a small circle, and with a sensitive and shy nature which prevented him from doing himself complete justice; but he was very capable of holding his own on occasion, and in his disposition, as I knew it, there was no want of moral courage, nor any trace of effeminacy.

How far he may have unconsciously exaggerated such failings in the revelation of his earlier self, or what the influence of such an experience as he relates may have done to strengthen the moral fibre, are points on which I can express no opinion, any more than I can pledge myself to the credibility of the supernatural element of his story.

It may be that only in the boy's overwrought imagination, the innocent Child-spirit came back to complete the work of love and pity she had begun in life; but I know that he himself believed otherwise, and, truly, if those who leave us are permitted to return at all, it must be on some such errand as Marjory's.

Douglas Cameron's life was short, and in it, so far as I am aware, he met no one who at all replaced his lost ideal. Of this I cannot be absolutely certain, for he was a reticent man in such matters; but I think, had it been so, I should have known of it, for we were very close friends. One would hardly expect, perhaps, that an ordinary man would remain faithful all his days to the far-off memory of a child-love; but then Cameron was not quite as other men, nor were his days long in the land.

And if this ideal of his was never dimmed for him

by some grosser, and less spiritual, passion, who shall
say that he may not have been a better and even a
happier man in consequence.

.   .   .   .   .   .

It is not without an effort that I have resolved to
break, in the course of this narrative, the reserve
maintained for nearly twenty years. But the chief
reason for silence is removed now that all those are
gone who might have been pained or harmed by what
I have to tell, and, though I shrink still from reviving
certain memories that are fraught with pain, there
are others associated therewith which will surely bring
consolation and relief.

I must have been about eleven at the time I am
speaking of, and the change which—for good or ill—
comes over most boys' lives had not yet threatened
mine. I had not left home for school, nor did it seem
at all probable then that I should ever do so.

When I read (I was a great reader) of Dotheboys
Hall and Salem House—a combination of which
establishments formed my notion of school-life—it
was with no more personal interest than a cripple
might feel in perusing the notice of an impending
conscription ; for from the battles of school-life I was
fortunately exempted.

I was the only son of a widow, and we led a
secluded life in a London suburb. My mother took
charge of my education herself, and, as far as mere
acquirements went, I was certainly not behind other

boys of my age. I owe too much to that loving and careful training, Heaven knows, to think of casting any reflection upon it here, but my surroundings were such as almost necessarily to exclude all bracing and hardening influences.

My mother had few friends; we were content with our own companionship, and of boys I knew and cared to know nothing; in fact, I regarded a strange boy with much the same unreasoning aversion as many excellent women feel for the most ordinary cow.

I was happy to think that I should never be called upon to associate with them; by-and-by, when I outgrew my mother's teaching, I was to have a tutor, perhaps even go to college in time, and when I became a man I was to be a curate and live with my mother in a clematis-covered cottage in some pleasant village.

She would often dwell on this future with a tender prospective pride; she spoke of it on the very day that saw it shattered for ever.

For there came a morning when, on going to her with my lessons for the day, I was gladdened with an unexpected holiday. I little knew then—though I was to learn it soon enough—that my lessons had been all holidays, or that on that day they were to end for ever.

My mother had had one or two previous attacks of an illness which seemed to prostrate her for a short period, and as she soon regained her ordinary health, I did not think they could be of a serious nature.

U

So I devoted my holiday cheerfully enough to the illumination of a text, on the gaudy colouring of which I found myself gazing two days later with a dull wonder, as at the work of a strange hand in a long dead past, for the boy who had painted that was a happy boy who had a mother, and for two endless days I had been alone.

Those days, and many that followed, come back to me now but vaguely. I passed them mostly in a state of blank bewilderment caused by the double sense of sameness and strangeness in everything around me; then there were times when this gave way to a passionate anguish which refused all attempts at comfort, and times even—but very, very seldom—when I almost forgot what had happened to me.

Our one servant remained in the house with me, and a friend and neighbour of my mother's was constant in her endeavours to relieve my loneliness; but I was impatient of them, I fear, and chiefly anxious to be left alone to indulge my melancholy unchecked.

I remember how, as autumn began, and leaf after leaf fluttered down from the trees in our little garden, I watched them fall with a heavier heart, for they had known my mother, and now they, too, were deserting me.

This morbid state of mind had lasted quite long enough when my uncle, who was my guardian, saw fit to put a summary end to it by sending me to school forthwith ; he would have softened the change for me by taking me to his own home first, but there was illness of some sort there, and this was out of the question.

I was neither sorry nor glad when I heard of it, for all places were the same to me just then ; only, as the time drew near, I began to regard the future with a growing dread.

The school was at some distance from London, and my uncle took me down by rail ; but the only fact I remember connected with the journey is that there was a boy in the carriage with us who cracked walnuts all the way, and I wondered if he was going to school too, and concluded that he was not, or he . would hardly eat quite so many walnuts.

Later we were passing through some wrought-iron gates, and down an avenue of young chestnuts, which made a gorgeous autumn canopy of scarlet, amber, and orange, up to a fine old red-brick house, with a high-pitched roof, and a cupola in which a big bell hung, tinted a warm gold by the afternoon sun.

This was my school, and it did not look so very terrible after all. There was a big bow-window by the pillared portico, and, looking timidly in, I saw a girl of about my own age sitting there, absorbed in the book she was reading, her long brown hair drooping over her cheek and the hand on which it rested.

She glanced up at the sound of the door-bell, and I felt her eyes examining me seriously and critically,

and then I forgot everything but the fact that I was
about to be introduced to my future schoolmaster, the
Rev. Basil Dering.

This was less of an ordeal than I had expected ;
he had a strong, massively-cut, leonine face, free and
abundant white hair, streaked with dark grey, but
there was a kind light in his eyes as I looked up
at them, and the firm mouth could smile, I found,
pleasantly enough.

Mrs. Dering seemed younger, and was handsome,
with a certain stateliness and decision of manner
which put me less at my ease, and I was relieved to
be told I might say good-bye to my uncle, and wander
about the grounds as I liked.

I was not surprised to pass through an empty
schoolroom, and to descend by some steep stairs to
a deserted playground, for we had been already told
that the Michaelmas holidays were not over, and
that the boys would not return for some days to come.

It gave me a kind of satisfaction to think of my
resemblance, just then, to my favourite David Copper-
field, but I was to have a far pleasanter companion
than poor lugubrious, flute-tootling Mr. Mell, for as I
paced the damp paths paved with a mosaic of russet
and yellow leaves, I heard light footsteps behind me,
and turned to find myself face to face with the girl I
had seen at the window.

She stood there breathless for an instant, for she
had hurried to overtake me, and against a background

of crimson creepers I saw the brilliant face, with its soft but fearless brown eyes, small straight nose, spirited mouth, and crisp wavy golden-brown hair, which I see now almost as distinctly as I write.

'You're the new boy,' she said at length. 'I've come out to make you feel more at home. I suppose you don't feel *quite* at home just yet?'

'Not quite, thank you,' I said, lifting my cap with ceremony, for I had been taught to be particular about my manners; 'I have never been to school before, you see, Miss Dering.'

I think she was a little puzzled by so much politeness. 'I know,' she said softly; 'mother told me about it, and I'm very sorry. And I'm called Marjory, generally. Shall you like school, do you think?'

'I might,' said I, 'if—if it wasn't for the boys!'

'Boys aren't bad,' she said; 'ours are rather nice, I think. But perhaps you don't know many?'

'I know one,' I replied.

'How old is *he*?' she wished to know.

'Not very old—about three, I think,' I said. I had never wished till then that my only male acquaintance had been of less tender years, but I felt now that he was rather small, and saw that Marjory was of the same opinion.

'Why, he's only a baby!' she said; 'I thought you meant a *real* boy. And is that all the boys you know? Are you fond of games?'

'Some games—very,' said I.

'What's your favourite game ? ' she demanded.

'Bezique,' I answered, ' or draughts.'

'I meant *out*door games; draughts are indoor
games—*is* indoor games, I mean—no, *are* an indoor
game—and *that* doesn't sound grammar! But haven't
you ever played cricket? Not ever, really? I like it
dreadfully myself, only I'm not allowed to play with
the boys, and I'm sure I can bat well enough for the
second eleven—Cartwright said I could last term—
and I can bowl round-hand, and it's all no use, just
because I was born a girl! Wouldn't you like a game
at something? They haven't taken in the croquet
hoops yet; shall we play at that ? '

But again I had to confess my ignorance of what
was then the popular garden game.

'What do you generally do to amuse yourself,
then ? ' she inquired.

'I read, generally, or paint texts or outlines.
Sometimes '—(I thought this accomplishment would
surely appeal to her)—'sometimes I do woolwork ! '

'I don't think I would tell the boys that,' she
advised rather gravely; she evidently considered
me a very desperate case. 'It's such a pity, your not
knowing any games. Suppose I taught you croquet,
now? It would be something to go on with, and
you'll soon learn if you pay attention and do exactly
what I tell you.'

I submitted myself meekly to her direction, and
Marjory enjoyed her office of instructress for a time,

until my extreme slowness wore out her patience, and
she began to make little murmurs of disgust, for
which she invariably apologised. 'That's enough for
to-day!' she said at last, 'I'll take you again to-
morrow. But you really must try and pick up games,
Cameron, or you'll never be liked. Let me see, I
wonder if there's time to teach you a little football.
I think I could do that.'

Before she could make any further arrangements
the tea-bell rang, but when I lay down that night in
my strange cold bed, hemmed round by other beds,
which were only less formidable than if they had been
occupied, I did not feel so friendless as I might have
done, and dreamed all night that Marjory was teaching
me something I understood to be cricket, which, however, was more like a bloated kind of backgammon.

The next day Marjory was allowed to go out walking with me, and I came home feeling that I had
known her for quite a long time, while her manner to
me had acquired a tone even more protecting than
before, and she began to betray an anxiety as to my
school prospects which filled me with uneasiness.

'I am so afraid the boys won't like the way you
talk,' she said on one occasion.

'I used to be told I spoke very correctly,' I said,
verdantly enough.

'But not like boys talk. You see, Cameron, I
ought to know, with such a lot of them about. I tell
you what I could do, though—I could teach you most

of their words—only I must run and ask mother first
if I may. Teaching slang isn't the same as using it
on my own account, is it ? '

Marjory darted off impulsively to ask leave, to
return presently with a slow step and downcast face.
'I mayn't,' she announced. 'Mother says "Certainly
not," so there's an end of that ! Still, I think myself
it's a decided pity.'

And more than once that day she would observe,
as if to herself, 'I do wish they had let him come to
school in different collars ! '

I knew that these remarks, and others of a similar
tendency, were prompted by her interest in my welfare,
and I admired her too heartily already to be offended
by them : still, I cannot say they added to my peace of
mind.

And on the last evening of the holidays she said
'Good-night' to me with some solemnity. 'Everything will be different after this,' she said ; 'I shan't
be able to see nearly so much of you, because I'm not
allowed to be much with the boys. But I shall be
looking after you all the time, Cameron, and seeing
how you get on. And oh ! I do hope you will try to
be a popular kind of boy ! '

.   .   .   .   .   .

I'm afraid I must own that this desire of Marjory's
was not realised. I do not know that I tried to be—
and I certainly was not—a popular boy.

The other boys, I now know, were by no means

bad specimens of the English schoolboy, as will be evident when I state that, for a time, my deep mourning was held by them to give me a claim to their forbearance.

But I had an unfortunate tendency to sudden floods of tears (apparently for no cause whatever, really from some secret spring of association, such as I remember was touched when I first found myself learning Latin from the same primer over which my mother and I had puzzled together), and these outbursts at first aroused my companions' contempt, and finally their open ridicule.

I could not conceal my shrinking dislike to their society, which was not calculated to make them more favourably disposed towards me; while my tastes, my expressions, my ways of looking at things, were all at total variance with their own standards.

The general disapproval might well have shown itself in a harsher manner than that of merely ignoring my existence—and it says much for the tone of the school that it did not; unfortunately, I felt their indifference almost as keenly as I had dreaded their notice.

From my masters I met with more favour, for I had been thoroughly well grounded, and found, besides, a temporary distraction in my school-work; but this was hardly likely to render me more beloved by my fellows, and so it came to pass that every day saw my isolation more complete.

Something, however, made me anxious to hide this from Marjory's eyes, and whenever she happened to be looking on at us in the school grounds or the playing fields, I made dismal attempts to appear on terms of equality with the rest, and would hang about a group with as much pretence of belonging to it as I thought at all prudent.

If she had had more opportunities of questioning me, she would have found me out long before; as it was, the only occasion on which we were near one another was at the weekly drawing lesson, when, although she drew less and talked more than the Professor quite approved of, she was obliged to restrict herself to a conversation which did not admit of confidences.

But this negative neutral-tinted misery was not to last; I was harmless enough, but then to some natures nothing is so offensive as inoffensiveness. My isolation was certain to raise me up an enemy in time, and he came in the person of one Clarence Ormsby.

He was a sturdy, good-looking fellow, about two years older than myself, good at games, and, though not brilliant in other respects, rather idle than dull. He was popular in the school, and I believe his general disposition was by no means bad; but there must have been some hidden flaw in his nature which might never have disclosed itself for any other but me.

For me he had displayed, almost from the first,
one of those special antipathies that want but little
excuse to ripen into hatred. My personal appearance
—I had the misfortune to be a decidedly plain boy—
happened to be particularly displeasing to him, and,
as he had an unsparing tongue, he used it to cover
me with ridicule, until gradually, finding that I did
not retaliate, he indulged in acts of petty oppression
which, though not strictly bullying, were even more
harassing and humiliating.

I suspect now that if I had made ever so slight
a stand at the outset, I should have escaped further
molestation, but I was not pugnacious by nature, and
never made the experiment; partly, probably, from a
theory on which I had been reared, that all violence
was vulgar, but chiefly from a tendency, unnatural
in one of my age and sex, to find a sentimental
satisfaction in a certain degree of unhappiness.

So that I can neither pity myself nor expect pity
from others for woes which were so essentially my
own creation, though they resulted, alas! in misery
that was real enough.

It was inevitable that quick-sighted Marjory should
discover the subjection into which I had fallen, and
her final enlightenment was brought about in this
manner. Ormsby and I were together alone, shortly
before morning school, and he came towards me with
an exercise of mine from which he had just been
copying his own, for we were in the same classes,

despite the difference in our ages, and he was in the habit of profiting thus by my industry.

'Thanks, Cameron,' he said, with a sweetness which I distrusted, for he was not as a rule so lavish in his gratitude. 'I've copied out that exercise of yours, but it's written so beastly badly that you'd better do it over again.'

With which he deliberately tore the page he had been copying from to scraps, which he threw in my face, and strolled out down to the playground.

I was preparing submissively to do the exercise over again as well as I could in the short time that was left, when I was startled by a low cry of indignation, and, looking round, saw Marjory standing in the doorway, and knew by her face that she had seen all.

'Has Ormsby done that to you before?' she inquired.

'Once or twice he has,' said I.

'And you let him!' she cried. 'Oh, Cameron!'

'What can I do?' I said.

'I know what *I* would do,' she replied. 'I would slap his face, or pinch him. . I wouldn't put up with it!'

'Boys don't slap one another, or pinch,' I said, not displeased to find a weak place in her knowledge of us.

'Well, they do *something*!' she said; 'a real boy would. But I don't think you are a real boy, Cameron.

I'll show you what to do. Where's the exercise that
—that *pig* copied? Ah! I see it. And now—look!'
(Here she tore his page as he had torn mine.)

'Now for an envelope!' and from the Doctor's
own desk she took an envelope, in which she placed
the fragments, and wrote on the outside in her round,
childish hand: 'With Marjory's compliments, for
being a bully.'

'He won't do that again,' she said gleefully.

'He'll do worse,' I said in dismay; 'I shall
have to pay for it. Marjory, why didn't you leave
things alone? I didn't complain—you know I
didn't.'

She turned upon me, as well she might, in
supreme disdain. 'Oh! what a coward you are! I
wouldn't believe all Cartwright told me about you
when I asked—but I see it's all true. Why don't
you stick up for yourself?'

I muttered something or other.

'But you *ought* to. You'll never get on unless,'
said Marjory, very decidedly. 'Now, promise me
you will, next time.'

I sat there silent. I was disgusted with myself,
and meanly angry with her for having rendered
me so.

'Then, listen,' she said impressively. 'I promised I would look after you, and I did mean to, but
it's no use if you won't help yourself. So, unless
you say you won't go on being a coward any more, I

shall have to leave you to your own way, and not take the least interest in you ever again.'

'Then, you may,' I said stolidly; 'I don't care.' I wondered, even while I spoke the words, what could be impelling me to treat spirited, warm-hearted Marjory like that, and I hate myself still at the recollection.

'Good-bye, then,' she said very quietly; 'I'm sorry, Cameron.' And she went out without another word.

When Ormsby came in, I watched him apprehensively as he read the envelope upon his desk and saw its contents. He said nothing, however, though he shot a malignant glance in my direction; but the lesson was not lost upon him, for from that time he avoided all open ill-treatment of me, and even went so far as to assume a friendliness which might have reassured me had I not instinctively felt that it merely masked the old dislike.

I was constantly the victim of mishaps, in the shape of missing and defaced books, ink mysteriously spilt or strangely adulterated, and, though I could never trace them to any definite hand, they seemed too systematic to be quite accidental; still I made no sign, and hoped thus to disarm my persecutor—if persecutor there were.

As for my companions, I knew that in no case would they take the trouble to interfere in my behalf; they had held aloof from the first, the general opinion (which I now perceive was not unjust) being that 'I deserved all I got.'

And my estrangement from Marjory grew wider and wider; she never spoke to me now when we sat near one another at the drawing-class; if she looked at me it was by stealth, and with a glance that I thought sometimes was contemptuously pitiful, and sometimes half fancied betrayed a willingness to return to the old comradeship.

But I nursed my stupid, sullen pride, though my heart ached with it at times. For I had now come to love Marjory devotedly, with a love that, though I was a boy and she was a child, was as genuine as any I am ever likely to feel again.

The chance of seeing her now and then, of hearing her speak—though it was not to me—gave me the one interest in my life, which, but for her, I could hardly have borne. But this love of mine was a very far-off and disinterested worship after all. I could not imagine myself ever speaking of it to her, or picture her as accepting it. Marjory was too thorough a child to be vulgarised in that way, even in thought.

The others were healthy, matter-of-fact youths, to whom Marjory was an ordinary girl, and who certainly did not indulge in any strained sentiment respecting her; it was left for me to idealise her; but of that, at least, I cannot feel ashamed, or believe that it did me anything but good.

And the days went on, until it wanted but a

fortnight to Christmas, and most of us were thinking of the coming holidays, and preparing with a not unpleasant excitement for the examinations, which were all that barred the way to them now. I was to spend my Christmas with my uncle and cousins, who would by that time be able to receive me; but I felt no very pleasurable anticipations, for my cousins were all boys, and from boys I thought I knew what to expect.

One afternoon Ormsby came to me with the request that I would execute a trifling commission for him in the adjoining village; he himself, he said, was confined to bounds, but he had a shilling he wanted to lay out at a small fancy-shop we were allowed to patronise, and he considered me the best person to be entrusted with that coin. I was simply to spend the money on anything I thought best, for he had entire confidence, he gave me to understand, in my taste and judgment. I think I suspected a design of some sort, but I did not dare to refuse, and then his manner to some extent disarmed me.

I took the shilling, therefore, with which I bought some article—I forget what—and got back to the school at dusk. The boys had all gone down to tea except Ormsby, who was waiting for me up in the empty schoolroom.

'Well?' he said, and I displayed my purchase, only to find that I had fallen into a trap.

When I think how easily I was the dupe of that

not too subtle artifice, which was only half malicious,
I could smile, if I did not know how it ended.

'How much was that?' he asked contemptuously,
'twopence-halfpenny? Well, if you choose to give a
shilling for it, I'm not going to pay, that's all. So
just give me back my shilling!'

Now, as my weekly allowance consisted of three-
pence, which was confiscated for some time in advance
(as I think he knew), to provide fines for my mysteri-
ously-stained dictionaries, this was out of the question, as I represented.

'Then go back to the shop and change it,' said
he; 'I won't have that thing!'

'Tell me what you would like instead, and I will,'
I stipulated, not unreasonably.

He laughed; his little scheme was working so
admirably. 'That's not the bargain,' he said;
'you're bound to get me something I like. I'm not
obliged to tell you what it is.'

But even I was driven to protest against such
flagrant unfairness. 'I didn't know you meant that,'
I said, 'or I'm sure I shouldn't have gone. I went
to oblige *you*, Ormsby.'

'No, you didn't,' he said, 'you went because I told
you. And you'll go again.'

'Not unless you tell me what I'm to get,' I
said.

'I tell you what I believe,' he said; 'you never
spent the whole shilling at all on that; you bought

x

something for yourself with the rest, you young swindler! No wonder you won't go back to the shop.'

This was, of course, a mere taunt flung out by his inventive fancy; but as he persisted in it, and threatened exposure and a variety of consequences, I became alarmed, for I had little doubt that, innocent as I was, I could be made very uncomfortable by accusations which would find willing hearers.

He stood there enjoying my perplexity and idly twisting a piece of string round and round his fingers. At length he said, 'Well, I don't want to be hard on you. You may go and change this for me even now, if you like. I'll give you three minutes to think it over, and you can come down into the playground when I sing out, and tell me what you mean to do. And you had better be sharp in coming, too, or it will be the worse for you.'

He took his cap, and presently I heard him going down the steps to the playground. I would have given worlds to go and join the rest at tea, but I did not dare, and remained in the schoolroom, which was dim just then, for the gas was lowered; and while I stood there by the fireplace, trembling in the cold air which stole in through the door Ormsby had left open, Marjory came in by the other one, and was going straight to her father's desk, when she saw me.

Her first impulse seemed to be to take no notice, but something in my face or attitude made her alter her mind and come straight to me, holding out her hand.

'Cameron,' she said, 'shall we be friends again ? '

'Yes, Marjory,' I said ; I could not have said any more just then.

'You look so miserable, I couldn't bear it any longer,' she said, 'so I *had* to make it up. You know, I was only pretending crossness, Cameron, all the time, because I really thought it was best. But it doesn't seem to have done you much good, and I did promise to take care of you. What is it ? Ormsby again ? '

'Yes,' I said, and told her the story of the commission.

'Oh, you stupid boy ! ' she cried, 'couldn't you see he only wanted to pick a quarrel ? And if you change it now, he'll make you change it again, and the next time, and the next after that—I know he will ! '

Here Ormsby's voice shouted from below, 'Now then, you, Cameron, time's up ! '

'What is he doing down there ? ' asked Marjory, and her indignation rose higher when she heard.

'Now, Cameron, be brave ; go down and tell him once for all he may just keep what he has, and be thankful. Whatever it is, it's good enough for *him*, I'm sure ! '

But I still hung back. 'It's no use, Marjory, he'll tell everyone I cheated him—he says he will ! '

'That he shall not!' she cried; 'I won't have it.
I'll go myself, and tell him what I think of him, and
make him stop treating you like this.'

Some faint glimmer of manliness made me ashamed
to allow her thus to fight my battles. 'No, Marjory,
not you!' I said; 'I will go: I'll say what you want
me to say!'

But it was too late. I saw her for just a second
at the door, my impetuous, generous little Marjory,
as she flung back her pretty hair in a certain spirited
way she had, and nodded to me encouragingly.

And then—I can hardly think of it calmly even
now—there came a sharp scream, and the sound of a
fall, and, after that, silence.

Sick with fear, I rushed to the head of the steps,
and looked down into the brown gloom.

'Keep where you are for a minute!' I heard
Ormsby cry out. 'It's all right—she's not hurt;
now you can come down.'

I was down in another instant, at the foot of the
stairs, where, in a patch of faint light that fell from
the door above, lay Marjory, with Ormsby bending
over her insensible form.

'She's dead!' I cried in my terror, as I saw her
white face.

'I tell you she's all right,' said he, impatiently;
'there's nothing to make a fuss about. She slipped
coming down and cut her forehead—that's all.'

'Marjory, speak to me—don't look like that; tell

me you're not much hurt!' I implored her; but she only moaned a little, and her eyes remained fast shut.

'It's no use worrying her now, you know,' said Ormsby, more gently. 'Just help me to get her round to the kitchen door, and tell somebody.'

We carried her there between us, and, amidst a scene of terrible confusion and distress, Marjory, still insensible, was carried into the library, and a man sent off in hot haste for the surgeon.

A little later Ormsby and I were sent for to the study, where Dr. Dering, whose face was white and drawn as I had never seen it before, questioned us closely as to our knowledge of the accident.

Ormsby could only say that he was out in the playground, when he saw somebody descending the steps, and heard a fall, after which he ran up and found Marjory.

'I sent her into the schoolroom to bring my paper-knife,' said the Doctor; 'if I had but gone myself— ! But why should she have gone outside on a frosty night like this?'

'Oh, Dr. Dering!' I broke out, 'I'm afraid—I'm afraid she went for me!'

I saw Ormsby's face as I spoke, and there was a look upon it which made me pity him.

'And you sent my poor child out on your errand, Cameron! Could you not have done it yourself?'

'I wish I had!' I exclaimed; 'oh, I wish I had!

I tried to stop her, and then—and then it was too late.
Please tell me, sir, is she badly hurt ? '

' How can I tell ? ' he said harshly ; ' there, I can't
speak of this just yet : go, both of you.'

There was little work done at evening preparation
that night; the whole school was buzzing with curiosity
and speculation, as we heard doors opening and
shutting around, and the wheels of the doctor's gig as
it rolled up the chestnut avenue.

I sat with my hands shielding my eyes and ears,
engaged to all appearance with the books before me,
while my restless thoughts were employed in making
earnest resolutions for the future.

At last I saw my cowardice in its true light,
and felt impatient to tell Marjory that I did so, to
prove to her that I had really reformed; but when
would an opportunity come? I might not see her
again for days, perhaps not at all till after the
holidays ; but I would not let myself dwell upon such
a contingency as that, and, to banish it, tried to
picture what Marjory would say, and how she would
look, when I was allowed to see her again.

After evening prayers, read by one of the as-
sistant-masters, for the Doctor did not appear again,
we were enjoined to go up to our bedrooms with as
little noise as possible, and we had been in bed some
time before Sutcliffe, the old butler, came up as
usual to put out the lights.

On this occasion he was assailed by a fire of

eager whispers from every door: 'Sutcliffe, hi! old
Sutty, how is she?' but he did not seem to hear,
until a cry louder than the rest brought him to our
room.

'For God's sake, gentlemen, don't!' he said, in
a hoarse whisper, as he turned out the light; 'they'll
hear you downstairs.'

'But how is she? do you know—better?'

'Ay,' he said, 'she's better. She'll be over her
trouble soon, will Miss Marjory!'

A low murmur of delight ran round the room,
which the butler tried to check in vain.

'Don't!' he said again, 'wait—wait till morning.
. . . Go to sleep quiet now, and I'll come up first
thing and tell you.'

He had no sooner turned his back than the
general relief broke out irrepressibly; Ormsby being
especially demonstrative. 'Didn't I tell you fellows
so?' he said triumphantly; 'as if it was likely a
plucky girl like Marjory would mind a little cut like
that. She'll be all right in the morning, you see!'

But this confidence jarred upon me, who could
not pretend to share it, until I was unable to restrain
the torturing anxiety I felt.

'You're wrong—all of you!' I cried, 'I'm sure
she's not better. Didn't you hear how Sutcliffe said
it? She's *worse*—she may even be dying!'

I met with the usual treatment of a prophet of
evil. 'You young muff,' I was told on all sides, 'who

asked your opinion? Who are you, to know better than anyone else?'

Ormsby attacked me hotly for trying to excite a groundless alarm, and I was recommended to hold my tongue and go to sleep.

I said no more, but I could not sleep; the others dropped off one by one, Ormsby being the last; but I lay awake listening and thinking, until the dread and suspense grew past bearing. I *must* know the truth. I would go down and find the Doctor, and beg him to tell me; he might be angry and punish me—but that would be nothing in comparison with the relief of knowing my fear was unfounded.

Stealthily I slipped out of bed, stole through the dim room to the door, and down the old staircase, which creaked under my bare feet. The dog in the yard howled as I passed the big window, through which the stars were sparkling frostily in the keen blue sky. Outside the room in which Marjory lay, I listened, but could hear nothing. At least she was sleeping, then, and, relieved already, I went on down to the hall.

The big clock on a table there was ticking solemnly, like a slow footfall; the lamp was alight, so the Doctor must be still up. With a heart that beat loudly I went to his study door and lifted my hand to knock, when from within rose a sound at which the current of my blood stopped and ran backwards—the terrible, heartbroken grief of a grown man.

Boy as I was, I felt that an agony like that was sacred; besides, I knew the worst then.

I dragged myself upstairs again, cold to the bones, with a brain that was frozen too. My one desire was to reach my bed, cover my face, and let the tears flow; though, when I did regain it, no tears and no thoughts came. I lay there and shivered for some time, with a stony, stunned sensation, and then I slept—as if Marjory were well.

The next morning the bell under the cupola did not clang, and Sutcliffe came up with the direction that we were to go down very quietly, and not to draw up the window-blinds; and then we all knew what had happened during the night.

There was a very genuine grief, though none knew Marjory as I had known her; the more emotional wept, the older ones indulged in little semi-pious conventional comments, oddly foreign to their usual tone; all—even the most thoughtless—felt the same hush and awe overtake them.

I could not cry; I felt nothing, except a dull rage at my own insensibility. Marjory was dead—and I had no tears.

Morning school was a mere pretence that day; we dreaded, for almost the first time, to see the Doctor's face, but he did not show himself, and the arrangements necessary for the breaking-up of the school were made by the matron.

Some, including Ormsby and myself, could not

be taken in for some days, during which we had to remain at the school: days of shadow and monotony, with occasional ghastly outbreaks of the high spirits which nothing could repress, even in that house of mourning.

But the time passed at last, until it was the evening of the day on which Marjory had been left to her last sleep.

The poor father and mother had been unable to stay in the house now that it no longer covered even what had been their child ; and the only two, besides the matron and a couple of servants who still remained there, were Ormsby and I, who were both to leave on the following morning.

I would rather have been alone just then with anyone but Ormsby, though he had never since that fatal night taken the slightest notice of me ; he looked worn and haggard to a degree that made me sure he must have cared more for Marjory than I could have imagined, and yet he would break at times into a feverish gaiety which surprised and repelled me.

He was in one of these latter moods that evening, as we sat, as far apart as possible, in the empty, firelit schoolroom.

'Now, Cameron,' he said, as he came up to me and struck me boisterously on the shoulder, ' wake up, man ! I've been in the blues long enough. We can't go on moping always, on the night before the holidays, too! Do something to make yourself sociable—talk, can't you ?'

'No, I can't,' I said ; and, breaking from him, went to one of the windows and looked vacantly out into blackness, which reflected the long room, with its dingy greenish maps, and the desks and forms glistening in the fire-beams.

The ice-bound state in which I had been so long was slowly passing away, now that the scene by the little grave that raw, cheerless morning had brought home remorselessly the truth that Marjory was indeed gone—lost to me for ever.

I could see now what she had been to me ; how she had made my great loneliness endurable ; how, with her innocent, fearless nature, she had tried to rouse me from spiritless and unmanly dejection. And I could never hope to please her now by proving that I had learnt the lesson ; she had gone from me to some world infinitely removed, in which I was forgotten, and my pitiful trials and struggles could be nothing to her any more !

I was once more alone, and this second bereavement revived in all its crushing desolation the first bitter loss which it so closely followed.

So, as I stood there at the window, my unnatural calm could hold out no longer ; the long-frozen tears thawed, and I could weep for the first time since Marjory died.

But I was not allowed to sorrow undisturbed ;

I felt a rough grasp on my arm, as Ormsby asked me angrily, ' What's the matter now ? '

' Oh, Marjory, come to me ! ' I could only cry ; ' I can't bear it ! I can't ! I can't ! '

' Stop that, do you hear ? ' he said savagely, ' I won't have it ! Who are you to cry about her, when—but for *you*—— '

He got no farther ; the bitter truth in such a taunt, coming from him, stung me to ungovernable rage. I turned and struck him full in the mouth, which I cut open with my clenched hand.

His eyes became all pupil. ' You shall pay me for that ! ' he said through his teeth ; and, forcing me against a desk, he caught up a large T-square which lay near ; he was far the stronger, and I felt myself powerless in his grasp. Passion and pain had made him beside himself for the moment, and he did not know how formidable a weapon the heavily-weighted instrument might become in his hand.

I shut my eyes : I think I rather hoped he would kill me, and then perhaps I might go where Marjory was. I did not cry for help, and it would have been useless if I had done so, for the schoolroom was a long way from the kitchen and offices of that rambling old house.

But before the expected blow was dealt I felt his grasp relax, and heard the instrument fall with a sudden clatter on the floor. ' Look,' he whispered, in a voice I did not recognise, ' *look there* ! '

And when I opened my eyes, I saw Marjory standing between us !

She looked just as I had always seen her: I suppose that even the after-life could not make Marjory look purer, or more lovely than she was on earth. My first feeling was a wild conviction that it had all been some strange mistake—that Marjory was not dead.

'Marjory, Marjory!' I cried in my joy, 'is it really you? You have come back, after all, and it is not true!'

She looked at us both without speaking for a moment; her dear brown eyes had lost their old childish sparkle, and were calm and serious as if with a deeper knowledge.

Ormsby had cowered back to the opposite wall, covering his face. 'Go away!' he gasped. 'Cameron —*you* ask her to go. She—she liked you. . . . I never meant it. Tell her I never meant to do it!'

I could not understand such terror at the sight of Marjory, even if she had been what he thought her; but there was a reason in his case.

'You were going to hurt Cameron,' said Marjory, at length, and her voice sounded sad and grave and far-away.

'I don't care, Marjory,' I cried, 'not now you are here!'

She motioned me back: 'You must not come nearer,' she said. 'I cannot stay long, and I must

speak to Ormsby. Ormsby, have you told anyone ? '

' No,' he said, shaking all over, ' it could do no
good. . . . I thought I needn't.'

' Tell *him*,' said Marjory.

' Must I ? Oh, no, no ! ' he groaned, ' don't make
me do that ! '

' You must,' she answered, and he turned to me
with a sullen fear.

' It was like this,' he began ; ' that night, when
I was waiting for you down there—I had some string,
and it struck me, all in a moment, that it would be
fun to trip you up. I didn't mean to hurt you—only
frighten you. I fastened the string across a little
way from the bottom. And then '—he had to
moisten his lips before he could go on—' then *she*
came down, and I tried to catch her—and couldn't—
no, I couldn't ! '

' Is that all ? ' asked Marjory, as he stopped short.

' I cut the string and hid it before you came.
Now you know, and you may tell if you like ! '

' Cameron, you will never tell, will you—as long
as he lives ? ' said Marjory. ' You must promise.'

I was horrified by what I had heard ; but her eyes
were upon me, and I promised.

' And you, Ormsby, promise me to be kinder to
him after this.'

He could not speak ; but he made a sign of assent.

' And now,' said Marjory, ' shake hands with him
and forgive him.'

But I revolted : ' No, Marjory, I can't ; not now—when I know this ! '

' Cameron, dear,' she said, ' you won't let me go away sorry, will you ? and I must go so soon. For my sake, when I wish it so ! '

I went to Ormsby, and took his cold, passive hand. ' I do forgive him, Marjory,' I said.

She smiled brightly at us both. ' And you won't forget, either of you ? ' she said. ' And, Douglas, you will be brave, and take your own part now. Good-bye, good-bye.'

I tried to reach her. ' Don't leave me ; take me with you, Marjory—dear, dear Marjory, don't go ! ' But there was only firelit space where she had stood, though the sound of her pleading, pathetic voice was still in the air.

Ormsby remained for a few minutes leaning against a desk, with his face buried in his arms, and I heard him struggling with his sobs. At last he rose, and left the room without a word.

But I stayed there where I had last seen Marjory, till the fire died down, and the hour was late, for I was glad to be alone with the new and solemn joy that had come to me. For she had not forgotten me where she was ; I had been allowed to see her once more, and it might even be that I should see her again. And I resolved then that when she came she should find me more worthy of her.

From that night my character seemed to enter

upon a new phase, and when I returned to school it was to begin my second term under better auspices.

My cousins had welcomed me cordially among them, and as I mastered the lesson of give and take, of respecting one's self in respecting others, which I needed to learn, my early difficulties vanished with the weakness that had produced them.

By Ormsby I was never again molested ; in word and deed, he was true to the promise exacted from him during that last strange scene. At first, he avoided me as being too painfully connected with the past; but by degrees, as he recognised that his secret was safe in my keeping, we grew to understand one another better, although it would be too much to say that we ever became intimate.

After he went to Sandhurst I lost sight of him, and only a few months since the news of his death in the Soudan, where he fell gallantly, made me sorrowfully aware that we should never meet again.

I had a lingering fancy that Marjory might appear to me once more, but I have long since given up all hope of that in this life, and for what may come after I am content to wait.

But the charge my child-friend had undertaken was completed on the night she was allowed to return to earth and determine the crisis of two lives ; there is nothing now to call the bright and gracious little spirit back, for her influence will remain always.

Spottiswoode & Co. Printers, New-street Square, London.

WORKS BY F. ANSTEY.

ILLUSTRATED EDITIONS

OF

POPULAR WORKS.

Handsomely bound in cloth gilt, each volume containing
Four Illustrations. Crown 8vo. 3s. 6d. each.

———◦◦———

THE SMALL HOUSE AT ALLINGTON. By ANTHONY TROLLOPE

FRAMLEY PARSONAGE. By ANTHONY TROLLOPE.

THE CLAVERINGS. By ANTHONY TROLLOPE.

TRANSFORMATION : a Romance. By NATHANIEL HAWTHORNE.

DOMESTIC STORIES. By the Author of 'John Halifax, Gentleman.'

THE MOORS AND THE FENS. By Mrs. J. H. RIDDELL.

WITHIN THE PRECINCTS. By Mrs. OLIPHANT.

CARITÀ. By Mrs. OLIPHANT.

FOR PERCIVAL. By MARGARET VELEY.

NO NEW THING. By W. E. NORRIS.

LOVE THE DEBT. By RICHARD ASHE KING ('Basil').

WIVES AND DAUGHTERS. By Mrs. GASKELL.

NORTH AND SOUTH. By Mrs. GASKELL.

SYLVIA'S LOVERS. By Mrs. GASKELL.

CRANFORD, and other Stories. By Mrs. GASKELL.

MARY BARTON, and other Stories. By Mrs. GASKELL.

RUTH ; THE GREY WOMAN, and other Stories. By
Mrs. GASKELL.

LIZZIE LEIGH ; A DARK NIGHT'S WORK, and other Stories.
By Mrs. GASKELL.

London : SMITH, ELDER & CO., 15 Waterloo Place.

POPULAR NOVELS.

Each Work complete in One Volume, Crown 8vo.
price Six Shillings.

NEW GRUB STREET. By GEORGE GISSING.

EIGHT DAYS. By R. E. FORREST, Author of 'The Touchstone of Peril.'

A DRAUGHT OF LETHE. By ROY TELLET, Author of 'The Outcasts' &c.

THE RAJAH'S HEIR. By a New Author.

THE PARIAH. By F. ANSTEY, Author of 'Vice Versâ' &c.

THYRZA. By GEORGE GISSING, Author of 'Demos' &c.

THE NETHER WORLD. By GEORGE GISSING, Author of 'Demos' &c.

ROBERT ELSMERE. By Mrs. HUMPHRY WARD, Author of 'Miss Bretherton' &c.

RICHARD CABLE: the Lightshipman. By the Author of 'Mehalah,' 'John Herring,' 'Court Royal,' &c.

THE GAVEROCKS. By the Author of 'Mehalah,' 'John Herring,' 'Court Royal,' &c.

DEMOS: a Story of Socialist Life in England. By GEORGE GISSING, Author of 'Thyrza' &c.

A FALLEN IDOL. By F. ANSTEY, Author of 'Vice Versâ' &c.

THE GIANT'S ROBE. By F. ANSTEY, Author of 'Vice Versâ' &c.

OLD KENSINGTON. By Miss THACKERAY

THE VILLAGE ON THE CLIFF. By Miss THACKERAY.

FIVE OLD FRIENDS AND A YOUNG PRINCE. By Miss THACKERAY.

TO ESTHER, and other Sketches. By Miss THACKERAY.

BLUEBEARD'S KEYS, and other Stories. By Miss THACKERAY.

THE STORY OF ELIZABETH ; TWO HOURS ; FROM AN ISLAND. By Miss THACKERAY.

TOILERS AND SPINSTERS. By Miss THACKERAY.

MISS ANGEL; FULHAM LAWN. By Miss THACKERAY.

MISS WILLIAMSON'S DIVAGATIONS. By Miss THACKERAY.

MRS. DYMOND. By Miss THACKERAY.

LLANALY REEFS. By Lady VERNEY, Author of 'Stone Edge' &c.

LETTICE LISLE. By Lady VERNEY. With 3 Illustrations.

London : SMITH, ELDER, & CO., 15 Waterloo Place.

www.ingramcontent.com/pod-product-compliance
Lightning Source LLC
Chambersburg PA
CBHW031339070726
47496CB00017B/1324